Thick as Thieves

Thick as Thieves

Patrick Quinn

Crown Publishers, Inc.
New York

Published by Crown Publishers, Inc., 201 East 50th Street, New York, New York 10022. Member of the Crown Publishing Group.

Random House, Inc. New York, Toronto, London, Sydney, Auckland

CROWN is a trademark of Crown Publishers, Inc.

Manufactured in the United States of America

Design by Cindy Dunne

Library of Congress Cataloging-in-Publication Data

Quinn, Patrick, 1957–
    Thick as thieves / Patrick Quinn. — 1st ed.
        1. Thieves—Illinois—Chicago—Fiction.   2. Chicago (Ill.)—
Fiction.   I. Title.
PS3567.U3485T47   1995
813'.54—dc20
94-28424
CIP

ISBN 0-517-70009-3

10 9 8 7 6 5 4 3 2 1

First Edition

For Ed, the best man in the world

Acknowledgments

My thanks to Tony Schraut and David Randall,
for that serendipitous street-corner conversation.

"For it is not possible for many men to lose their property and fortunes in one city, without drawing many along with them into the same vortex of diaster."

CICERO

Thick as Thieves

1

THE WAITRESS was young and blond and pretty. She delivered the drinks, Scotch and soda for Riles, double bourbon for Mackin, and smiled at Riles. "Anything else?"

Riles smiled back. "We're okay, but keep an eye on us." He watched her as she walked across the small space to a harried-looking businessman sitting alone at another table. "Just look at that," he murmured. "And me a happily married man."

They were sitting in a terminal bar in O'Hare. It was Friday afternoon. Mackin watched a 737 taxi past the outside wall of windows. The fact that Riles had left his bodyguard at the office confirmed that he was there to discuss a job. "So what do you need, Frank?" Mackin pitched his voice low. He had flown into Chicago—unwillingly, which was the way he always flew—that afternoon at the other man's request.

"I need a favor." Riles looked across the table. "I need a hand."

Mackin smiled again. "You leave a message on my voice mail at nine this morning and ask me to meet you ASAP, I figured you needed something. Tell me all about it."

Riles looked out the window at the runways gleaming in the chill autumn sunlight. Mackin knew that Riles was a heavyweight in the Chicago outfit, a guy with a lot of contacts in gambling, prostitution, and loan-sharking, but that wouldn't be what Riles wanted to talk about. Mackin wasn't a connected guy, he didn't even live in Chicago, and he never had anything to do with Riles's day-to-day work. Mackin was from Kansas City. He was a thief.

"There's this guy," Riles said quietly. His hand went to his collar and he unconsciously checked the knot in his tie. The tie was silk, a dark red splashed with quiet blue. He was wearing it over a white shirt and dark gray suit. He wasn't like the other wiseguys Mackin knew. Riles knew how to dress. "Name's Pointy Williams, out of town. Black guy, good-sized crew. He has a score, needs some help. He called me. I owe the guy a small one."

Mackin sipped his bourbon. "How do you owe him?"

"I had a problem with our dark brothers on the South Side." Riles shrugged. "No big thing, a beef about a couple of clubs that didn't want to pony up their ante. Williams made a few phone calls, straightened everything out. It would be of service to me if you would help him."

There was no threat in Riles's voice. Mackin knew that this conversation was strictly a request. Riles had sent a lot of business Mackin's way in the past, jobs where Mackin had made a lot of money. That spring, Riles had turned Mackin on to a Milwaukee cold-storage warehouse that was holding four semi-trailers full of furs. Mackin and a three-man crew busted the place on a Saturday night—he liked to work on weekends—stripped the furs out of the trailers, and packed them into another truck that they dropped off in front of Riles's Chicago office Sunday afternoon. Since then, Riles had paid Mackin installments totaling almost $90,000 as his end of the score.

"So what's the deal?" He wanted to help Riles out, but he wasn't going to commit himself unless he knew more.

"Williams has a line on a printing plant." Riles sipped his drink and leaned back in his chair. He glanced at Mackin's drink and looked over at the bar. The waitress was watching him, and he pointed at Mackin's glass and winked. She winked back. "He needs a pro to bust it."

Mackin drained his glass. "A printing plant?" He shook his head. "What's it print? Money?"

"Just about. Food stamps; he says like a quarter mil worth."

"I've never done food stamps." Mackin looked thoughtful. "They're not the first thing that comes to mind when you think about highly liquid instruments, if you know what I mean."

The waitress delivered his drink and he smiled at her, but she was already looking critically at Riles's half-empty glass. "Time for you to get with the program, mister," she said accusingly. Riles winked again and she laughed. The businessman across the bar raised his glass and she walked away.

Mackin stared out the windows at a big United jet rolling awkwardly through a wide runway turn. A deep-pitched rumbling from the engines penetrated the bar. "I'll need some time to set it up, get some people out there."

Riles sighed. "That's the bad part. It has to go down this weekend. It's Labor Day, and the plant will be closed for three days. The stamps are in an on-site warehouse. Tuesday morning they'll be moved to a state warehouse."

"Shit." Mackin scowled and shook his head. "I don't even know this guy, Frank."

"It's a fluff job, Mackin. It's a fucking printing plant, for

Christ's sake. A Cub Scout den could take it down. He only needs you because the stamps are in a storage building with reinforced walls and a steel door, so you'll need a burning bar to pop it. Williams doesn't have anyone who can run a burning bar, but he'll have a couple of guys there to give you a hand."

"Shit," Mackin said again. A bad feeling tickled the back of his brain. "I don't like running into this kind of thing half-cocked."

"Help me out on this thing, Mackin."

"How does the money work?"

"You fly out there today, take a look at the plant, bust it over the weekend and fly home. Twenty grand, cash on the spot." Riles emptied his glass. "Pure fluff. Found money."

"I'll take a look at it." Mackin waved the waitress off. "I'll go out there and check it out. If I don't like it, I'm outta there."

"Fair enough." Riles reached into his suit jacket, removed a ticket envelope, and pushed it across the table. "Your plane leaves in forty minutes. You got everything you need?"

Mackin smiled in spite of himself. "I brought a bag. I had a feeling you wanted me to go somewhere."

Riles grinned. "Feeling, my ass. You've always got a bag."

Mackin picked up the ticket and put it in his pocket. "What's your end on this, Frank?"

"I told you, I owe the guy one." He put on a look of hurt bewilderment. "This is a favor."

Mackin stared across the table. Riles held the stare for a moment, then laughed. "All right, all right. It's grocery stores."

"I don't get it."

Riles shifted in his chair. "The reason you don't hear about this kind of score going down every day is that, like you said, food stamps aren't negotiable, at least not by just anyone. I mean, sure, you could like sell 'em on the street for fifty percent face or some shit like that, but that's way too much work, too much exposure. The only people who can turn the goddamn thing into real money are grocery stores."

"So you're in the grocery business now?" A small smile played around Mackin's lips.

"Long story." Riles shook out a cigarette and lit it with a gold gas lighter. "Guy named Hookright—can you believe that? Hookright?—he inherits this chain of grocery stores, sixteen of 'em, from his grandfather or some such shit. Consolidated Food and Produce. Well, Mr. Hookright is what you could call a fuckup with major appetites. He likes to play. Cards, dice, coke, broads. Lots of coke, lots of broads."

He pointed to the ticket folder on the table. "Guy's only got one store in Illinois. Most of his shit is in Pointy's territory. Four of the biggest stores are in Pointy's town. Pointy gets to know this Hookright, which isn't unusual, 'cause out there if you like to do the kind of shit Hookright likes to do, you get to know guys like Pointy Williams."

"I think I see where this is going." Mackin lit a cigarette of his own. "I just don't see where Chicago comes in."

Riles shrugged. "Hookright needed some money, more than Pointy had laying around. Coke guys always end up needing money. There are some *paisans* out there, but they're old Mustache Pete guys. They loan-shark a little, gamble a little, sit around in the afternoon and tell each other lies about fucking over J. Edgar Hoover, y'know? They aren't the kind of guys you go to when you need to borrow one hundred forty large in a hurry. Hookright went to Pointy, and Pointy called us."

Mackin's smile was growing. "This clown Hookright borrowed a hundred and forty thousand dollars from you guys? Oh my God. Is he still alive?"

"Hell, yes." Riles put on a look of mock hurt. "What do you

think we are? He's still got his penthouse apartment, a red sports car, a pile of coke on his coffee table, and a nineteen-year-old hardbody named Michelle keeping him happy."

"And you got yourself a chain of grocery stores."

"You are talking, Mr. Mackin, to the executive vice president of Consolidated Food and Produce, Inc. Unofficially, of course. Show some respect."

Mackin shook his head in admiration. "You're unbelievable, Frank. Truly unbelievable. Grocery stores."

Riles sighed. "It's a ball-breaker business, Mackin. Really a ball-breaker. Grocery stores operate on a margin so small you need a microscope and CP-fucking-A to see it. This affordable-food-for-the-masses shit is bleeding us to death. But one thing grocery stores can do is turn food stamps in to the state for money. So we need some food stamps. Pointy turned us on to this deal. He gets a piece, too. He's the broker for the score. I told him you were the best."

Mackin nodded. "What did he need the money for?"

Riles raised his eyebrows in question.

"The grocery guy, Hookright or Hookup or whatever," Mackin said. "Why was he in such a hurry for a hundred forty gs?"

"I didn't mention that?" Riles looked down at the table and slid his glass in circles. "He got a call from one of his coke buddies, had a chance to buy into a real estate development in Florida, but he had to move in forty-eight hours. Kind of a shady deal, I suppose. Place called Mariner Estates West, outside Lauderdale. The money behind it is buried pretty deep." His face was expressionless.

"You goddamn pirate." Mackin struggled not to laugh. Mariner Estates West was Frank Riles's own project. "You loaned the money to yourself."

"Hey." Riles raised his hands. "What the little coked-up piece of shit doesn't know won't hurt him, right?"

Mackin stood up. "I'll call you one way or the other. Drinks are on you." He turned to go.

Riles looked serious. "Mackin. Be careful. Treat Williams with respect. He's a major street player, and he whacked four or five guys getting there. Don't underestimate him."

Mackin nodded. He still felt the tickle, but he remembered the Milwaukee score and the $90,000 and decided it wouldn't hurt to check out the warehouse. He walked out of the bar and into the terminal. His plane left in thirty minutes.

Riles ordered another drink and chatted up the waitress. Her name was Sarah, and she lived in Downers Grove. So did Riles.

"You like it out there?" he asked. "I live on the North Side, myself." Riles lied about casual things frequently, fluently, and without much thought. It had become a reflex over the years. On those rare occasions when someone caught him at it, he told another lie to explain himself, and then another, if he had to. He thought of telling the truth the way he thought of taking a cold shower, as something to be avoided whenever possible.

But he didn't tell professional lies if he could avoid it, and he hadn't lied to Mackin. Mackin was a serious earner, a stand-up guy, and he was taking a hell of a chance walking into this thing on short notice. Mackin had made Riles a lot of money over the years, and Riles made it a practice to treat people who made him a lot of money with respect.

The public address system announced that Mackin's flight was boarding. When Sarah went to attend to her other cus-tomer, Riles walked to the pay phones in the concourse and called Pointy Williams's office. The phone was answered on the first ring.

"Yeah." The voice at the other end was quiet.

"Reeves?"

"Who's asking?"

"Chicago." Riles lit another cigarette. The concourse was filled with preoccupied people, all of them walking rapidly and staring at a point just above the heads of the people around them.

"This is Reeves," the quiet voice said. Riles thought he heard a note of caution in the other man's voice.

"Tell Williams our guy is on the way. Everything set at your end?"

"Everything be cool. We're ready to rock." There was something off center in Reeves's tone.

"I hope so," Riles snapped. "This guy is all business. I'd hate to be around if he thought he was walking into some half-assed mess."

"I'll tell Pointy." There was a subdued click as Reeves replaced the handset in the cradle.

Riles stared at the phone for a moment, then swore softly. He walked back to the bar and finished his drink. He flirted with Sarah, but he wasn't serious. He hadn't lied to Mackin about that, either. He was a happily married man.

2

MACKIN took down Felton Industrial Printing with a two-man crew and a burning bar. The crew was local talent, guys Mackin had never seen before. One guy, muscle named Danny, was the driver. The other, a kid who called himself Scooter, told Mackin right away that he'd never worked a big job before—he had a full-time gig as a welder in a body shop. Mackin groaned inwardly. It definitely wasn't the way he liked to work, but he didn't see any overwhelming obstacles. The warehouse was hardly a bank. The stamps were locked in a steel-walled storeroom for the weekend, guarded only by a retired suburban cop.

They hit the plant at three o'clock Sunday morning. Danny went over the fence, put the guard to sleep, and opened the gate. The three of them taped heavy paper over the windows in the warehouse, and Mackin and Scooter went through the door to the storage room with the burning bar in fifteen minutes. The kid did just fine. They had the truck loaded and were gone in less than an hour. Mackin found out later that the security guard had to be hospitalized for dehydration and shock after his relief found him bound and gagged when he came to work Monday.

Pointy Williams met him at five-thirty Sunday morning at an all-night coffee shop. He knew Mackin as Paul Moffitt.

"How'd it go?" Williams was sitting in a back booth, the remnants of an omelette on a plate in front of him. He was wearing a long, light raincoat. Mackin saw a starched white shirt collar and a yellow tie that looked like silk under the raincoat. A slightly taller, much heavier black man stood easily against the back wall of the shop next to the rest-room doors, his hands clasped loosely in front of him. He was wearing a Detroit Pistons warm-up jacket and a plug hat. He didn't take his eyes off Mackin. "He just Beano-D," Williams said. "Don't pay no mind to him. How'd it go?"

"Satin." Mackin dropped a ring of keys on the table. "The merch is in the truck, the truck is in the garage, the garage is locked, and I sent the boys home." He pushed his single bag, a light vinyl duffel, across the cushioned bench, sat down next to it, and ordered coffee from a passing waitress. "I had Danny drop me off at a convenience store down the street. He thought I was supposed to pay the two of them. I told them you'd take care of it. Today."

Williams grinned. "Man, that Danny can have an attitude sometimes. Pretty reliable for a white boy, though. He break bad on you?" His voice was low and smooth, almost musical.

"Not really." Mackin stirred his coffee. It was still dark outside, and cool. The coffee shop was tucked in a corner of the

Brickyard, that part of the city that used to be its industrial heart. Over the past two decades the Brickyard had sunk into a squalid mess of abandoned warehouses, rusted railroad tracks, and low-income housing. Mackin didn't have any trouble believing that Pointy Williams swung a lot of weight in the Brickyard. "You owe me some money."

"Chill, baby." Williams's grin didn't falter. "Pointy got you covered." He pulled a long envelope out of the inside jacket of his brown sports coat and set it on the table next to the keys. "Car's in the lot, red Toyota. The keys are under the floor mat."

Mackin picked up the envelope and lowered it to his lap. He glanced down and riffled through the inch-thick stack of bills inside. All C-notes, nonsequential, all new. He put the envelope in his pocket and rose. "Pleasure doing business with you."

"Stick around, homes." Williams looked pained. "Get yourself some sleep, let Pointy show you some fun in his city tonight."

"No, thanks." Mackin drained his coffee. "Business elsewhere."

"Riles said you don't fuck around." Williams shrugged. "You in such a all-fired hurry, how 'bout you give those keys to my man Beano and let him drive you to the airport?"

Mackin glanced at Beano-D, then back at Williams. "No, thanks," he said again. "It's been fun. I'm out of here. I'll leave the car in long-term parking at the airport." He nodded at Williams and walked out of the diner.

Williams swiveled his head to Beano-D. "Long-term parking, homes." He was still smiling.

Beano-D smiled back. "That sumbitch be headed for *forever*

parking," he said, and both of them laughed. The counterman looked over at the booth, then turned back to the morning paper.

The Toyota, about three years old, was parked in the corner of the lot. Mackin automatically checked the tag to make sure it was valid, threw his bag in the front seat, and pulled out of the parking lot. He was twenty blocks from the airport interstate entrance ramp. He made ten before the cops pulled him over.

The moment he saw the red light in his mirror, he began to review his driving, wondering why they had stopped him. A lot of people in Mackin's line of work ended up in the joint because of traffic stops, but he was a careful, low-profile driver. He immediately pulled the Toyota to the curb. A hint of sunrise showed in the eastern sky.

He cursed himself for not checking the headlights and taillights before he left the lot; one of them was probably burned out. He rolled down the window, put both hands on the wheel, and waited for the officer to approach the car. He wasn't very worried. The driver's license and credit cards in his wallet, all in the name of Paul Moffitt, were clean. A .45 automatic was in the duffel bag, but there wasn't any reason for the cops to search the bag.

Mackin's internal alarm began to ring when he realized that the car behind him was unmarked, a plain Chevy sedan. Both doors of the car opened at the same time. Mackin saw to his shock that both officers were crouched behind the doors, their revolvers leveled at the Toyota. An amplified voice boomed from the loudspeaker on the car: *"Climb out of the driver's side window feet first immediately! Lay facedown on the street with your arms spread wide! Move!"*

Mackin glanced at the duffel bag, but instantly dismissed the thought. They had him cold. He awkwardly pushed his feet out the window and dropped to the pavement.

"Eat some street, asshole! Arms wide now!"

Mackin spread-eagled himself on the asphalt. He heard one of the cops approaching him from behind. A rough hand pressed against the back of his head and shoved his face into the grit of the street. He felt a metallic circle push into his neck. "One move, asshole, you're history," the cop rasped. The other officer moved into Mackin's line of sight, his revolver pointed directly at Mackin's head from ten feet away. He was in plainclothes. "Just take it easy, friend," he said. "You know the drill."

Mackin's alarm bells were screaming. He wondered why he'd been pulled over by plainclothesmen. He wondered why they thought he knew the drill. The cop behind him frisked him roughly and thoroughly, then lifted one of his arms from the pavement and pulled it behind his back. "I'm gonna cuff you now, pal," the voice said. "Don't make this hard." Mackin felt the handcuffs slip around his wrist and click into place. The cop pulled his other wrist back and cuffed it, tight but not too tight, then lifted him to his feet. It was hard going; Mackin was a big man and the second officer made no move to help. As soon as Mackin was up, the cop spun him around and bent him over the hood of the Toyota.

"You want to tell me what this is all about, Officer?" Mackin was relaxed and unresisting. He already had an idea about what was going on.

The cop behind him lifted Mackin's leather wallet, then shoved his hand under Mackin's chest and removed the white envelope from Mackin's jacket. He glanced through the wallet and the envelope, then smiled and nodded at his partner. "You're driving a stolen car, Mr. . . . Moffitt," the cop said. He was about forty, a large man in a cheap suit showing the start of a beer gut. "I'm Sergeant Kendall, that's Officer Macnamara." He pulled the keys and the duffel bag from the car. "You're also carrying a large amount of cash. You are one suspicious character, Mr. Moffitt, and we're going to ask you to have a seat in our vehicle while we check you out."

Kendall grabbed Mackin's arm just over the elbow and hustled him to the Chevy. He pushed the handcuffed man in the backseat. "Just wait here, Mr. Moffitt. Soon we'll be back for a little chat."

Mackin leaned back in the seat and watched as the cops conducted their search. Macnamara, smaller and trimmer than Kendall, broke into a huge grin as he pulled the .45 from Mackin's bag. Both officers turned and glanced at the Chevy. Their lips were moving, but Mackin could hear nothing from inside the car.

He was enraged. He nurtured the anger, watching it swell into a crimson cloud inside his mind but not letting it out of control. Anger was a tool to be used like a burning bar. Pointy Williams had set him up, putting him into a stolen car and arranging for a pair of friendly cops to be waiting for him. Mackin was hardly surprised when he saw Kendall remove a brown paper shopping bag from the trunk of the Toyota. The paunchy cop removed a tightly wrapped cellophane package from the bag, and again both cops smiled.

It was a rip-off, Mackin realized. Neither officer had told him he was under arrest or read a Miranda warning; neither had so much as shown him a badge. No other cops had appeared, though more than enough time had passed for backup to show. It was definitely a rip-off. Pointy had used him to take down the printing plant, then given him up to a couple of crooked cops. The goddamn car was a time bomb. Pointy would have to pay for that.

The only question was whether or not the cops intended to kill him.

The policemen stopped smiling. Mackin saw Macnamara lift one leg and plant his foot on the bumper of the Toyota. The detective lowered one hand to his ankle and brought it up holding a gun, a small, blue-steel revolver. He slipped the gun into the side pocket of his jacket.

"Throwdown." Mackin's voice sounded loud in the quiet of the closed car, but the two detectives couldn't hear him. "Son of a bitch. A throwdown."

He wondered where the little gun had come from, and what crime he would be tied to when they found it on his body. He pulled away from the car seat and forced his fingers under his belt at the small of his back. A small lockpick rested in a special pocket of the belt. He popped the cuffs in less than ten seconds, kicked them under the seat, and put his hands behind his back.

The two detectives walked back to the car and climbed into the front seat. Kendall shut off the flashing red light on the dash. "Here's what we got, Mr. Moffitt," Kendall said easily. His smile fed Mackin's anger. "That Toyota was stolen from a downtown parking lot three days ago, so we got grand theft auto."

Macnamara held up the cellophane package. Mackin saw that it was full of white powder. "I'd guess this will test out to be blow." Macnamara's voice was higher than Kendall's. "So we got possession with intent to sell." He hefted Mackin's .45 in his other hand. "And this will go down as an illegal concealed weapon, so from where I sit it looks like your ass pretty much belongs to us."

Mackin stared at the two men in the front seat. He hated cops. "You were tipped," he finally said. He kept the rage out of his voice. "Pointy tipped you."

"It's a cold world, Mr. Moffitt," Kendall said. "It's hard to know who to trust anymore. Let's just say that Pointy owed us one." He raised the white envelope over the seat. "You are in some serious deep shit, but I think maybe we can work something out."

Mackin sighed. "Like maybe you guys keep what's in the envelope, and I walk."

"We're not that cruel, Mr. Moffitt." Kendall removed a single hundred-dollar bill from the envelope and dropped it in Mackin's lap. "Officer Macnamara and I will be happy to drop you off at the bus station, so long as you promise to be on the next bus out of the city."

Mackin pretended to think it over. The two cops were relaxed, confident that they were in absolute control of the situation. Almost ten minutes had passed since he'd seen the red light in the mirror, and not a single car had appeared on the street. The sky to the east was rapidly lightening. He finally nodded and pasted a weak grin on his face. "It doesn't look like I have much choice, does it?"

"Not really," Macnamara said, and Mackin hit him savagely on the side of his head with a balled fist. Macnamara's head bounced off the passenger side window and his eyes rolled up. Mackin reached over the seat, picked up the .45, snapped the safety down, and shot Kendall twice in the chest. The big sergeant never had time to react. Macnamara was groaning and fumbling for the gun in his jacket. Mackin shot him twice, too, then grabbed the envelope from the seat. The blood hadn't reached it. Macnamara was still breathing, his hands twitching in his lap, his eyes wide open in agony. "Fuck you," Mackin said to the bleeding man. "You're a dead motherfucker. Happy Labor Day."

He pulled out a handkerchief, picked up the handcuffs, carefully wiped them clean, and dropped them back on the floor. Then he ran the cloth over the backseat. He reached into Kendall's smoking, blood-soaked jacket and found the leather wallet, then opened the door and stepped out of the car. The street was still deserted. The Toyota's keys were in the open trunk lid. He closed the trunk, picked up his duffel bag from the street, and slipped behind the wheel. There was blood on his right hand and the right sleeve of his jacket. He took off the jacket, turned it inside out, and used it to wipe his hand clean, then rolled it up and put it in his bag. His ears were ringing from the explosions in the Chevy. The street was still deserted in the half-light of early morning. He started the car and drove away.

He knew he needed to get out of the city fast. The car was hot, and as soon as Williams heard about the two dead cops, the Paul Moffitt ID would be hot, too. He drove directly to the city center, praying that he wouldn't run into a black-and-white with nothing better to do than run the tag on the Toyota. Traffic was light, and in ten minutes he was in the business district. He parked the Toyota on a downtown street, looked around quickly, and wiped down the steering wheel, gearshift, and the window handle.

He pulled on a pair of thin leather gloves from his duffel bag. He locked the car, running his gloved hand thoroughly across the Toyota's door handle, put a quarter in the meter, and walked casually down the sidewalk. It was just past seven, and the city was starting to wake up and come alive.

He found a half-filled diner six blocks from where he'd parked the car. He bought a newspaper from the rack outside the door. Once inside he went to the men's room, removed his gloves, washed his hands thoroughly, and examined himself in the mirror. Other than needing a shave, he looked fine. He was dressed casually, but his clothes were nice and no one would mistake him for a bum. He walked out and sat at the counter. "Just coffee," he said to the waitress. She didn't give him a second glance. Mackin opened the paper and pretended to read. He noticed with satisfaction that his hands weren't shaking. The problem was getting out of town in a hurry without attracting attention or leaving a paper trail, and he settled down to think it through.

In fifteen minutes he had a plan he thought would work. He smiled at the waitress. "I changed my mind. I think I'll have breakfast after all." He leafed through the paper looking for book reviews.

3

A CONSTRUCTION WORKER working holiday overtime on a high-rise job found the Chevy. Detective Sgt. Milos Petrone stared thoughtfully at the carnage inside the car. "Fuck me running," he said to no one in particular.

It was bad. Cop killings were always bad. This was the worst cop killing in the city's history. A uniformed officer putting up yellow crime-scene tape was openly crying, and Larry Whittier, another Homicide detective, was slamming his hand repeatedly on the hood of their car. "Goddammit," he said flatly, over and over. "Goddammit." He was crying, too. More than a dozen officers were at the scene already, and Petrone knew that number would double as word of the shootings went out. Reporters had already started to gather on the street.

Petrone was shaken, as shaken as anyone there, but it didn't show. He had mastered the art of self-control when he was still in uniform working the Brickyard and knee-deep in the horrors of the worst part of the city. Still, this was one of the worst he'd seen.

Kendall and Macnamara were slumped on either side of the front bench seat of the Chevy. The seat and the dash were covered with blood, and half of Kendall's jacket had smoldered away. "Contact shots," Petrone muttered. "From a big fucking gun, too." He saw two expended brass cartridges on the floor of the front seat, and he suspected the crime-scene technicians would find two or three more. He had a lot of questions, not the least of which was what the two officers were doing together. Kendall was assigned to Narcotics, Macnamara to Vice, and as far as Petrone knew, the two had never worked together.

" 'Scuse me, Sarge." A crime-scene photographer named Walker tapped Petrone on the shoulder. "Could you step away from this side of the car for a sec?"

Petrone nodded and walked over to Whittier. He put his hand on the crying man's shoulder. "Tighten up, Larry," he said soothingly. "We got work to do."

Whittier made a visible effort to pull himself together. After a moment he nodded and exhaled violently. "Some cocksucker is going down hard for this one," he said grimly. "Real hard."

The two detectives walked back to the Chevy. "I got a door-to-door going," Petrone said. "I don't think we'll get much there, though. There's no one around this part of the city before seven. It's all commercial, and half the businesses down here have been closed for years."

He pointed at the cellophane package on the front seat. "We have some very serious problems here, Larry," he said quietly. "I don't think that's sugar."

"What the fuck are you talking about?" Whittier said angrily.

"You telling me you think these guys were dirty? Jack Kendall *worked* narcotics, for chrissakes. He was probably undercover."

"In an unmarked city unit? C'mon, Larry." Petrone shook his head. "I'm not saying anything yet, except that I got a lot of questions about this."

He walked around the car. "There's a dollar bill on the backseat," he said, peering through the window. "No, wait. It's a hundred. And it looks like there's a set of cuffs on the floor. This is weird."

One of the uniforms walked over from his black-and-white. "Both their COs are on their way, Sergeant." He stared into the car for a moment and looked away. "Dispatch says they had no radio transmissions. They're both scheduled off yesterday and today."

"Thanks." Petrone nodded absently. He waved the crime-scene technicians and the representative from the medical examiner's office over to the Chevy. "It's all yours." He shook his head. "Weird," he repeated.

Thom Walker snapped the last of his photographs and stared at the interior of the car for a moment. A civilian, he worked on contract with the police department and dreamed of the day when he could stop taking pictures of mangled bodies for the cops and start taking them for a daily newspaper. He had worked out an arrangement with a reporter named Maloney from the *Times*, who sometimes pitched him a hundred bucks for fresh information. He wondered what was in the cellophane-wrapped package on the car seat and decided that when he got back to the darkroom, he should make some extra prints.

Mackin was the first customer of the day in Hilliard's Men's Apparel. He purchased a quiet brown sports coat, a red tie, and a black leather briefcase. He paid with a pair of the hundreds from the white envelope. He had run an electric razor over his face and shaved off his mustache in the men's room at the diner. No one seemed to have noticed. With the addition of the coat, tie, and briefcase, Mackin looked like a moderately successful businessman. He found a phone booth, called TWA's toll-free number, and booked a one-way ticket to New York in the name of Paul Moffitt. As he gave the operator the number of the Visa card in Moffitt's name, he noticed his driver's license was missing. That made the possibility of Pointy Williams passing the name to the police moot. They'd have it on their own soon. That was all right. The reservation to New York had no purpose other than to muddy the water.

He briskly walked two blocks to the downtown Marriott and strode into the lobby. It was eight-thirty in the morning and a line of people were checking out of the hotel. Mackin pretended to study the rack of tourist information near the front desk.

He watched three people check out before he found one who looked right. A heavyset man in a nice suit dropped a key and a credit card in front of the desk clerk. "Samuels," he said. "I'm checking out of four twelve." The clerk ran the credit card through the desk register and handed the slip to Samuels for his signature. Samuels was studying an airline ticket folder. "When does the next airport shuttle leave?"

The clerk glanced at his watch. "Fifteen minutes, Mr. Samuels." He pointed to the front doors. "Right outside."

The businessman nodded. "Thanks. Gotta be in Cleveland by five this afternoon." He picked up his suitcase and walked away.

Mackin watched him leave the hotel, then walked across the lobby to the travel booth. He fashioned a rueful smile for the pretty girl behind the counter. Her name tag read ELAINE.

"Good morning, Elaine," he said. "I'm Mr. Samuels, in four

twelve. I just called my office, and I'm afraid I'm in a bit of a pickle."

She returned his smile. "Change of plans?" she asked solicitously.

Mackin heaved an internal sigh of relief. She didn't seem to know Samuels. The businessman's ticket folder had been creased and a little worn; Mackin was fairly certain he'd picked up his tickets out of town. " 'Fraid so." He set his briefcase down and leaned on the counter. "I was supposed to go to Cleveland today, but now they want me in St. Louis right away. Unhappy client. Can you help me out?"

"I just bet we can, Mr. Samuels." She began punching the keys on the computer terminal in front of her. "I've got a nonstop on United that leaves at eleven-forty," she said after a moment. "That gives you just enough time to get to the airport and check in. Will that work?"

"Perfect." Mackin smiled. "You've saved my life, Elaine. Let me have a one-way."

"That will be three hundred and thirty-seven dollars on the nose for business class. Should I put that on your credit card?"

"I'll pay cash." Mackin opened his wallet and pulled out four bills. This was the danger point. Airline regulations required any ticket sold for cash to be verified with identification, but Mackin was betting that Elaine would let it slide for a guest whose credit card number was already in the hotel's computer.

"Fine," she said, still staring at the screen. The printer on her desk began to rattle out the ticket. "Should I cancel your ticket to Cleveland, Mr. Samuels?"

"Oh, no. My office is calling our travel agency." He accepted his change and the ticket. "Thanks so much, Elaine. You've been a terrific help. Really."

He bought a magazine in the hotel gift shop and put it in

the briefcase. Then he wrapped the wallet and the remainder of the Moffitt identification in the plastic bag from the gift shop, put it in his pocket, and got on the airport shuttle. He sat three seats behind Mr. Samuels.

Mackin dropped the plastic bag in a trash can on the sidewalk in front of the airport. He checked the duffel and the briefcase through to St. Louis. The .45 was wrapped in a shirt inside the briefcase.

He found a vacant pay phone on the concourse and called a number in Kansas City. The gruff voice that answered sounded sleepy.

"What the hell . . . 'Lo."

"This is Mackin. I'm hot. Have someone pick me up in front of the United terminal at Lambert at three-thirty this afternoon."

The voice was suddenly awake. "Rodney will be there."

Mackin hung up. Three hours after his exchange with Elaine he was in the air on his way to St. Louis. He tried to relax on the plane. He glanced through the magazine he'd bought and pushed the packaged airline lunch around on his tray, but he hated to fly. Planes were too confining for Mackin.

The events of the morning ran through his head like a looped videotape. It wasn't the first time Mackin had killed, but he'd never killed a cop before, let alone two of them. Common sense said he'd have to lie low for a while, which meant that he wouldn't be able to earn. Common sense didn't enter into the picture when he thought about Pointy Williams. Pointy had payback coming.

He gritted his teeth and hung on to the armrests as the plane landed. A passing stewardess smiled sympathetically and patted his shoulder as she headed to her seat in the back. He was sweating when the plane finally pulled up at the gate.

Rodney was waiting on the sidewalk outside the terminal. He was a black man of medium height, stocky and powerful looking. He had his hands shoved in the pockets of a brown leather jacket. His eyes touched on Mackin for a moment, then flitted over the crowd behind and around him.

"How hot are you?" There was no tension in Rodney's voice.

"I think I'm all right. I just had to get outta Dodge in a hurry."

Rodney relaxed and removed his hands from the pockets of the jacket. "Car's over there," he said, inclining his head toward a nearby parking lot. "Bo said you ran into some trouble."

Mackin glanced around as they walked through the lot. No one was near. "I had to kill a couple of cops."

Rodney's expression didn't change. "Sounds like the cops had the trouble. I had a phone put in the car. You can call Bo from the highway." He looked at his watch. "Tell him we'll get to the club around seven-thirty."

Mackin wondered if the police had found the Moffitt driver's license yet.

Pointy Williams had a very bad Labor Day weekend.

As soon as Mackin left the coffee shop, Williams sent Beano-D and a crew to the garage to move the truck and the food stamps. Once the stamps were secure he planned to take his mother and a girl to the lake for a picnic. His mother made the best potato salad in the world, and Pointy was a pretty fair hand on the grill.

Pointy did most of his business out of an office in a building next to Grovner's Pawn and Loan, a big hockshop on Amsterdam Street between the Brickyard and downtown. Carl Grovner was married to Pointy's sister. Pointy thought Carl was a useless shit, but Emily loved him and Pointy had to find something for him. Carl was too stupid to be a successful lawbreaker, so

Pointy kept him legitimate. On paper the two buildings were owned by entirely separate corporations, which was enough of a legal distinction to keep the cops from screwing around with Carl's federal firearms license.

"You got a good living here," Pointy told his brother-in-law. "You keep it clean, run this by the numbers. You fuck this up, start buying hot merchandise or fucking around with illegal guns, I'll cut your dick off." Of course, Pointy made sure that the registration cards for a few of the guns that came through the shop disappeared. It never hurt to have a few extra pieces lying around.

Pointy's third-floor office was done in quiet pastels. Pointy liked peaceful colors, understated elegance, ripples instead of splash. He'd made a big noise coming up in his teens and twenties, decked out in gold chains and driving a fire-engine-red Caddy, but at thirty-six Pointy had arrived. He didn't need the noise anymore. Now he drove a gray Volvo and owned half of the best French restaurant in town.

He was at his desk—Scandinavian, done in off-white with natural wood trim—when Dink Reeves told him about the cops. Technically, Dink was vice president of Williams Entertainment, the corporation that ran most of the vending, pinball, and video machines in the Brickyard. In reality, Dink was Pointy's number one guy. What Beano-D and his crew were for muscle, Dink was for brains. His office was next to Pointy's, and he was in it by seven-thirty every morning.

Dink knocked and stuck his head through the door that joined their offices. "Police scanner says someone aced a couple guys in a car down the Brickyard. Shot 'em all to pieces."

Pointy looked up. "Yeah?" He opened the cashbox in the

bottom drawer of his desk and transferred a stack of C-notes to his wallet. "Shit happens. People be fucking crazy these days."

"Scanner says these guys are cops."

Pointy's holiday went to hell right then. "Shit." He hurried into Dink's office in time to hear one of the uniforms at the scene identify Kendall. "Shit!" he shouted. "Get Beano here! That crazy honky killed a couple of fucking cops, man. He'll be on his way here next! Shit."

"He don't know where here is," Dink said calmly. "He ain't never been here."

"I don't fucking care 'bout that. This mother is crazy, man. Get me some people here *now*."

"Cool. I'm on it." Dink picked up his phone. Dink had never been thrilled about the idea of ripping off the thief. It wasn't professional. Dink was very professional.

Pointy returned to his desk and pulled a .38 Smith & Wesson from the back of the bottom drawer. He didn't like to carry heat; he felt he was above that. Guns weren't the sort of accessories you carried into a French restaurant. This was different. He checked the load and shoved the gun in his belt. He walked out and locked the door to the stairs.

"Beano on his way," Dink said. "He's bringing some people."

"All right, all right." Pointy went back to his office, sat down at his desk, and immediately howled and stood up. The barrel of the .38 had jammed into his scrotum. "Mother*fucker!*" he shouted. He pulled the pistol out of his pants and set it on the desk.

Dink watched his employer without expression. Pointy had been enjoying himself a little too much in the past couple of years, Dink thought, spending a little too much time with the girls, doing a little too much blow, taking a little too much for granted. He wasn't taking care of business. "You best chill, Pointy. We got us a problem bigger than this honky."

"What you mean?"

"Them cops was ours, homes. If Moffitt didn't steal the blow, they going to find two dead cops with a kilo of coke. There'll be some serious heat around here."

"There be some serious fucking heat right here in this office if that crazy bastard blows through that door with a gun," Pointy muttered. He was starting to calm down.

"I don't 'spect a guy just lit up two police gonna be hanging round. If he's alive, he be outta this town in a heartbeat."

Pointy nodded. "Could be." He thought for a moment. "When Beano and his people get here, you go out and find out what's going on. Find out if they got the honky. If they didn't, call someone we know and give them Moffitt's name."

"No sweat. Probably ain't his real name, though. The guy came highly recommended as a pro."

"I know." Pointy scowled at the door. "Get me that Italian son of a bitch in Chicago on the phone. And call my momma and tell her the fucking picnic's canceled."

4

PETRONE found the license two minutes after the pathologist turned over Kendall's clothes. It was eleven-thirty in the morning. The license was in the side pocket of Kendall's suit coat. He handled it with tweezers, bagged it, and gave it to the lab for prints.

It had been a rough morning. Petrone, Whittier, and a policewoman had broken the news to Kendall's widow, a small woman with a pinched face who began wailing as soon as she saw Whittier's expression. Petrone gazed curiously around the living room as the policewoman tried to comfort Mrs. Kendall. He noticed a silver serving set displayed on a mahogany sideboard. A home entertainment center, complete with a big-screen color television, sat in one corner of the room. He looked down at his shoes. The carpet was a thick-pile pastel that looked like real wool.

"Jesus, that was rough," Whittier said as they drove back downtown. Petrone knew that Whittier and Kendall socialized. The two detectives had worked together in narcotics for a couple of years. Whittier had only been in Homicide for ten months.

"Yeah, rough." Petrone was staring out the window. "I wonder if Mrs. Kendall has a job." Whittier glared at him and they finished the trip in silence.

Police headquarters was a madhouse. Three camera crews were already set up on the steps, and Petrone and Whittier had to push through dozens of reporters to get through the doors. "No comment," Petrone repeated calmly as they shouldered through the pack of barking journalists. "No comment."

The dead men's commanding officers could offer no explanation for the two officers' presence on the street together. They weren't working any investigation that could have linked the two of them. Petrone detected a hint of reserve in both lieutenants, especially Kendall's CO. He made a mental note to speak to Pete Tenesco in Internal Affairs before lunch.

The driver's license was a puzzle. He ran the name and license number through the National Crime Information Center computer and came up empty; there were no wants, warrants, or criminal history on the name. The address on the license was for a residence in Grand Rapids, Michigan, but the Grand Rapids police had never heard of Moffitt and told Petrone that the address was in fact that of the local Wal-Mart. He issued a pickup order for Paul Moffitt. Whoever he was.

The print technician returned the license just after twelve. "One clean thumb lift off the back. I'll run it through Printek, but don't hold your breath. It's tough to match a single."

Petrone nodded glumly. "Appreciate it. Hell, it's probably mine."

"It's not." The technician grinned. "I checked. You did good, Sergeant."

Petrone stared at the license photo intently. It showed a fortyish white male—the license said he was forty-one—with slightly curly brown hair cut just over his ears. It was an unremarkable face except for the eyes. Even through the steel-rimmed glasses—Petrone wondered if they were real or just accessories—the eyes were blank and cold, and Petrone caught a hint of arrogance in their flat stare at the camera. He turned the license over to the photo techs and asked for blowups of the picture.

He was at his desk reading the preliminary crime-scene reports when Pete Tenesco, the Internal Affairs chief, stuck his head through the office door.

"Got a minute, Milos?" Tenesco was carrying a pair of fat file folders.

Petrone swung his feet off his desk and pointed to an empty chair. "I was just going to call you," he said without surprise. "I have a feeling that you're going to tell me something I don't want to hear."

Tenesco pushed the files across the desk. "They were both dirty," he said without preamble. "We've been investigating them for three months, along with some others. They were working for Dink Reeves, which means they were working for Pointy Williams. Cheapjack stuff, mostly. Tip-offs about upcoming raids, information about ongoing gambling investigations, occasional services as security for big dope deals. We were going to put it in front of the grand jury next month."

Petrone sighed. "Reeves is a new player, but Pointy I know. He's whacked one or two people along the way, probably ordered a few more. I was at Kendall's house this morning. He had some toys not normally found in the home of a cop making thirty-nine thou a year."

Petrone opened the top file. It was Kendall's. Most of the sheets inside were surveillance photographs and wiretap transcripts. He shut the file. "I think we'll probably pick Mr. Reeves up for a talk." He stared levelly across his desk at Tenesco. "Pete, I'm going to ask you a very bad question. . . ."

"Whittier isn't involved. At least, not as far as we can tell. The investigation started when he was still in narco, and we found no evidence linking him to Kendall other than an occasional game of spades with the wives."

Petrone nodded. One less shitstorm on the horizon. He tapped the files. "Will I find the name Paul Moffitt anywhere in these?"

Tenesco crinkled his forehead in thought, then shook his head emphatically. "No. Never heard it before. You got something?"

Petrone told him about the driver's license. "There isn't much else. They were each shot twice. We found brass from four .45 shells in the car. No prints on the casings, not even smears. The guy wipes his shells before he fills his magazines, that's a pro. There was a kilo of coke on the seat between them. The lab thinks it's probably street shit, stepped on ten or fifteen times."

Petrone shook his head. "A couple of uniforms found a watchman at a factory a couple of blocks from the Chevy who says he saw a red car with one guy in it driving out of the area around six. He thinks the car was an import. That's all we have."

Petrone's phone buzzed. He picked it up, listened for a moment, grunted, and hung up. He looked bleakly at Tenesco. "The chief wants us in his office in five minutes. Big meeting. He says we have a major public-relations problem on our hands."

"No shit." Tenesco nodded. "He's bright, the chief is. He picks right up on shit like that."

"I guess that's why he makes the big bucks." Petrone stood up. "Let's go."

The chief ordered Petrone to handle the press conference. "I'll be there, but you do the talking," he said shortly. "Just tell them the usual." He'd spent a very uncomfortable twenty minutes briefing the police commissioner and the mayor and was, Petrone decided, ready to shit all over the first subordinate who looked at him sideways.

Petrone wondered what exactly was "the usual" for a double-cop killing. "I'd like to keep back the Moffitt ID for now."

"Keep back whatever the fuck you want, Milos." The chief scowled and lit a cigarette. The heavy glass ashtray on his desk was already overflowing. "Just give them enough to get most of them the hell out of here. You can't turn around out there without knocking down a goddamn reporter."

Petrone nodded.

"The mayor tells me he doesn't want this to turn into a media circus." The chief let out a sour laugh and shook his head. "I got two detectives with a kilo of coke between them shot to shit in an unmarked in the fucking Brickyard, don't even know what the fuck they were doing there, and he wants to avoid a media circus. Sweet Mother of God."

"How do we handle the Internal Affairs stuff?"

"Don't be an asshole, Milos." The chief stared at him. "We don't say word one about that. For the moment, these guys are dead fucking heroes. We'll worry about the Internal Affairs shit tomorrow. Or next month, or whenever. Besides, there are some angles on that you don't know about yet."

"Terrific. Okay." Petrone thought about Nick Maloney, the police reporter from the *Times*. Most of the print reporters assigned to the police beat were the next thing to rookies, and the TV people generally couldn't find their own ass with both hands and a Seeing Eye dog, but Maloney had close to twenty years as a crime reporter and was damn good at it. He stayed with it because he liked it and because over the years he had managed to get a couple of books out of it. Trying to shine Nick Maloney would be very tough. "When are we on?"

"Fifteen minutes. Print people gotta make deadline." The chief stubbed his cigarette and picked up his pack. "Shit. I'm out."

Later, Petrone decided that the press conference could have been worse. The first five minutes were complete chaos, with reporters all shouting questions at the same time. Petrone stood silently next to the chief at the podium, watching a department communications specialist hand out black-and-white glossy portrait shots of Kendall and Macnamara. Petrone didn't move until an uneasy silence fell over the assembled multitude. He noticed that Maloney stood at the back of the room.

The communications specialist read a carefully phrased statement that could have been edited down to "Two detectives were found shot to death this morning." As soon as he finished reading, chaos erupted again. Petrone waited patiently for order. A woman from the local ABC affiliate, ignoring the informal protocol that granted Maloney the first question on the basis of seniority, asked Petrone what kind of case the two detectives had been working on.

Stupid question, Petrone thought. "I can't offer any information that might compromise an ongoing investigation," he said blandly. He stared earnestly at the red lights of the cameras and wondered if his tie was straight. In the next ten minutes he provided the same basic answer to the same basic question four more times.

"No, there are no suspects at this time," he said in response to the next question. "We are pursuing a number of promising leads."

"What kind of weapon was used in the shooting?" The question came from a kid on the *Argus-Record*.

"Preliminary indications are that the two officers were killed with a large-caliber handgun. Both men were shot twice."

"Recover any slugs?" the kid asked.

Petrone realized to his surprise that he didn't know. "I haven't heard from the lab people yet," he said truthfully. "We'll provide details on the weapon as soon as they're available." He made a mental note to call the lab right away.

Maloney finally spoke up. "Sergeant, can you explain what the detectives were doing together in a department car on a day that both were scheduled off duty?"

Oh, shit, Petrone thought. Careful, careful. Maloney's contacts in the department were the best in town. "Again, Nick, I can't really comment on an open investigation." He fought the urge to put his hands in his pockets.

A murmur broke out among the reporters. Maloney smiled.

The chief stepped to the podium. "That's it, people. We'll have another press briefing at eight tomorrow morning." He and Petrone ignored the shouted questions that followed, and in a minute the herd thundered out of the room.

Maloney was waiting in the hall when Petrone started back to his office.

"I really don't have any time, Nick. Don't you have a deadline or something?" Petrone felt a dull sense of impending doom.

"I had a kid here to handle this." Maloney was tall, thin to the point of being cadaverous, with flat brown hair that Petrone suspected was dyed. A network of fine lines were etched between his nose and mouth, and pronounced bags were under his eyes. He took off his glasses, old-fashioned horn-rims, and used them to point back at the briefing room. "I didn't expect you guys to give up much."

"We gave you what we have, Nick." Petrone started to edge around the reporter. "I really gotta get back at it."

"I have the coke, Milos." Maloney dropped his notebook into the pocket of his jacket. "A kilo on the seat between them."

"Oh, shit," Petrone groaned. "I have to ask you to sit on that for a little bit, Nick."

"And if I do?"

Petrone thought quickly. Maloney was so close to the Internal Affairs probe that he might trip over it at any moment. Time for damage control. "All right. I'm going to be here for hours, but I'll call you at your apartment when I get home. I may have some things for you."

"Fair enough." Maloney peered at the detective. "They were dirty, weren't they, Milos?"

"I'll call you tonight, Nick." Petrone stepped around the reporter and hurried to his office. Everything was going to hell.

Rodney dropped Mackin outside Showalter's Show Lounge. Mackin had told him the story of the setup while they were on the road. "You need anything, you call."

Mackin looked in through the window. "You coming in?"

"Gotta date." Rodney put the car in gear and smiled. "She's better lookin' than you, Mackin."

"I may go back there, Rodney."

"Call me." His tone was noncommittal. The car pulled into traffic.

Mackin walked into the cool darkness of the bar and sat at a table in the back. The jukebox blared Guns N' Roses. A nude girl twisted languidly on the stage. The bartender, a bleached blonde in a tank top, hotshorts, and high heels, looked up from a crossword puzzle and came around the bar.

"Getcha something?" She looked thirty-five, thin and attractive. Mackin had never seen her before.

"Double bourbon, rocks." He looked around the almost empty club. "Jimbo around?"

She tossed her head toward the door next to the stage. "In the back. Want I should get him?"

Mackin nodded. "Tell him Mackin is here."

She opened the door and said something on her way back to the bar. A few seconds later Jimbo Showalter walked out of the office and joined him at the table. He was a big man, about fifty years old with a massive gray mustache and a salt-and-pepper fringe of hair around a shiny bald spot. He was showing a little weight, but Mackin knew that Showalter was still his own best bouncer. The bartender put a pair of drinks in front of them.

"Thanks, Maggie." Showalter's voice was deep and a little rough with smoke and Scotch. He stroked the back of her thigh as she turned away, and she offered a little shake.

Mackin laughed. "You doing her, Bo?"

Showalter smiled. "Sooner or later I do 'em all, Mackin. You know that. It's in the goddamn job description." He drained his drink in one extended swallow and leaned back. "Her name's Maggie. Been here a while, you haven't been in. Welcome home."

"I had a little problem."

"I heard." Showalter lowered his voice. "Riles called here an hour ago shitting cinder blocks."

Mackin sipped his bourbon and looked across the table. "What did he say?"

"He said the client called this morning and told him that you flipped out and blew two cops away on the street." Showalter sounded bored. "He said the client told him that you were a stone-crazy, psycho, murdering son of a bitch, and if you ever went back there, you'd be dead before you had time to park your car."

Showalter raised his glass toward the bar. "He was grumpy. He wants you to call him right away."

Mackin waited until Maggie deposited another drink in front of Showalter. "It was a setup," he said quietly. "The client, this black fucker named Pointy Williams, put me in a stolen car and had a couple of dirty cops waiting for me. I'm pretty sure they planned to whack me. I don't know what the fuck he was thinking of. I guess he wanted the twenty grand to go toward his payroll."

Showalter raised an eyebrow. "You hang on to the money?"

"Goddamn right I hung on to the money." Mackin finished his drink. "But it got real messy. There's a piece in that briefcase that's hotter than a five-hundred-dollar whore. Make it disappear."

Showalter nodded. "Anything else?"

"Yeah. There's some money in there, too. I need another gun, new ID, and credit cards."

"The paper will take a couple of days. I'll have the gun later tonight. Come by around ten." Showalter pulled a set of keys out of his pants pocket. "Your car is in the back."

A pair of dancers, a redhead and a blonde, walked into the bar. They both hugged Showalter on their way to the dressing room. Mackin grinned. "You got it made, you know that?"

"It's tough being me, Mackin." Showalter squeezed the redhead's backside as she walked away. "Takes up all my time. You going home?"

"For now." Mackin eyed the bartender and raised his empty glass. "Maybe I'll take Maggie with me."

"Be my guest." Showalter stood up with the briefcase. "So you're living the quiet life for a while?"

"Tonight all I'm interested in is taking some time to get to know your new bartender," Mackin said easily. "Maggie, right?"

"Maggie Raynor." Showalter grinned. "And no, I'm not doing her. You got a clear field of fire. She's a good kid."

Mackin watched as Maggie poured a drink. "Not too good, I hope."

Showalter leaned closer. "You had a big weekend. I think maybe you should think some more about taking some time off before you go back there."

"Can't let people start thinking they can turn me up, Bo." Mackin watched Maggie walk from the bar. He smiled. "Bad for business."

Sarah Petrone eyed the tomato critically for a moment, then shaved two thin slices from it with a knife from the butcher block on the kitchen counter. She set the tomato slices on her sandwich, used the knife to slather on some mustard, and cut the sandwich in half. She put a handful of potato chips on a paper plate, added the sandwich, and carried the plate and a glass of milk into the living room. It was a little before eleven P.M., and she'd only been home from work for an hour.

Her husband was sitting in his favorite chair near the picture window. Cold autumn rain drummed on the glass. Milos had a faraway look in his eye and was pinching his lower lip between his thumb and index finger. She sat down on the couch and balanced the paper plate on her knees. "You sure you don't want a sandwich, babe?"

Petrone looked up, distracted, then smiled. "No, thanks. I ate. You were late tonight."

"You're hopeless, Milos." She took a big bite from the sandwich and talked around it. "Quarterly audit. I told you. I have to work all weekend." Sarah Petrone was a vice president of one of the city's largest banks. "It happens every three months, remember?"

Petrone laughed. "I are a detective, huh? How's it going?"

"It's an audit. It's like watching paint dry, only more so." She drank some milk and looked critically at her husband of eighteen years. "I saw you on TV at work. You want to talk about it?"

He sighed. "I don't know. It was messy. Jack Kendall and Louis Macnamara. I think you met Kendall at the DARE benefit dinner last year. Good-sized fella, little bit of a pot on him, talked a lot about his cabin on the lake?"

Sarah squinted in recollection. "Vodka cranberry, brown suit, bad haircut, you didn't like him much."

"That's him." Petrone caught himself. "That *was* him. It looks like they were both working for a gangster type from the Brickyard named Williams."

"Pointy Williams." Sarah was nodding. "Not a good person."

Petrone stared at his wife wide-eyed. "How in hell do you know anything about Pointy Williams?"

"He *banks* with us, babe." Sarah took another bite from her sandwich. "The U.S. attorney has been expressing interest in Williams's bank records lately. I think Uncle Sam wants to put him away."

Petrone grinned. "You never cease to amaze me. We don't have a hell of a lot, but it looks like they were killed in some kind of drug deal gone bad. I think we have a picture of the killer." He told her about the driver's license.

He pushed himself out of the chair. "Now I have to call Nick Maloney and open negotiations to try to prevent him from putting a department-corruption story on the front page, at least until after we've got everything under control. Working with that guy is like trying to do a deal with the Vatican."

Sarah smiled. "You poor thing. And all he's ever done for you is put you in that book about the Townsend Lake Strangler and make you out to be the world's greatest detective."

"I guess I should be grateful. At least he's accurate."

5

IN MARCH 1984, a high school cross-country runner was training in the park surrounding Townsend Lake on the western
edge of downtown when he discovered the body of Caroline
Elaine Moore, age nineteen. She had been strangled with her
own panty hose. An autopsy revealed she had been raped prior
to her murder. Milos Petrone caught the squawk in Homicide,
Nick Maloney had it for the *Times*. Twenty-two weeks and four
bodies later, Maloney watched from a police surveillance van as
Petrone arrested Karl Randolph Dennerman, thirty-one, as the
killer left his apartment for his job at a suburban hospital.

Maloney earned his privileged position in the van across the
parking lot from Dennerman's apartment because the anonymous phone tip that identified the killer as a hospital orderly
had come to him at home and not to the police. He'd played
the tape for his editors and taken it to Petrone.

The caller was a woman. "Don't ask me who I am," she began nervously. "I have a friend named . . . well, I have a friend who went out with this guy. It was almost three years ago. He works at a hospital, he's like a male nurse or an attendant or something, and I think his name was Rick or Randy or something like that; anyway it started with an *R*. I never heard his last name."

Maloney sat silently in a red armchair in his living room, watching the tape roll on his recorder. Like all good reporters, he was an excellent listener. As with many good reporters, a tape recorder was always connected to his phone.

"She went out with him 'cause she'd just broken up with her boyfriend." The woman spoke in a low contralto. Maloney couldn't hear any background sound; her voice might have come from a vacuum. "She met him at a jazz club. He seemed nice, I guess. He took her to a Kenny Loggins show the first night. They went out two or three times. The last time they ended up at the lake. They started kissing and stuff, and he got . . . strange, I don't know. He put one of his hands on her throat, and when he kissed her, he started to squeeze a little bit. Susan didn't like that and she pushed his hand away. Then he got kind of crazy; she said his eyes got real weird and he grabbed her. . . ."

Maloney stared at his tape recorder. "What happened then?" he gently prompted.

He heard her take a deep breath. "He, he raped her, right there in the car. She said it was awful, he was saying things to her. He kept a hand on her throat the whole time, and at the end he was squeezing real hard and she couldn't breathe. A police car drove through the park right in the middle of the whole thing, and he didn't even stop. When he was done, he told her never to tell anyone what happened. He said he knew where she lived, and that no one went to prison for very long for rape, and that if she called the police and he went to jail, he'd spend all his time thinking about coming back to see her, and he pushed her out of the car and just drove away." She finished in a rush, as if the telling were less terrible when done quickly.

"Where's your friend now?"

"She moved. She went to Minnesota and moved in with her mom for a while. She's in therapy. She said his name was Randy or something, and that he worked at the hospital."

"What kind of car did Randy drive?" Maloney asked, but the woman hung up. The tape of the conversation was fifty-three seconds long.

"It could be nothing," Maloney said to Petrone the next morning. "Hell, it's the fifth call I've received at home since the first killing, although I admit it's a lot more coherent than most of them."

"I like it a lot more than the guy who told you Walter Mondale was committing the murders to discredit the Reagan administration," Petrone said. "I like it a lot more than that."

"We'll probably never find Susan, whoever she is." Petrone rewound the tape and played it again. "That part right there"— he pointed at the recorder—"about the police car driving through the park and our boyo carrying right on with his work, that scares the hell out of me. That sounds like a very bad, very cool customer. That sounds like our guy all the way." He looked up at the reporter. "What do I have to do to keep this out of tomorrow's paper?"

"We're cooperating, Milos. Short of cutting our own throat, anyway. My editors ask—please note that this is a request and not a demand—that I be allowed a high level of access to the investigation, and that you don't sell us out to the goddamn television sharks when you collar the bastard."

"Done," Petrone said promptly. "Your story. Here's what makes this interesting. You know VICAP, the FBI outfit that works serial killers?"

"Violent Criminal Apprehension Program." Maloney nodded. "I don't think they've actually caught one yet."

"They're claiming a piece of Wayne Williams down in Atlanta—"

"Everyone's claiming a piece of that little prick," Maloney interrupted. "Williams went down 'cause he dumped what may or may not have been a body off a bridge in front of what amounted to every police officer in the southeastern United States."

Petrone was shaking his head. "Not the point, Nick. The VICAP guys aren't really shoe-leather murder cops, but they're doing some really interesting work on psychological profiling. They've been working on our boyo since we found the second body, and one of the things they've suggested is that our guy has some kind of tie to the medical profession."

Maloney raised an eyebrow. "Like maybe a male nurse?"

"Like maybe a male nurse."

The Townsend Lake Strangler had killed four victims at the time of the telephone tip. He killed one more, a fourteen-year-old named Sarah Genvieve Lawson, before Petrone and the task force made it to Mathauss Memorial Hospital and learned that a personable young orderly named Karl was known to his friends as Randy. Exactly 117 days after Dennerman was sentenced to five consecutive life terms in the state penitentiary, and three weeks after *Reader's Digest* named Milos Petrone

Detective of the Year, Maloney presented Petrone with a copy of *Death at the Shore: The Townsend Lake Strangler*. The paperback was inscribed on the flyleaf. *If you'd let the bastard run up his score a little bit*, Maloney had written, *we'd all be rich and famous now*. And Petrone had smiled and said, "Walter Mondale would've made a better story."

Now Nick Maloney sat in that same aged, red Queen Anne chair staring at the small color television in his living room. A cable channel was airing another in the endless series of John Kennedy assassination "exposés." Occasionally his eyes would shift to the telephone on the table next to the chair. A motley pile of documents, photographs, and sheets of handwritten notes lay scattered on the floor near his feet. It was shortly before midnight.

Maloney's apartment was in an old downtown brownstone reclaimed from the fringe of the Brickyard by 1980s yuppies; his landlord was also his lawyer. The building was close enough to the river to allow him to walk to the shore in about five minutes, but far enough away from the water to keep the rent reasonable. Maloney had no objections to gentrification. He had spent two years of his childhood in the South Bronx and saw nothing ennobling about living in a slum.

A serious-looking man on the TV screen was using a pointer to indicate a manhole cover in Dealey Plaza that he believed marked the location of either the third or fourth shooter in the assassination; Maloney had lost count of exactly how many people this particular exposé was arguing had killed the president. He made a clicking sound of disgust and shook his head.

He answered the phone on the first ring. It was Petrone.

"How much you got, Nick?" the detective asked without preamble. He sounded tired.

"Jesus, Milos, you ought to turn your TV to channel four. There's a talking head on right now who says the entire staff of the Federal Trade Commission was in Dealey Plaza to kill the president 'cause of the steel thing."

"Not tonight, Nick. I've got a couple of murders of my own to worry about, and they aren't the kind that interest Oliver Stone. So what do you got?"

Maloney leaned over and pawed at the pile of paper at his feet. "I told you this afternoon, Milos," he said easily, "I've got the cocaine in the car with 'em. I know it was a day off for both of them, that they usually took days off together, and that they weren't working on anything for the department. I've got enough to write a six-take story for page one that says the two of them went down in a dope deal gone bad, and I don't think my editor will have any problem with it." He pulled a copy of one of the crime-scene photographs out of the pile.

"Yeah, well, it could be more complicated than that. There's all sorts of shit coming down, Nick. If it were as simple as a couple of bad cops, I could probably live with your story, but I don't think it's that simple." The detective fell silent.

"I've got what I've got, Milos." Maloney looked critically at the photograph. In black and white, the blood spread across the front seat of the car looked black, as if someone had poured tar over the two dead men. "If there's a reason for me not to write a six-take story about a dope burn, tell me what the reason is."

Petrone sighed. "Look, you were right about them being dirty. IA was going to put both of them in front of a grand jury next month and start cutting them up in little pieces, and there's more, a lot more, but until you and I work something out, I never said that."

Maloney grinned. He'd spent an hour with the city editor and managing editor of the *Times* working out an arrangement. "Same deal as before, Milos?"

"Same as before." There was relief in Petrone's voice. "You sit on this a few days, and what you end up with will make it worth your while."

Maloney's grin widened. "We need to meet."

Petrone groaned, "Not *tonight*, Nick. I'm married, for Christ's sake. Sarah just walked in the house, asked me who the hell I am. Tomorrow. I'll call you tomorrow."

"Don't fuck me with the TV people, Milos."

"Nick," Petrone said earnestly, "hear me on this: I would turn in my badge and gun and take up another career sucking off sheep for a dollar a head before I gave those ghouls the time of day."

"My best to Sarah, Milos."

At the other end of the line, Petrone gently hung up the phone.

Sarah stared at him with disapproval. "That last bit about sheep just might be the most disgusting thing I've ever heard come out of your mouth."

He smiled. "Let's go to bed and see if I can top it."

"Baa, baa, baby."

6

MAGGIE RAYNOR started stripping because it was easy and she needed money in a hurry. She was nineteen years old the first time and had been married to Billy Raynor for three months. They lived in Chula Vista, California, just outside San Diego.

Dancing was Billy's idea. He knew a couple of strippers. Billy ran with a fast crowd; it was one of the things about him that attracted Maggie. He was trying to start an automotive body shop, and she wanted to help. One of Billy's friends got her a job in a big club called the Red Garter.

"We kind of frown on dancers fucking the customers," the club manager told her. "That's why I prefer married girls. Joint like this is always a headline away from a prostitution bust, anyway." A dancer named Caitlin made it explicit: "You don't have to sleep with anyone, honey," she said, waving a languid arm to include the entire club interior. "Just wiggle that butt of yours in their lap for two or three minutes, let 'em cop a feel or two, and they'll give you twenty bucks. In here, the more you put out, the more you bring in."

Over the next four months Maggie gave her husband more than ten thousand dollars in cash. Billy used the money for a down payment on a hydraulic lift and a full set of shop tools.

"I don't think I want you dancing anymore," he told her the night he bought the gear. "We don't need the cash that bad."

"One more month," Maggie told him. "I want a new car." She could tell he was unhappy. He'd come into the Garter two or three times after she started working there, but never stayed long. Maggie wasn't too concerned. The job had given her her first taste of financial independence, and she liked the feeling of strength that came with it.

Two weeks later Billy walked into the Garter and saw her kissing a customer in a dark corner of the club. He turned and walked out without speaking to her. That night they fought.

"It's only for another couple of weeks," she said, but he wasn't mollified.

"You look just like a whore in there." He was a little bit drunk.

"You didn't say anything like that when I was giving the money to you," she shot back, and then he hit her. She left him and a year later they were divorced; by then Billy was on probation for running a chop shop.

She never saw him again and rarely thought of him. The Garter paid for the divorce and a new Mustang, and once the marriage was dissolved she got an agent and went on the road for a few years. There had been men along the way, some of them good, others not, none of them really memorable. A guy in Los Angeles offered to marry her, but he produced pornographic movies for a living and wanted her to appear in them. He told her he'd make her a "star" and seemed honestly surprised when she declined.

She'd told Mackin none of this because he hadn't asked. She wondered if he ever would.

"You got a regular girl?" she asked. She was up on one elbow in Mackin's bed. It was seven o'clock in the morning. She had come home with him the night before when he picked up his briefcase from Showalter.

"Just you, angel." Mackin was pulling on a pair of chino slacks. His hair was still wet from the shower. He wasn't lying. His life didn't allow much time for relationships. He smiled when she laughed.

"Aren't you a smooth-tongued bastard," she said. "I kind of like you."

"Then get your beautiful ass out of that bed and make me some coffee." He bent over and kissed her quickly, then walked to the closet and found a shirt.

Maggie pushed the covers back and swung her feet to the floor. She was thirty-four, with long legs, a slim waist, and small, proud breasts. Mackin had been right, the blond hair came out of a bottle, but it was full and thick and smooth. She put on Mackin's bathrobe. "Where's the coffee?"

"Refrigerator," he said absently. He put on a pair of leather loafers, no socks, and picked up a brush. He had slipped out of bed while she was still sleeping. "I kind of like you, too," he said as she padded out of the bedroom.

She turned, but he was in the bathroom and out of sight.

She walked into the kitchen and started the coffee. Mackin's apartment was in a quiet suburban subdivision, an upper-class community withdrawn from the rigors of the city. He had used an electronic key card to open the security gate when they arrived. He lived in a corner unit with two bedrooms.

Maggie hadn't really looked around the night before—they both had other things on their minds and never even managed to turn on the lights—but in the sunlight she saw that the apartment was furnished with antiques. A cherrywood buffet, lovingly restored, was centered on one wall. The sofa and matching chair were overstuffed Victorians done in a subdued floral print. A grandfather clock almost seven feet tall sat stolidly in the far corner, and one wall was lined entirely with oak bookcases.

She walked to one of the bookcases and removed a volume from the top shelf. It was obviously old. The dust jacket was old and a little stiff and protected by a clear plastic wrapper. She looked at the title. *An American Tragedy,* by someone named Dreiser.

"That's a signed Dreiser first." Mackin was watching her from the bedroom door.

"You have a beautiful place." She put the book back on the shelf. "What's a signed first?"

He smiled. "A first edition signed by the author."

"You collect books?"

"A little bit." Mackin walked into the kitchen. "Where's that coffee?"

She followed him into the kitchen and put her arms around him from behind. "Coming up." She was a couple of inches shorter, and she nestled her head against the back of his neck. "I had fun last night."

"So did I." He opened a cabinet and removed two coffee cups. "Cream is in the refrigerator. Sugar's on the breakfast bar."

The kitchen was immaculate. "You're a neat freak," she said accusingly.

"So they say." He sat down and lightly thumped his coffee cup on the bar. "Service, wench."

"I got your service, mister." She brought the coffeepot to the bar and watched him pour. He drank it black.

She filled her cup. She liked his smile. "What do you do, Mackin?"

He shrugged. "I'm an independent contractor. Kind of a consultant. Some real estate, that kind of thing."

She remembered exploring his body the night before. Even in the moonlight she could tell the puckered depression in his back was a scar from a bullet wound.

She had asked Bo Showalter about his friend when Mackin left the club the first time. "It's like this, baby," Bo said casually. "There's guys that think they're hard guys. There's guys that aren't hard guys and know it. And there's hard guys. Mackin is a hard guy."

Then Showalter grinned. "And so am I."

She sipped her steaming coffee and wondered what kind of consulting Mackin did.

The fingerprint technician was waiting in Petrone's office. "Tell me you love me." He was sitting on the corner of Petrone's desk.

"You're shitting me." Petrone stared at him, his coat half-removed.

"Gotta hit on the thumbprint from the license." The technician waved a computer printout.

Petrone's face split in a wide smile.

"It ain't much." The technician glanced down at the report.

"It matches a partial lift from a vault job in Atlanta four years ago. Miracle we made it. The partial was the only print Atlanta came up with."

"Better than nothing." Petrone finished pulling off his coat and hung it over the back of his chair. "Hell of a lot better than nothing."

The technician grinned. "Welcome to the computer age, Sarge."

"We can't do shit with those stamps," Dink Reeves said. He was in Pointy Williams's office. Pointy was at his desk and Beano-D was sitting next to the door. A shotgun was leaning on Beano's chair.

"Tell me 'bout it." Pointy had cooled off once he realized that the thief wasn't going to be charging up the stairs at any moment. Now he was all business. A little late, Dink thought. "Looks like I'm out twenty grand. Fuck."

"Twenty-two," Dink said. "Scooter and Danny went a grand each."

"Shit." Pointy rapped his knuckles lightly on his desk. "Plus our end of the stamps. Maybe we can move them cross-state or something."

Dink shook his head. "Chicago was our only grocery connection, and they sure as fuck don't want 'em now. I don't think we should be making no waves, Pointy. Things be hot at the moment. Probably oughtta just burn 'em."

"Goddamn crazy motherfucker. Quarter million stamps good as cash, and they be no better than toilet paper to me." Pointy stood up and shrugged. "Lose 'em, Dink. I ever get my hands on that thief, I'll shoot him two hundred fifty thousand fuckin' times."

Reeves pulled a cigarette out of the pack in his shirt pocket. His cigarettes were extralong and wrapped in brown paper. They smelled faintly of cinnamon. People only laughed at them once. "I don't get why you did it, Pointy."

"Did what?"

"Why you tried to shake down the thief. He goes home pissed off, he calls Riles, we get the fuckin' Italians all over our ass. I don't see no percentage for us."

"He wasn't supposed to go home." Williams walked to the window and shoved his hands into his pockets. "Kendall and Macnamara were gonna put him back in the Toyota and do the fucker. They keep the twenty gs, leave the coke, it looks like a dope burn or some shit. We call Riles, tell him his boy went out playing with the wrong people and got himself killed. Whose fault is that? That thief ain't no made man, he ain't no Italian. Just be a bad break. I thought it was a good way to build some bridges with the goddamn police. They were being jerk-offs lately."

Dink nodded. He thought it was the craziest idea he'd ever heard come out of Pointy Williams's mouth. "They ain't gonna be jerkin' anyone off no more. I think we best just chill shit for a while, Pointy." He lit the cigarette with a flat black lighter. "Cops got their balls in an uproar over Kendall and Macnamara. Maybe you oughtta split for a little bit."

"Yeah. Gotta point." Williams nodded. "There any way that cocaine can come back on us?"

"I'll handle it. It'll be cool. They figure out those guys worked for us, I'll probably have to go downtown. I'll talk to Simons."

Ralph Simons was the attorney of record for Pointy's operation.

"We have another problem," Dink said.

Pointy scowled.

"Riles is very unhappy," Dink said. "He says that he provided a service in good faith. He thinks we fucked him over, made him look bad. I think maybe this Moffitt guy is a friend of his."

"What the fuck am I supposed to do about that?"

"I don't think we want anybody in Chicago pissed off at us. I think maybe we should work something out."

Pointy jumped out of his chair. "How am I supposed to work it out when I can't move the stamps? I'm supposed to just be signing checks over to some greaseball in Chicago? How much? Ain't I lost enough on this deal already?"

"Riles is a connected guy. He *is* a made man. Not a guy to fuck around with. Them Chicago Italians ain't like our Italians. They still kill people."

Pointy sat quietly for a moment, then sighed. "Shit. Work something out. This is killing me."

Dink nodded. "He also said this thief is a stand-up badass," he said carefully. "He said this guy's liable to come back looking for trouble."

From next to the door, Beano-D laughed.

"I hope he does," Pointy snapped. "I'll kill the son of a bitch myself." He walked over to a large plant in a heavy brown ceramic pot sitting beneath the window overlooking Amsterdam Street. "I think I'll take Cassandra to Miami for a week or two. Get some beach. You be okay?"

"No problem." Dink smiled. "I'll handle things."

Petrone stared out his office window and grimaced. It was the day after the press conference.

Item: A plainclothesman in Vice was told by one of his

regular street informants that a man named Paul Moffitt was the shooter in the cop killings.

Item: Someone using Moffitt's name had reserved a first-class seat on a flight to New York at about the time Petrone and Whittier had reached the Chevy the day before, but no one had picked up the ticket.

Item: The thumbprint on the Moffitt driver's license matched a latent left at the scene of a bank robbery in Atlanta. It was a very professional piece of work, a full crew that burned into the vault over the weekend and walked out with $373,000 in cash and bearer bonds and an undetermined amount of money and jewels from rifled safety-deposit boxes. Thanks to a tip, Atlanta PD picked up two guys from the crew in less than a month. They were both experienced, they both kept their mouth shut, and they both had alibis. They walked. Word on the street was that the job had been put together by a guy from out of town.

"You really need to talk to this insurance guy," the detective in Atlanta Robbery told him. "Hang on, let me find it. . . . John Lockhart, Allied-Commercial Reinsurance. He's in Hartford."

Petrone called him. Lockhart was an insurance investigator. He didn't have good news. "If this guy is in your city on a holiday weekend," he told Petrone, "you're about to hear of a big, big score. I'll be on the next plane."

Item: After twenty-four hours of turning the city upside down, there was no indication at all that Paul Moffitt, whoever he was, was anywhere to be found.

Petrone sighed and called the chief. "I think we better give the Moffitt picture to the media," he said. Downstairs the dispatcher was sending the first black-and-white units to Felton Industrial Printing.

7

MACKIN had a Keogh plan.

He spent ten or twelve days a year keeping himself legal. The second bedroom of his apartment was his office, and the four-drawer, fireproof filing cabinet next to the desk contained a complete paper history for Score, Inc., the company that provided Mackin with his visible living. The name was Bo Showalter's idea. It had taken ten years for Mackin to put it all together—a couple of small apartment buildings, an auto body shop, a small piece of Showalter's bar. He had never committed a crime in Missouri. He filed his taxes scrupulously each year; on paper he never made more than $48,000 a year.

Except for Showalter's, all of Mackin's holdings were out of town. He was almost invisible in Kansas City, one anonymous businessman among thousands. Three or four times a year he sat down at his personal computer and began the laborious process of moving money from a bank in Belgium through a pair of Delaware shell corporations into Score, Inc. All of his securities holdings were administered through the overseas bank.

A construction contractor recommended by Showalter had installed a false wall in the back of Mackin's bedroom closet. Behind it, Mackin kept a half dozen clean weapons, ammunition, and his get-out bag—a packed suitcase with a clean set of identification, credit cards, and $50,000 in cash. None of the guns had been purchased in Mackin's name, and none had ever been used in the commission of a crime. The .45 Mackin had used in the Chevy had come from the closet, and the replacement Showalter provided took its place.

"Eddie has the paper at the club," Showalter told him over the phone. "He'll be there tonight. He'll want money."

Mackin called Maggie. "You working tonight?"

"Just until eight." She was pleased that he called. She hadn't seen him since she'd left his apartment.

"Ever been to Rayz?"

"A couple of times. I like to dance."

"I'll pick you up at the club. Be nice to me, and I'll feed you."

"Very nice." She laughed. "I promise."

It was just after noon. Mackin got in his car, a two-year-old Bronco, and drove to a suburban mall. A bank of public telephones were inside the doors. He called a number in Chicago.

"This is Mackin. Ask Frank Riles to call me." He read the number from the front of the phone. It rang in three minutes. "Mackin."

"I had no fucking idea, Mackin." There was exasperation in the other man's voice. "I thought Williams was a straight-up guy. I've worked with him on one or two things, he's never pulled a stunt like this. The fucker used me. He used us. You want, I'll drop a dime and he'll be dead tomorrow morning."

"I'll take care of whatever needs to be done, Frank." Mackin automatically scanned the busy mall. A teenager in a black T-shirt picked up the phone two positions away and dropped a quarter in the slot. Ragged white letters across the front of the shirt read EITHER YOU ROCK OR YOU SUCK. Mackin grinned. "I may have to go back and talk to Pointy, work this thing out."

"I got no problem with that, Mackin. I'll send flowers."

"I'll need some information on Pointy's business, Frank. Help me out?"

"Anything you need, Mackin."

"I'll be up day after tomorrow." Mackin hung up the phone. As he walked out the door of the mall, he heard the kid in the T-shirt say, "Oh, baby, that ain't *right*," into the phone.

"You rob a bank, you don't really hurt the bank," Lockhart said. He had come straight to Petrone's office from the airport. His luggage was on the floor. Petrone guessed he had already seen fifty, but he carried it very well. Ex-FBI, Petrone thought. Bureau guys all carry it well. "And you don't really hurt the insurance company. You hurt the reinsurance company. That's us."

The night before, all four local evening newscasts led with updates on the police shootings, followed by stories on the robbery at the printing plant. Petrone had watched the video of the security guard being wheeled into an ambulance on a gurney. A detective sergeant named Hamilton was handling the job for Robbery. Petrone and Lockhart were to meet with him in an hour.

Lockhart's briefcase was an extralarge model with extended flaps that closed over the handle. "Insurance companies farm out their risk to reinsurance companies," he said. He removed a pack of cigarettes from the briefcase.

"Sounds like how bookies lay off bets." Petrone pushed an ashtray across the desk.

"Exactly. Take that Atlanta job, three hundred seventy-three thousand dollars. The insurance carrier took a hit for ten percent. We took a hit for almost three hundred and fifty grand."

"Ouch."

"On the basis of MO, I've got this character down for five, maybe six major scores in the past four years. I haven't had a chance to work back any further, but I suspect he's been around for a lot longer than that. He's a very cool customer, very professional." He looked down at the blowup of the license photo. "I can't believe you actually got a picture of him."

"I want the son of a bitch for killing two cops."

"Can't figure that. This guy doesn't strike me as the type to run a red light and flip out. Like I said, a very cool customer."

"It doesn't look like a blown-up traffic stop." Petrone described the crime scene.

"Shakedown?" Lockhart stubbed his cigarette.

"Possible. I can't figure the money and the handcuffs. Kendall, at least, was too smart to let a suspect talk his way out of cuffs. And I can't figure the gun. They were shot with a .45. Where the hell did that come from?"

Petrone stood up and stretched. He'd slept only three hours the night before. "If this guy did the printing plant and the shooting, we're looking at a one-man fucking crime wave."

Whittier knocked and entered the office. He'd spent the past hour with Pete Tenesco, examining the Internal Affairs files on Kendall and Macnamara. His eyes were dull. "I didn't know, Milos. Honest to God."

"I know, Larry."

"We still gotta take this guy down."

"Absolutely."

Dink Reeves was making the rounds. One by one, he stopped at the whorehouses, the street corners, the crack houses, talking in low tones to a collection of pimps, dealers, and gamblers. His message was always the same: "Things heating up over this cop thing. Pointy be out of town. Keep things quiet a little bit." Beano-D was at his side, silent and watchful.

A three o'clock in the afternoon, as the two of them walked down a cracked sidewalk in the Brickyard, a black-and-white jerked over to the curb in front of them. Two uniformed cops shot out of the car and walked toward them. Both of them had their hands on their gun butts. Reeves and Beano-D stood quietly, watching them.

"Want to talk to you downtown, Reeves," one of the cops said.

Beano-D vaguely remembered a scene from a television movie he'd watched recently. "You got a warrant?"

The second cop stared at him through mirrored sunglasses. "One more fuckin' word out of you, shitbird," he said in a bored voice, "I'll put you down like an old rug."

Reeves raised a hand. "No problem." He turned to Beano. "Call Simons. Tell him to meet me downtown, and tell him I don't want to wait." He walked to the black-and-white, opened the door, and climbed into the backseat.

They drove him to the station in silence and deposited him in an interview room. The bulletin board on the wall was covered with grainy black-and-white surveillance photos of Reeves together with Kendall and Macnamara. Dink ignored them. After thirty minutes, Petrone and Tenesco walked into the room.

Picking up Reeves was Petrone's idea. "If the shooting was because of a shakedown, and the shakedown was related to the printing-plant job, then Reeves knows something," he had said.

"Iffy," Tenesco had replied. "Very iffy. We don't have much leverage. With Kendall and Macnamara dead, I'm not sure we can make corruption charges against Reeves stand up for the grand jury."

Dink was sitting with his arms crossed. "I'm not saying a word until my lawyer gets here," he said calmly.

"He's right behind us," Petrone said. He and Tenesco sat down across the table. "We got a little problem, Dink," Petrone said easily.

Reeves sat quietly.

"We know that Kendall and Macnamara were working for you," Tenesco said. He didn't bother to raise his voice. The good-cop-bad-cop routine was so well known that it didn't even work on stupid hoods, let alone someone as streetwise as Dink Reeves. "Now they're dead. We thought maybe you could help us out."

Ralph Simons bustled into the room. "Hello, Milos," he said cheerfully. "Detective Tenesco. What seems to be the problem here?"

"Your client had a relationship with the two detectives killed over the weekend," Tenesco said flatly. "We're hoping he can help us out."

"I see." The lawyer looked from the detective to Reeves. One index finger tapped against his lip.

"We just want to talk," Petrone said.

"Can I have ten minutes, please?" Simons opened the door of the interview room like an usher. "Thank you," he said pleasantly as the detectives walked out.

He looked at Reeves. "Tell me about it."

Reeves pointed to the pictures on the bulletin board. "Pulled me off the street. The cops did some business for me. I don't know anything about them getting shot."

Simons examined the photos. "Do they have concrete evidence of the officers accepting money in return for criminal acts?"

"All I've seen so far is those pictures, but they ain't really talked to me yet."

Simons stroked his chin.

"These two cops," Dink began, "they took care of some—"

Simons held up his hands, palms out. "Don't tell me." He walked over and opened the door. "Come in, gentlemen."

The detectives filed into the room.

"Are you planning to charge my client with respect to the shootings?" Some of the pleasantness had left the attorney's voice.

"Christ, no," Petrone said. "We just want to talk."

"Planning to charge Mr. Reeves with respect to the alleged bribery?"

Tenesco glanced at Petrone. "Not at this time," Tenesco said shortly.

"My client assures me that he has no information about the death of the detectives." Simons spread his hands on the table. "I think that, in the absence of any charges, we'll be leaving."

"One second." Petrone shook out a cigarette. "Let me run this past you, Dink. We have a professional thief come to town, take down more than two hundred thousand dollars in food stamps. We have evidence—hard evidence—that the thief was in the car with the dead detectives. We know that you and the detectives did some business."

Simons stood up. "Then I think, Detective Petrone, you should be looking for your thief." He touched Reeves on the shoulder, and the two of them walked to the door.

"See you around, Ralph," Petrone said to the lawyer's back. "Appreciate all the help."

Salvatore Capetti pinched his fingers in the pliers and swore violently under his breath. He was hanging a bird feeder from the elm tree in his backyard. The elm was huge, more than eighty years old, with a massive green canopy that kept the back of Capetti's two-story house cool in the heat of Chicago's summers. Now the leaves had started to turn. Capetti was standing halfway up an aluminum stepladder, wiring the bird feeder to the lowest branch with the remnants of a coat hanger.

"I have the stock certificates for Consolidated with me," Riles said. He was holding the legs of the ladder. Raymond, his driver and bodyguard, was in the kitchen having coffee with Capetti's wife, Maria.

"Those you should probably take to the accountant." Capetti twisted the wire one last time. "There. That will make Maria happy." He carefully stepped down the rungs of the ladder. He was sixty-seven years old. "It makes her sad to see the birds with nothing to eat."

Riles stepped away from the ladder. "There's a problem."

Capetti sighed. "I think maybe I ought to see that chiropractor you talk about." He put his hands in the small of his back and stretched. "Always there are problems, Francis. What is it this time?"

"The food stamp score. Williams tried to rip off the thief, and it all went to hell." Riles briefly described his conversations with Williams and Mackin.

Capetti grinned. "Which one is lying? Or are they both?"

"Williams, I think," Riles said carefully. "Mackin is a straight-up operator, a professional. Drugs aren't his thing, and there is no way on God's earth he'd ice two guys just to kill time. Williams probably planned it from the beginning. His guy Reeves sounded kind of hinky over the phone when I called to let them know the deal was down. I think Williams thought he could cut some corners with us."

"Not smart." Capetti shook his head. "Williams is greedy, Francis. Greedy people make mistakes. But he has been our friend in the past, is that not so?"

"Sure." Riles nodded. They walked to the flower beds that lined the back fence of the yard. "We've done some good business. The thing is, Mackin's been good to us, too. He's real pissed off. He's not being real rational about this, if you know what I mean. He wants to go back and even things up."

Capetti lowered himself carefully to his knees. "This time of year, everything goes dormant, dies." He extended a bony finger and prodded a plant that was listless and barely green. Riles had no idea what kind of plant it was. "How much are we out?"

"Consolidated's out maybe a quarter mil because there is no fucking way we want anything to do with those stamps. That's not real money, though. We would've had to trickle the stamps through the system so slow that we barely would've noticed the income. Direct, short term, we're not hurt."

Capetti grasped Riles's hand and slowly pulled himself to his feet. "Our pride, Francis. Only our pride. Does this friend of yours want our help?"

Riles shook his head. "Not direct. Mackin handles things on his own. He's gonna want some information."

"Will he kill Williams, do you think?"

"Hard to say." They turned and walked toward the house. "I think he wants to knock Williams down a few notches. He's a thief, Sal. He'll probably rip Pointy off."

"This is what you do. You give the thief what he wants. We owe him that because he has been our friend. Then you call Mr. Pointy Williams and ask him to make a gesture to us because of the stamps. Not the full amount, of course. Just a token. For our pride."

Riles nodded. Raymond appeared silently on the back porch. "Start the car, Ray. We're through."

Capetti frowned at the tree. "It's sad, Francis. I think the Dutch elm is taking it. This time next year it will be dead."

8

MACKIN walked into Showalter's Lounge at a quarter till eight. Bo was nowhere in sight. Maggie was behind the bar serving the beginning of the evening rush, a mostly blue-collar crowd that drank lots of beer. A couple of the dancers were carrying fishbowls through the crowd, collecting money for the jukebox. Mackin smiled. The jukebox was wired so that it didn't require money; the girls split the cash from the fishbowls backstage.

"Look at you," Maggie said. "You're almost . . . respectable."

Mackin was wearing a sports coat, black flecked with gray, over black slacks. His shirt was white with French cuffs, and his tie was very thin and very red. He smiled. "We won't get through the door at Rayz, you don't change," he said.

Maggie was wearing her usual work uniform, which meant she wasn't wearing much. "Just you wait till I get off. I've got an outfit in the back." She put a double bourbon on the bar in front of him and went back to work.

As soon as her relief showed up, she cashed out and vanished. She reappeared in fifteen minutes wearing a deep purple minidress, dark hose, and black high heels. A heavy gold brooch was pinned over her left breast, and she'd piled her hair up in a carefully arranged twist. Mackin smiled as every head at the bar turned to watch her walk past.

"I approve." He lifted his glass. "I think I'll consent to be seen with you now."

She hit him on the shoulder. "I'm starving. Take me somewhere nice."

Mackin nodded. "We'll eat. I expect you'll need your energy before the night is over." He drained his glass and took her elbow. They walked out to the Bronco.

He took her to Mitchell's, a small, elegant downtown restaurant. They ate a leisurely dinner. Maggie told him that she was from San Diego.

"California?" He looked quizzical. "I thought good little Midwestern girls went west, not the other way around."

She grinned. Mackin was learning to like her grin. "I worked out there as a dancer for a few years, got tired of it. Last year I met this guy, kind of a jerk, actually. He came out here for some kind of job a couple months ago, and I followed him. He dumped me."

She didn't sound overly upset. "So I got a job with Bo. I haven't decided what I'm going to do. I like tending bar, but the real money is up onstage, and I think my days of wearing my panties on my head are over."

Mackin lit cigarettes for both of them. "He was a fool."

"Bo?" She looked shocked.

"The guy that dumped you."

She smiled. "Thanks. I think so, too."

He handed her cigarette across the table. "And as far as I'm concerned, you can wear your panties on your head anytime you want."

They finished their dinner over small talk.

"How would you like to drive up to Chicago with me for a couple of days?" he asked casually as the waiter cleared the table.

"When?"

"Day after tomorrow." He sipped his coffee.

"I have to work." She sounded disappointed.

"We can probably get around that." He eyed her over the wineglass. "I'd enjoy your company. Show you the town."

"I've never been there. It's a date." She smiled, reached across the table, and covered his hand with her own.

They left the restaurant and drove to Rayz. The small parking lot of the club was completely packed, and Mackin had to leave the Bronco a couple of blocks away.

Rayz was, at least for the moment, the hottest club in Kansas City. A line of hopeful, well-dressed entrants was always at the door. Tonight the line snaked down the sidewalk. Mackin led Maggie to the front of the line. A doorman with a shaved head who looked like three hundred pounds of bored menace eyed the two of them without interest. He wore jeans and a sleeveless denim jacket. His massive arms were covered with tattoos. A velvet rope barred the open doors behind him.

"Full house tonight," he said. "Might have to wait awhile. Line forms at the rear."

"I'm here to see Eddie. He's expecting me."

"You're Mackin." The doorman nodded, straightened up, and lifted one end of the rope. "Eddie's at his table."

A young man with dark hair near the front of the line stepped up. He was wearing an expensive pastel suit and had his arm around a blond girl's waist. The blonde was pretty and drunk. "Hey," he said angrily, "we've been waiting out here for almost half an hour. Who the hell does this guy—"

The doorman's head swiveled lazily and he stared into the man's eyes. "Why don't you shut the fuck up and get back in line," he said calmly.

Mackin slipped a folded twenty into the pocket of the doorman's jacket. "Appreciate it."

Maggie grinned as they stepped into the club. Behind her, she heard the doorman's bored voice. "Put your money away and don't be an asshole," he was saying to the man with the blonde.

Milos Petrone and John Lockhart were standing in the security storeroom of Felton Industrial Printing. It was a large, one-story warehouse with a cracked concrete floor and cinder-block walls. Half a dozen pallets stacked with taped cardboard cartons were shoved against one wall. A pile of empty pallets was in the center of the room. Crumpled sheets of brown wrapping paper, torn cardboard, and wadded shipping tape were scattered across the floor. The storeroom's single, steel-reinforced door lay in a pile of greasy, black ash on the floor where it had fallen. The door had been painted bright red, but heat from the burning bar had made the paint blister and peel. It was eleven P.M.

"Like opening a walnut with a goddamn jackhammer." Leonard Hamilton, a detective sergeant in Robbery, was staring at the warped door. "Overkill."

Lockhart was examining the scorched doorjamb. "Embedded interior security hinges. You want to dick around for an hour and a half, you drill. You want to get the damn job done, get the hell outta here, you burn."

Petrone pointed to the cartons against the wall. "Our boyos miss some, Len?"

Hamilton snorted. "No way, Milos. Those are blank community-college transcript forms. When they load the cartons off the press, they tape an example of what's inside to the top of the box. Labeled for your convenience. The thieves didn't even have to cut 'em open to check."

Petrone gazed around the room. "I don't suppose you found shit on toast, did you?"

"No prints, no partials," Hamilton said. "Night watchman didn't even hear the guy who sapped him, let alone see him. We don't know for sure how many of them there were, for chrissakes. We got a partial tire track that probably came from a van or light truck, but we won't know if it's from one of the printer's vehicles until tomorrow. It probably doesn't make any difference, because it ain't much of a partial. There were two impressions from athletic shoes in the ashes. The first uniform on the scene smeared one of them. The other is an Adidas. I figure there are two hundred twenty-seven billion shoes in town that'll match it."

Hamilton pulled a briar pipe, dull with age, from his jacket pocket and clamped it between his teeth. "Expect an arrest momen-fucking-tarily, Milos. Count on it." The two detectives stared at each other and burst into sour laughter.

Petrone looked at Lockhart, who had finished his examination of the doorjamb. "You hungry? Let's eat."

Half an hour later they were in a booth in an all-night restaurant. Petrone was methodically destroying a platterful of chicken-fried steak and mashed potatoes. Lockhart stared dubiously at his hamburger and fries. Petrone had picked the restaurant. It was a little past midnight.

"Where's your partner?" Lockhart said. "Whittier?"

"Not my partner," Petrone said around a mouthful of potatoes. He swallowed and dabbed a napkin at his lips. "Christ, I've been hungry for days. Growing boy. We're both in Homicide, but we're not really partners. He's at a wake." He drained half his coffee and leaned back in the booth. "Kendall's wake. Look, John—you mind I call you John? . . . Good. Look, Larry is no rocket scientist, but he's a pretty good cop. It's just that he's decided to treat this thing like *Hamlet* or *Macbeth* or something, y'know? He's a little bit crazy right now, 'cause Kendall was a friend of his and Kendall's wife is a friend of his wife and they all used to sit around on Wednesday nights playing cards. Now he's found out that Kendall was a corrupt piece of dogshit, and that makes Whittier and his wife look like fools, so he's gonna run around like Duncan and slay the slayer. At least, that's what he talks about doing when he's not tearing his hair and gnashing his teeth and screaming imprecations at the stormy night sky." He burped, then gestured to the waitress for more coffee.

Lockhart barked out a sharp laugh. "You're a cold son of a bitch, Milos."

Petrone shook his head. "I'm a realist. So anyway, Larry isn't going to be much use to us on this thing, at least not for a while. You gonna eat that burger?"

Lockhart grimaced. "I'm still waiting to see if it moves. Tell me about this Pointy Williams guy. You figure he set up the printing-plant job?"

"Probably. I guess." Petrone looked thoughtful. "It's just a bit out of Pointy's league, if you know what I mean. Food stamps aren't like cash. Unless you plan to stand around on street corners hawking them to the homeless, you've got to have some sophisticated means to convert them into real money. Pointy's still pretty much a street guy. A smart guy, sure, but still street."

The waitress filled their coffee cups. "Pointy's been top dog in the black underworld for maybe ten years," Petrone said. "He likes to think he's a traditionalist. We haven't had an influx of Los Angeles gang-bangers yet, and if you could talk to Pointy straight-up about it, he'd probably tell you he wouldn't stand for it, all that driving around town, popping caps at random, shooting babies. That's not Pointy's idea of taking care of business. At least not nowadays."

"He sounds old-fashioned," Lockhart said.

Petrone scowled. "He's anything, he's old-fashioned scum. We're like anyplace else. Most of the violence in this town is black on black, and a hell of a lot of it is dope related. That's Pointy's world, that's what he does. Maybe his guys don't wear colors and call press conferences, but he's still a fucking parasite in the body of the black community. Don't believe me, ask the pastors of about twenty African Methodist Episcopal churches on the South Side. Ask the pastors in the Brickyard."

His scowl faded. "Carl Ingers, the guy who put together the organization Pointy's got now, he was a different story. Ol' Carl *invented* black organized crime in this town, and he had flair. Don't get me wrong, he was scum, too, but he had more style all by himself than all the Italians I've ever met. I mean, Carl was a public relations Godzilla. It was the sixties. He owned a couple of city councilmen, he headed his own civil rights organization, he marched on City Hall, he built playgrounds in the Brickyard . . . he was amazing. A bad day for Carl was a day he couldn't get his name in the papers. And all the while you couldn't put down a bet or borrow a dime on the streets of this town without Carl Ingers getting his percentage. Pointy was his number three or four guy when he was coming up."

"What happened?"

"The eighties. Cocaine," Petrone said absently. "The world went to hell with cocaine. Coke changed everything. The old days, you put a good crew together, got out there and hustled, made book, ran whores, sold some pot, sold some smack, loan-sharked a little, ran the numbers, you could clear maybe two, three hundred grand a year. You pay your lawyers, your city councilmen, there's enough money for everyone to drive a nice car, have a nice downtown apartment, take care of business. The point is, those guys were *hustling*. They were scum, but they were hustling scum. In a sick way it was like having a job. Everyone was too busy to spend much time killing people. When coke took off, there were guys barely out of their teens who could clear a hundred gs in a week. They all went out and bought fucking machine guns and suburban mansions. Carl was just late getting with the program. We found him one Sunday afternoon in the front seat of his Lincoln with a couple of nine-millimeter slugs in his head. The kids call it 'two in the dome.' More bodies turned up over the next few days, and when it was all over, Pointy came out on top. But it's not like it was in the old days. You whack the top brains in any organization, you're going to set it back a few years. Pointy doesn't own any city councilmen yet, at least none that we know about. And Pointy just doesn't have Ingers's style."

Mackin held Maggie's hand as he led her through the crowd at Rayz. The entry contained an old-fashioned hatcheck room and a couple of small tables for patrons who wanted to talk instead of dance. The interior of the club was a large, square room. A horseshoe-shaped bar jutted from one wall, and five bartenders in black vests and white bow ties were trying to keep up with the demand. It was very dark. A slide projector flashed huge images from the sixties on one wall. As they entered the room, Maggie watched the picture snap from one of John Lennon to one of a Buddhist monk engulfed in flames. Four video screens suspended from the ceiling were showing *Modern Times*. Charlie Chaplin's lips moved soundlessly above the crowd. The room shook with the boom of a hypnotic Nine Inch Nails song, and the dance floor was covered with a swarm of surging bodies.

Maggie pulled Mackin's head down and raised her voice. "I'll bet there are eight hundred people in here." She almost shouted to make herself heard above the music. "That was pretty slick, the way you got us in."

"I have to see one of the owners. Business. He's got some papers for me." Mackin shouldered them expertly through the throng in the direction of a set of tables on a small riser against one wall. "Eddie's gay, by the way."

"So are half the guys here. It's okay with me. I'm into men, too." Maggie squeezed his hand.

Eddie Kesko was the dance-hall king of Kansas City. He also sold the best paper in the Midwest. He worked for only a handful of trusted clients and never handled politicals. He'd never been arrested. Tonight he was holding court at his usual table in the back corner of the club. He was very tall, with sunken, dark eyes and black hair swept directly back from his forehead. Maggie noticed that he had unusually large hands. He wore a white, double-breasted, silk sports coat and a pair of black-and-white-striped formal pants. He wasn't wearing a shirt.

A single gold chain, Maggie thought, would have rendered the effect ridiculous, but Kesko wore no jewelry. He was one of the most striking men Maggie had ever seen. He smiled as they approached the riser and waved them up.

Four young men, all handsome and all dressed in various states of urban hip, were seated with him. One of them rose as they approached the table and pulled a sliding partition from a slot in the wall. The partition screened them from the other tables and created what amounted to a semiprivate office. It also deadened the music enough to make conversation possible.

Mackin slid into the empty chair. He reached across the table and shook Kesko's hand. "Eddie Kesko, Maggie Raynor; Maggie, Eddie."

"Charmed." Kesko smiled at her. He had a beautiful smile, she noticed, and a deep, mellifluous voice. She guessed he was in his early thirties. It figures, she thought. He really is too good to be true. Kesko turned to the young man sitting at Mackin's left and raised an eyebrow. "Peter?"

The young man looked puzzled.

"Don't be such a fag, Peter." Kesko's smile took the edge from the words. "Give this enchanting lady your seat."

Peter rocketed out of his chair and began to splutter apologies. Maggie smoothed the back of her dress and sat down.

"My dear boy." Kesko directed the smile to Mackin. "Truly, we do not see enough of you." He turned to Maggie. "And we have never seen you with a date. I always suspected you of a secret life. So." He reached into a leather attaché at his feet, removed a manila envelope, and handed it across the table. "Business first. I think you'll find that complete."

Mackin didn't bother to open the envelope. He knew that it contained what Eddie called a "wallet set": driver's license, social security card, three or four credit cards, an insurance card, and miscellaneous documents such as library cards or association membership cards. "You've never let me down, Eddie. Could you have someone hold it in the checkroom for me? We're going to be here for a while." He removed a sealed, white, business-sized envelope from his jacket and passed it across the table. It contained $5,000 in fifty-dollar bills.

"Robert." One of the young men stepped to the table. Kesko pointed to the manila envelope. "Check that, would you please? And tell the bar that Mr. Mackin and Miss Maggie drink on the house."

Mackin stood and took Maggie's arm. Kesko reached out with his left arm, shoved the partition back into the wall, and smiled at them. "Welcome to my world. We really must get a new photo of you, Mackin. The mustache, you know."

Petrone looked at his coffee cup and waved to the waitress. "Food stamps, I don't know. I gotta figure there's a partner in this somewhere. I would've guessed Pointy was five, six years away from pulling something like this on his own. And the murder is completely out to lunch. Point *pays* cops, he doesn't kill 'em."

Lockhart shrugged. "The thief, this Moffitt character, could be the partner you're looking for. He's a sophisticated enough bastard. If you go by his history, though, it's not his style. He likes the quick in and out."

"Your turn," Petrone said. The waitress deposited a thermal jug full of coffee on the table. She muttered something about "cops" as she walked away. Petrone grinned. "Tell me about you. Tell me about Mr. Moffitt."

Lockhart shrugged. "Me, I'm simple. FBI. Retired when I was forty-four, got into the insurance racket. I like taking down thieves. I've been chasing this cocksucker for four years. He's the slickest I've ever seen, the slickest I've ever heard of. He's fucking good, is what he is. I think I actually ran across his handiwork when I was still with the Bureau, seven, eight years ago, but I can't prove it. We provided some support to the Naval Investigative Service and the locals after someone took down a Marine Corps armory in Charleston, South Carolina. Huge haul. Assault rifles, frags, concussion grenades, every conceivable kind of ammo. They must've needed a deuce-and-a-half to drive it away. Everyone was scared shitless, 'cause they also got four fifty-caliber machine guns and two cases of LAWs, but we recovered that stuff."

Lockhart picked up his hamburger, stared critically at it for a moment, then set it down and pushed his plate away. "That score went down over the Christmas weekend. They had to immobilize three separate security checkpoints inside and outside the building to make it work, and they had to do it damned fast, but they pulled it off."

"Burning bar?"

"Hell, no." Lockhart shook his head and picked up a french fry. "Walked in and drove the shit out through the front door. Two of 'em spent what must have been a hellish half hour in plain sight impersonating sentries. They only had a forty-five-minute start before the security people caught on, but that was enough. I don't know. Like I said, I can't prove it was the Moffitt guy, but the holiday weekend, the level of organization . . . my gut tells me it was."

"I think I want a piece of pie." Petrone was looking at the menu. "Inside job?"

"Oh, yeah. South Carolina Law Enforcement Department found

the LAWs and the fifties stacked in the basement of a retired top sergeant who liked to drink and talk. The SLED boys figured he knew it was all over. They found him in his kitchen with a bullet in his head and one of the stolen forty-fives in his hand. Moffitt, if the armory was his, has stayed away from federal reservations since then. I've got him down for two banks, two, maybe three jewelry stores. Last April someone punched their way into a bonded, refrigerated warehouse in Milwaukee and walked out with four hundred and fifty thousand dollars' worth of fur coats—that's retail, of course—and I have some questions about that one, too."

"He's a busy boy." Petrone ordered a piece of apple pie. "Whacking two cops, though, that's like starting a second career."

"Maybe not, Milos." Lockhart looked doubtful. "I wasn't all that sure the jarhead sergeant did himself. Two other Marines with less-than-stellar service records turned up dead around the same time, in what may or may not have been a boating accident. They had served with the top. I don't know. I think maybe you fuck Mr. Moffitt over, he kills you."

Petrone stabbed his fork into the slab of pastry and fruit. "I just hate guys like that. Don't you? I think I'll ask her to wrap that burger to go, if you don't want it."

9

STARING INTO the barrel of the pistol, Dink Reeves cursed himself for listening to Pointy about the four kilos. He wondered if Danny was still alive.

"I know you want me to lay low and shit," Pointy had snapped over the phone from Miami. "This is different. I've been working on this connection for six fuckin' months, Dink, and the deal has to go down now. This is high-grade Peruvian shit at wholesale prices, baby. The samples sent Cassandra to Mars. I'm telling you, she wanted to bop all night. Just handle it, man. I gotta do every fuckin' thing? The cash is in the safe." And then he hung up.

There had been $75,000 in the safe, and Dink had called the number on the message to set up the meet. "I got a real bad feeling about this," he told Beano-D. "Nigger offers to sell you four kilos for the price of three is probably not a good nigger.

Keep your eyes open." And he arranged for Danny to cover the back of the building, but it didn't look like it had made any difference. The seller hadn't wasted any time on preliminaries.

They were on the first floor of Walnut Towers, an abandoned apartment building in the Brickyard. Dink had taken that as an indicator of trouble, because that's not the kind of place serious players do deals. It was midnight. Dink guessed that Las Vegas—and *that* should've been a serious indicator, he thought bleakly, how the fuck could Pointy expect to do serious business with a clown who called himself *Las Vegas?*—had watched from the window as he and Beano-D walked up the sidewalk, because his muscle, whose name Dink didn't know, was waiting behind the door when they came in and shoved a pistol into the back of Beano-D's neck.

Las Vegas pulled his own piece, a big, chrome-plated revolver, and leveled it at Dink's head. "Where's the cash?" he said quickly. He was sweating, and the hand holding the gun was shaking slightly. He was young, Dink saw, maybe twenty-two or -three, and he was wearing sunglasses in the gloom of the vacant lobby. Style over substance, Dink thought. We aren't dead yet.

He slowly raised his hands to shoulder level. The butt of a pistol showed over his waistband. "Where's the shit, then? What's this all about?" He forced a stiff smile. There was still a chance that everyone could walk away from this. Assuming the kid had the dope. Assuming the kid didn't kill him. "You ain't crazy enough to think you can fuck with Pointy Williams and survive, are you? You ain't stupid enough to try to burn Pointy Williams? Just give us the shit, we give you the money, everyone's happy."

"Where's Pointy?" the kid said loudly. He shot a glance over his shoulder. "*Where the fuck is Pointy?*" He was yelling now.

"Pointy don't handle chickenshit like this himself," Dink said easily. "Right now he's back at his office deciding how many pieces he's gonna leave your momma in if you try to rip him off. So where's the coke?"

Las Vegas brought his other hand up, so that he had both fists balled around the grip of the shiny revolver. He took a deep breath, thumbed back the hammer of his gun, and found a smile. The revolver barrel wasn't shaking so much. At that moment Dink knew it was going down bad.

"Coke's in your fuckin' mind." Las Vegas giggled. *"In your fuckin' mind. The question is, where's the cash?"* He stepped forward, took one hand from his gun butt, snatched Dink's pistol, and stepped away.

"You be careful, now," Dink said. They were standing in line with the back doors of the lobby. If Danny was still alive and came through those doors, Dink would be directly in the line of fire. "Lot of guns in this room." He began to sidle to his left.

"Don't you move!" Las Vegas was fumbling with Dink's pistol with his left hand, trying to shove it into his jacket pocket. Should just drop it behind you, Dink thought. You got too much shit going on all at once, child. He wondered if it would make any difference. He fought the urge to turn his head and look at Beano-D.

Danny materialized like a ghost from the darkness at the back of the room. He was pointing his shotgun at the back of Las Vegas's head, which meant it was pointed at Dink's head, too. The muscle behind Beano-D started barking. *"Behind you, Vegas, 'hind you, man!"* and very clearly Dink saw Las Vegas's finger begin to tighten on the trigger of the chrome pistol, still leveled on his nose.

Dink dropped flat on the floor. Three guns fired almost simultaneously, the boom of Danny's shotgun reverberating below the sharp cracks of the thieves' pistols. Dink felt a stab of burning pain on his scalp and wondered if he was hit. He looked up in time to see Las Vegas buckle at the knees and collapse on top of him.

Beano-D had thrown himself backward and pinned the other punk to the wall with his body. The muscle's gun arm was extended over Beano's right shoulder, and he was trying to get another shot at Danny. Beano grabbed the gunman's right wrist in both hands, levered his left shoulder up, and pulled down hard. The punk's elbow snapped with a crack that sounded loud in the silence after the gunshots. The punk screamed and dropped his gun.

Dink heard Danny rack the action of the shotgun. He grunted and heaved Las Vegas off him. He rose to his knees and pried the chrome pistol from the kid's hand. He couldn't tell if Las Vegas was still alive, though judging by the immense amount of blood the kid had leaked all over him, it wasn't very likely. He shot him behind the ear anyway.

"Beano," Danny said. He wasn't hit and he didn't sound very excited. Beano was still holding the other kid against the wall with his body. The kid's arm hung over Beano's shoulder at a funny angle, and he was sobbing. Beano looked at Danny quizzically, then shook his head and pointed at his ear. He pulled his own pistol from a holster at the small of his back, turned around, stepped back, and shot the kid twice in the mouth.

"Sumbitch popped that cap right next to my ear." Beano's voice was loud. "I can't hear shit."

Danny swung the barrel of the shotgun around the room once, then raised the muzzle toward the ceiling. "Sorry if I took too long." Dink saw Danny was shaking as the reaction to the shooting set in. "Christ. There's another one in a Chevy in the alley. He had a gun on the seat next to him, but I couldn't tell if it was a burn or he was just back-door security. I thumped him pretty good when I heard the yelling and got here as quick as I could."

Dink shoved the chrome pistol into the pocket of his jacket. The gun was too big, and he turned it upside down so the barrel pointed straight up out of the pocket. He was covered with Las Vegas's blood. It had soaked through his shirt and jacket and was sticky on his back.

"I guess you did about great," he said to Danny. He was surprised at how loud their voices sounded in the wake of the gunfire. "Fuckers were gonna do us, sure as shit."

"Christ." Danny dropped to his haunches. "I never shot no one before. *Christ.*"

"Am I bleeding?" Dink reached a hand to the pain at the top of his head.

Danny looked up. "Jesus. I can't tell. You're covered in the shit, but I think most of it's his. Your head ain't bleeding."

Dink nodded. "We got to move now. Danny, go start the car. Wrap the shotgun in your jacket. Beano, you hearin' me?"

"I hear you." Beano-D was vigorously massaging his right ear with one hand. The other still held his gun. "It's just one side."

"Get all the guns, get their wallets and whatever. Don't waste no time. There's another one in a Chevy in the alley. Kill him and let's get the fuck outta here." Dink looked down at his blood-soaked clothes. "Pointy be buying me a new suit for this shit."

✳   ✳   ✳

Lockhart was staring at a cockroach that was sitting on top of the watercooler in Petrone's office. The roach was almost two inches long. "God Almighty," he said in a tone of wonderment. "That's the biggest bug I've ever seen in my life. We have rats in Hartford aren't that big."

"That's Debbie," Petrone said absently. He was at his desk, reading Lockhart's file on the Atlanta robbery for the fourth time. He had a meeting with the chief in half an hour.

"Debbie? You named a roach *Debbie?*" Lockhart turned the paper cup in his hand upside down and reached over the cooler. "How do you know it's a she?"

"Don't fuck with Debbie, now," Petrone said warningly. "She'll tear that cup to pieces, knock you on your ass, and do the cockroach tango on your face."

"God forbid." Lockhart tossed the cup in the wastebasket. "They say where you see one, there are thousands."

"She's the only one I've ever seen."

"You are a very strange man, Milos. In the short time I've known you, I've learned to worry about you."

"She's been hanging around for almost a year." Petrone closed the file, stood up, and reached for his jacket. "She's very low maintenance, y'know? Like a cat."

"What's this meeting about?"

"All very hush-hush. I'm not supposed to know yet. We're meeting in a *motel*, for God's sake. But, hey, you're an experienced investigator. Check out the lineup. I'm representing Homicide. Tenesco will be there from Internal Affairs. There's also gonna be people from the State Police, DEA, and the deputy director of the Chicago Effuh Beeuh Ayuh office." Petrone shouldered into his jacket. "Now, what would you make of that, Chief Inspector?"

"Motel? At night? *Feds?* Oh, goody." Lockhart's eyes were wide and he was beaming. "Wouldn't it be just swell, Detective Petrone, if all those high-powered law-enforcement types were going to tell you they had someone close to Mr. Pointy Williams?"

"Give the man from Connecticut a Kewpie doll." Petrone nodded. "Only thing that figures. Someone's under, and I'll bet they're under on Pointy."

"Do tell me all about it once it's over."

"Of course." Petrone opened the door to leave. "Why don't you and Debbie get to know each other while I'm gone? She's really a terrific roach."

Bo Showalter was sitting on Mackin's couch holding a tall water glass half-full of Scotch. A single ice cube, fading fast, clinked lightly against the glass every time he moved his hand.

"Go ahead, take her with you. So what is this? Love at first fuck? That's dead-on at twenty meters, by the way. Rear sights are locked in with epoxy."

Mackin was sitting at the breakfast bar. The .45 he'd received from Showalter was disassembled on a sheet of newspaper in front of him, and he was running an oil-soaked rag through the barrel with a cleaning rod. "It's a nice piece," he said absently.

"So's Maggie."

"Lighten up, partner." Mackin looked irritated. "I like her."

"Hell, I like her, too." Showalter drained his glass and stood up. "She's the best bartender I've ever had and she doesn't steal. She's got a nice ass, too." He walked into the kitchen and filled his glass from a bottle of Pinch on the counter. "You going to be talking to Riles?"

Mackin nodded.

"I don't suppose there's any way I can talk you into letting this thing lie for a while, is there?" Showalter planted his elbows on the bar across from Mackin. "Let this Williams fucker sweat for a few months, let the heat die down, maybe take a swing at that savings and loan in Little Rock? It's sitting down there like an apple ready to fall from the tree."

Mackin snapped the slide over the barrel of the pistol and set it down on the counter. He stared flatly into Showalter's eyes. "I'm going back, Bo. You don't want to come, don't come. I'm going back."

Showalter didn't flinch. "You go, I go. I'll call Rodney, *he'll* probably go. But no one's gonna tell you it's the most professional thing you've ever done. This Williams bastard will still be there next year, and the local John Laws won't be looking so hard for the guy that whacked two of their own. I like next year better, but if you want to go now, we'll go now."

Mackin turned back to the gun. He began wiping down the shells with the rag as a prelude to loading the magazine. "We go now."

10

PETRONE parked behind the suburban Best Western and walked up the back stairs to the door of the meeting room. The chief opened the door before he could knock. "C'mon in, Milos," he said shortly. "Some people here you should meet."

In fact, Petrone already knew most of them. Pete Tenesco was there. Daryl Mumford, the assistant special agent in charge of the Chicago FBI office, had worked with Petrone on a federal fugitive-apprehension sting two years earlier. Petrone had known Caroline Reese, a captain in the State Police, since their days at the state law-enforcement academy together more than fifteen years ago. The one person he didn't know was Richard Hardaway, who Mumford said was "liaising" for the Drug Enforcement Administration. Petrone generally had little regard for the activities of the DEA, but Hardaway seemed decent enough.

Petrone also remembered Janet Hassan. She had been one of his star pupils during his two-year term as an instructor at the academy six years before, and now she was sitting at the conference table between Reese and the chief. She had gone to the Staties, Petrone knew, and he remembered hearing that she had advanced from patrol officer to investigator. She shot him a strained smile as he sat down.

"Investigator Hassan." He smiled back at her. "That was good work you did last year, on that cigarette thing. I take it you're under on our friend Pointy."

"Jesus, Milos." Caroline Reese scowled and smiled at the same time. "How about you give us a chance to say hello?"

"Okay, people." The chief was chairing the meeting, and Petrone noticed the feds didn't seem to mind. "Most of you know Detective Sergeant Petrone, he's got the Kendall-Macnamara homicides, and right now that means he's got part of the printing-plant robbery, since all this seems to come back to Pointy Williams and his crew."

He turned to Petrone. "Milos, these people are the supervision for Operation Thunderstruck, which is a stupid fucking name that I didn't pick." The chief didn't look at anyone, but out of the corner of his eye Petrone noticed Hardaway shift in his chair. Janet Hassan raised a hand to her mouth and coughed. Her eyes said she was smiling. "Operation Thunderstruck is an undercover penetration of the illegal organization headed by Peter-aka-Pointy Williams. The penetration is being conducted by Investigator Hassan, who I guess you remember, of the State Police. Caroline is her supervisor. Daryl is representing the Bureau and the U.S. attorney's office, which is hoping to pull enough together to make a RICO indictment. Dick represents DEA, which believes Williams is the broker for as much as fifty percent of the illegal drugs in the city."

"That might be a little high," Petrone said.

The chief cut him off. "Let's agree that Pointy sells a lot of fucking dope, okay? I gotta file on Operation Thunderstruck in the safe in my office, it's three inches thick. You come upstairs tomorrow and take a look at it. We brought Pete into this thing a month ago, when Investigator Hassan witnessed a meeting between Williams and Sergeant Kendall during which money appeared to change hands. We're bringing you in now because Williams is the only solid direction we got on the Kendall-Macnamara shooting."

The chief leaned back. "That's what I got. Dick Hardaway and Daryl over there have a canned speech about how this operation is a model of federal and local cooperation that I imagine they're dying to give you, but it's nothing you haven't heard before. If you let her, Caroline will spend an hour telling you Thunderstruck is a classic example of why we ought to work more closely with her people and the attorney general's people, and you probably know that, too."

Petrone saw no visible reaction to the chief's remarks, which he guessed had cut the length of the meeting by two hours. He didn't bother to hide his smile. He addressed Janet Hassan. "Since we're having this meeting now, and not two days ago," he said easily, "I take it you weren't standing fifteen feet away with a camcorder when Kendall and Macnamara were shot."

"Unfortunately, no." Her smile was open now. She had always liked Petrone. "Actually, I'm not sure I have anything at all for you."

Petrone saw that she was very contained. She sat straight in her chair, a blank yellow legal pad set precisely on the table in front of her. She was wearing a plain blue business suit over a starched white blouse, which Petrone guessed was the closest thing to a uniform in her civilian wardrobe. Her gold badge was pinned to her left lapel. Yes, indeed, he thought. I'd want to be in uniform for a meeting like this, too. All these cops. All these old men.

"Williams knows me as Janet Howard," she said quietly. "I work as a hostess at Vingt-et-Un, a French restaurant Williams owns in midtown. We've been socializing for almost three months. I've put together a good overall picture of Williams's crew, but I frankly haven't witnessed much in the way of illegal acts. I don't have anything specific on the shootings."

"Electronic surveillance?"

She shook her head. "Nothing yet. I've been able to wear a wire on three occasions when I've met Williams, but most of what I've collected is in the form of general impressions."

"None of us are particularly thrilled at the pace of the investigation," Hardaway interrupted.

Petrone ignored him. "So give me your general impressions."

She looked thoughtful. "Williams is smart. He surprises me all the time with the things he knows about politics, particularly about city politics."

"He learned that from Carl Ingers," Petrone said.

She nodded. "He talks about Ingers often. He has an awful lot of free time. Dink Reeves seems to handle a lot of the day-to-day stuff."

"Dean-aka-Dink Reeves," the chief said. "He's a smart bastard, too."

"Williams left town immediately after the shootings," Hassan said. "He went to Florida. He wanted me to go with him. He took a girl named Cassandra Hughes with him when I said no."

"Coke whore," the chief said shortly. Petrone saw Hassan flinch slightly. "She's not important."

"I never saw the man from the driver's license," Hassan said.

"I never heard any discussion of the printing-plant robbery. I do know that Williams has been doing some kind of business with people in Chicago. This sounds crazy, but I think it has something to do with grocery stores."

"He's been talking about grocery stores?" Petrone leaned forward slightly.

"Once he made a joke about being in the grocery business. It wasn't very clear." Hassan paused, then continued tonelessly, "He sends me flowers several times a week, but they're never from a florist. They're always from a Benson's Grocery. One of his crew delivers them."

Silence fell. Richard Hardaway lifted his briefcase from the floor next to his chair and stood up. "That's what we have, Sergeant," he said. "Your chief will provide you with contact information for each of us. You understand that all of this must be kept strictly confidential."

"Oh, for Christ's sake," the chief snorted.

Hardaway looked at his watch. "I have to go." He walked quickly out of the room.

Several seconds of silence followed his departure. They heard Hardaway's car start in the parking lot. Mumford burst into laughter. "Priceless," he gasped. He reached over and clapped the chief on the back. "Priceless, Fred. Dick said a grand total of thirty-two words. I counted. Gotta be a record. Hell, if you'd let him, we'd be here all night."

"He's not a bad guy, you keep him quiet," the chief said equitably.

"I have a million questions that probably aren't of interest to anyone else here," Petrone said to Hassan. "Since we're safely exiled in suburbia, how about I buy you a cup of coffee somewhere?"

A cloud crossed Caroline Reese's face, but she said nothing. Hassan smiled. "I'd love a cup of coffee, Sergeant," she said quickly. "I have some questions for you, too." She stood and gathered her coat.

"Janet." Reese spoke quietly. "Your tin."

Hassan looked down at her lapel, then carefully unpinned her badge and handed it to the other woman. "And Milos," Reese said, "drink the coffee in the fucking car, okay?"

Milos Petrone walked out of a pancake house with two large styrofoam cups of coffee and handed them through the car window to Janet Hassan. He opened the driver's side door and slid behind the wheel.

"This whole area was open fields when I was growing up," he said, waving his arm to encompass the suburban sprawl around them. "A developer had come around in the forties and tried to put in a housing development, but he went broke. He did manage to get dirt roads bulldozed, and a bunch of us kids used to ride bikes out here."

Hassan handed him one of the cups and pulled the top off the other.

"By the time I got out of the army," he continued, "I got out in '71, late '71, a group of other developers had come through and started throwing houses up like mushrooms. I was only gone four years, but the place was unrecognizable when I got back."

"How long have you been with the department, Sergeant?" There was genuine interest in Hassan's voice. Petrone had been her most effective academy instructor.

"Milos. Call me Milos. Spent a couple years in college, got married." He uncovered his cup and sipped. "I joined in '73 and finished my degree at night." He smiled. "History, believe it or not. It probably wasn't the most practical decision I ever made, but having any degree is worth points with the department. I'd like to go to grad school after I retire."

Hassan smiled. "A thirty-year man?"

"I'll stick with it as long as I can keep up with the bad guys." He stared at her through the steam rising over the brim of his cup. "I was twenty-seven, a little bit older than you are now, the first time I worked under."

"This really isn't my first time," Hassan said quietly. "I spent about a week as a convenience-store manager on the cigarette sting."

She was referring to a State Police investigation from a year before that resulted in the arrest of a group that sold untaxed cigarettes. "I think that's why Captain Reese picked me for Thunderstruck."

"That, and the fact that you're an attractive black female."

Hassan eyed him without malice. "I can't really control that, Milos. All I can do is try to be a good cop. If that makes me an attractive black female cop, so be it, but I hope that people remember the good-cop part first."

"Point taken, Janet. You mind I call you Janet? . . . Okay." Petrone removed a chunk of bubble gum from his pocket and unwrapped it. "So this, tonight, is just between you and me, off the record. Here's where I'm at: This guy on the driver's license, this Paul Moffitt character, almost certainly killed Kendall and Macnamara and probably took down Felton Industrial Printing. The connection between those two events appears to be Pointy Williams. I got a guy in town named Lockhart who works for a big insurance company back east, and he wants Moffitt for being some kind of superthief able to leap tall Federal Reserve banks with a single bound. Mumford and Hardaway and Reese and all the rest of you in Thunderstruck, you want Pointy Williams on RICO, which as far as I'm concerned means you want him for being a generally bad person."

He popped the gum in his mouth and chewed vigorously for a moment. "All that is commendable, but it doesn't have much to do with me. I want Moffitt, whoever he is, for two counts of murder and the printing plant, and t'hell with whatever anyone else wants him for. If Williams had a piece of the printing plant, if he had anything at all to do with putting Moffitt in that car with Kendall and Macnamara, then I want that cocksucker for at least two counts of accessory to murder. Give me half a chance and I'll hang two counts of felony murder on him. I'm not real interested, at least not this week, in Pointy's drug business. You see where I'm coming from?"

He made an ineffectual effort to blow a bubble.

Hassan tried not to stare as the older man pulled pink gum off the end of his nose. "As I said, I've been at the restaurant for almost three months, and Williams started cruising me right away. He's well known among the employees as a Romeo, but he isn't pushy. He counts on his charm to win women over, and he has a *lot* of charm. He's taken me by his office several times. It's in a building he owns on Amsterdam, and it's nice. There are three locked file cabinets in there that I'd love to get a peek into, but we don't have enough for a solid warrant—yet. He just never talks about criminal activity with me. Early in our relationship, he made it clear that he could get me just about any kind of drugs or narcotics I was interested in, but that honestly seemed more a social offer than anything else. He never said he was a dope dealer, or anything like that."

She shrugged. "I haven't encouraged him. We're trying to come up with a sting that will make a RICO-based search warrant stand up, but I'm afraid that so far that would require me asking him for an amount of drugs not in keeping with what he thinks he knows about my character."

Petrone was nodding. He blew another bubble, successfully this time, and snapped it. "Mumford or Reese or someone will probably ask you this officially, but unofficially, I'd appreciate it if you'd keep your ears open about this grocery thing."

"You think it's important?"

"I'll know one way or the other tomorrow, but I gotta believe it has something to do with those food stamps. And the food stamps are our link to Mr. Moffitt, and I really want to get a piece of Mr. Moffitt's ass."

"It's hard for me to see Williams involved in the cop killings," Hassan said reflectively, "because it's so removed from the personality he shows me. I know he's completely criminal, of course, but I don't see that side of him."

She shook her head. "Hardaway, the DEA guy, he talks about how he's going to bust every single employee at the Vingt-et-Un, how they're all of them coke-dealing scum, and I just don't believe that's true. They're selling crepes, for heaven's sake, not drugs. Most of them seem to be trying to make a living, just like everybody else. And Cassandra, the girl your chief called a 'coke whore' . . . she's definitely got a serious substance-abuse problem, but it's not like she's turning tricks in the kitchen. She's a waitress."

Petrone looked across the car at her. "You like her."

Hassan nodded ruefully. "I do. She's funny and she's smart. She grew up in the Brickyard. That's her world. I grew up in the most boring, middle-class neighborhood in all of Ann

Arbor, Michigan. She talks about growing up in the projects; it's like a whole other country."

Petrone leaned back in the car seat and looked out the windshield. "First time I went under for any period of time was, well, it was a long time ago," he said quietly. "I was working Safe and Loft; we had a burglary ring hitting expensive houses out by the lake. I mean, we had a hell of a burglary problem anyway, but when the expensive people started getting their expensive things ripped off, that's when we got authorization for the sting."

He sipped his coffee. "Department set me up in a pawn shop downtown. Not in the Brickyard, because the people we were chasing were stealing shit that people in the Brickyard generally can't afford, even when it's hot. VCRs, for example, they were brand-new then, cost a thousand bucks apiece. Big-screen projection TVs, high-end stereo systems; they hit one place on Green Glen Road, I remember, and actually stole the goddamn furniture."

He grinned at the memory. "That was the home of a former city councilman. He was in California, had the family at Disneyland, these guys pulled a truck in front of the house and cleaned it out. My oh my, did the shit hit the fan."

"What happened?" Hassan was also smiling.

"Good guys won. It took a while. I was under almost nine months, running that hock shop for real, loaning money on the family TV. I was real popular with students because I'd give 'em good money for their bikes. It was two, three months before the thieves showed up. They were moving most of their stuff out of state, in Memphis and places like that, but they were handling so much product they needed outlets. I played it cool, made the right noises, didn't try to hurry anything, and before you knew it they thought I was the neatest thing since sliced white bread. We hung out together, partied, got a little drunk once or twice, they thought I was their friend."

"Were you?" Hassan was staring at the detective. "Were you their friend?"

"Near the end I didn't know. Outfit was headed by a guy named Mike Castleberry, he was a crazy man. Always looking for the next thrill, the next charge, the next score. Stealing was a joyful act for Mike. He thought of himself as some kind of Robin Hood because he only ripped off the well-to-do. He was smart, too. Excellent planner, no nerves. I really enjoyed being around him. The judge gave him eighteen years. He served a little more than seven, died in prison. Leukemia."

Petrone turned back to the young woman. "Hell of an operation, Janet. Commendations all around. I sailed into Homicide, made my career. We didn't get just the Castleberry outfit. In nine months of operation, that hock shop attracted what seemed like every burglar in town. We got twenty-six indictments out of that shop, made twenty-one of them stand up, but for months all I could think of was the way Mike looked at me when the uniforms walked in and I pulled out my badge. And I was wrong to feel that way, Janet. I really liked the guy, but he was a fucking hoodlum, a thief. So is Pointy Williams. You get a clear shot at a major indictment, you take that piece of shit down."

Hassan nodded. "I will, Milos. Don't worry. I will."

"Something else." Petrone's voice was light again. "This thing is looking pretty messy, especially since Walnut Towers. Being in the same building with Williams is now appreciably risky. You carry a weapon at the restaurant?"

She shook her head. "No gun, no badge. You saw how careful Captain Reese is."

"Yeah, well, I'll talk to her." Petrone tugged at his lower lip. "If you feel safe enough to occasionally wear a wire, you're probably okay to carry a little more. I think I'd feel better if you were armed."

11

WHENEVER THE SUBJECT came up, and in the past week it had come up often, Joe Macchi went to great lengths to explain to whomever he was talking to that his profound personal dislike of Pointy Williams had nothing to do with race. "I got no problems with spades, generally speaking," he would say. "Your average spade, he's had a rough time. You do what you gotta do to get by. I can unnerstand that."

Macchi had, in fact, occasionally done business with the Williams organization over the years, since Williams owned or controlled more than a dozen nightclubs that had been supplied with vending and pinball machines from Macchi's company, Momo Amusement. The company name was Macchi's way of paying tribute to his roots: he had started his career in Chicago working for Sam "Momo" Gianacana, a major power in Midwest organized crime in the years following Al Capone's imprisonment for income-tax evasion. Macchi had never personally met the "Great Man," as he thought of Capone, though at the age of twenty-one he had served as a driver in Capone's funeral procession.

That had been in 1947. Two years later, Macchi made his bones when he garroted a horseplayer who had welshed on a bet with Gianacana. By 1952 he was acting as Gianacana's occasional driver. In 1956 he had left Chicago and opened Momo Amusement; for the next twenty years he supervised a crew of almost two dozen and built a small but efficient criminal empire that provided him with a comfortable living.

"Those were the good times," he would tell Ricky Cento, who was now his driver. "Everybody worked together, y'know what I mean? Hell, in the sixties, we opened Vegas up like a fuckin' can of tuna. Us, the Chicago guys, and the Civella people in Kansas City, we were taking a million five a month out of Nevada alone. It was sweet, kid, as sweet as it gets."

Ricky Cento, who was twenty-eight and no kid, would nod and make admiring noises, even though he privately thought that his boss was living in a dream world. Cento knew that the Kansas City and Chicago mobs had, in fact, skimmed millions from several Las Vegas casinos before the Justice Department shut down the operation in the late 1970s, and he also knew that if Macchi had been involved in any significant way, he would probably have gone to prison with the rest of the skim organizers. Cento had had his doubts about his employer's veracity ever since he realized that one of Macchi's favorite stories, about testifying in front of the Kefauver Committee in 1952, was based on a single exchange between Macchi and the senator from Tennessee on a morning when Gianacana was scheduled to testify but had failed to immediately appear.

"You are Mr. Gianacana's driver?" Kefauver had asked Macchi, who nodded. "Where is your employer?"

"I think he's in the can," Macchi had replied.

"And *that* was his great fucking moment," Cento told his crew. "Talking toilets with a senator." Cento wasn't yet certain enough of his own power to show open disrespect to Macchi, but he was chafing under the restrictions imposed by the older man. Cento thought it was time he made his own mark, and he wanted to make it fast. It was clear to him that the key to quick success lay in narcotics, a business Macchi absolutely forbade. "It's been the one rule since the thirties," he would lecture his crew, most of whom were as old as he was. "Luciano himself made the decree: no drugs. I find any of my guys dealing drugs, I'll kill 'em personally."

There lay the nominal root of Macchi's discontent with Pointy Williams. "It's got nothing to do with the man's color, y'unnerstand," he was now saying into the phone. He and Cento were in Macchi's office at the amusement company. "I did business with Carl Ingers. I can do business with a nigger just like anyone else, and I *did* business with that fucker for four, five years."

He was talking to Frank Riles in Chicago. "I did business with him until he sent his boy Reeves over here to cancel the fucking rental agreements because the black bastard went and bought his own machines. It ain't even that, though. It's the fucking dope, Frank, the cocksucker's dealing dope all over the city—it ain't just the Brickyard. Hell, the other day one of his boys hit a couple of fucking *cops*. I ask you, how stupid can you get? Word is that Williams is getting a little shaky. . . ."

Cento was dividing his attention between Macchi's half of the conversation and the local morning news on the office TV.

He was six feet tall, with jet-black hair that fell over one eye and a crooked smile that the ladies loved. Cento had been working for Macchi for ten years. He had killed his first man when he was nineteen, a personal matter over the affections of a hooker named Ashley. As Macchi's driver he headed his own crew of four men his own age, and they were all starting to wonder when the old guard was going to get the fuck out of the way and let the next generation have some room to move.

"Yeah, Frank, yeah, I unnerstand." Macchi was fumbling with a new pack of cigarettes. "I got no trouble believing that at all, let me tell you. The man is lucky he got clear. Fuckin' spade will kill you soon as look at you, believe me."

He paused, listening intently. His right hand doodled on the legal pad in front of him. He wrote, *Williams cash business.* "Sure, whatever it takes. Mostly gambling, cars, whores, and dope. . . . Yeah, cars, top-line stuff like Lincolns and BMWs, his people snatch 'em right off the street, Williams sells 'em in fuckin' Saudi Arabia, Oman, places like that. He puts a couple dozen on a train for New York once a month; some of his spade buddies in Harlem ship 'em to the sand niggers. He's getting ten, twelve grand a pop, and he sure as fuck ain't sharing."

On the television, an impossibly blond anchorwoman was describing the shootings at Walnut Towers. Cento leaned forward.

Macchi wrote, *slots.* "The gambling is simple shit, Frank, like video poker and video slots. . . . In the clubs, yeah. . . . Fuck, he ain't running any numbers, Frank, no one's run numbers around here since the fucking state set up their fucking lottery. And they call us gangsters, can you believe it? But, hell, he's making a fortune off the machines. . . . I'll put together a package, get it out to you."

"Joe." Cento pointed to the television. "They found three niggers shot dead in one of the projects. Dope burn, they think."

Macchi nodded at his subordinate. "My man Ricky is telling me that they found three spades all shot up this morning, fucking drugs."

Cento winced inwardly at the sound of his name. He was sure that Frank Riles, whom Cento really did respect—Riles spoke for Sal Capetti, after all, and nobody fucked with Capetti—was on a pay phone, but Macchi acted like bugging hadn't been invented yet. Then again, he thought, why would anyone bug us? It's not like we're making any goddamn money.

Macchi had a cigarette out and was ineffectually attempting to strike a paper match. "Whatever you need, Frank. You'll have it tomorrow." Cento walked to the desk and lit Macchi's cigarette. The older gangster nodded his thanks. "Absolutely, Frank. You give my respects to Sal, okay? Tell him I tried that stuff he recommended on the roses, and it worked great. Ellen is thrilled. . . . Yeah. Same to you, guy."

Macchi replaced the receiver and leaned back in his chair. "Ricky, I need you to put together everything we got or can find out about Williams's operation." He quickly filled in the younger man on the details of the police shootings. "This thief, he's gonna pay Pointy a visit, get some back. Find out where he does his big volume on the video machines—"

"Ma Rainey's is the biggest. Joint in the Brickyard."

Macchi nodded absently. "Whatever. And find out where he keeps his cars before he ships 'em to New York."

"Warehouse out on the interstate frontage road." Cento gazed levelly at Macchi. He carefully kept his expression neutral, although he was inwardly stunned at the older man's ignorance. There was no denying it: Joe Macchi was getting old. "He leases it from us."

"Well, hell." Macchi scowled. "How'd I forget? I knew that. Anyway, put together a list of shit like that, get it to Riles tomorrow morning. I think maybe by this time next week, Mr. Pointy Williams is gonna have a full-time job covering his own ass."

Cento nodded and strode out of the office. His mind was racing furiously. On a personal level, Cento couldn't care less about Pointy Williams—he hadn't even met the man, and there was no denying that lately Williams had been acting as if his head were stapled up his ass—but professionally, Williams was nice to have around. For instance, Pointy's operation moved an awful lot of cocaine, rock and powder, and in the past year Cento had quietly grabbed a small piece of that action without Macchi's knowledge. On his own, Cento had established a mutually satisfactory working relationship with Dink Reeves, who was the kind of businessman Cento could respect.

"Fuck," Cento muttered to himself. He climbed into his car and sat for a moment, trying to envision the city without Williams's organization. There wasn't any chance that Macchi would take advantage of the black man's trouble to expand the Italians' business. "Old bastard's basically retired," he said to himself.

Which didn't mean shit, really, because his current orders didn't really come from Joe but from Frank Riles, which meant Cento's job was to salute and say, "Yessir." It wouldn't take him long to put together the information the man in Chicago wanted. Still, it probably wouldn't hurt to cover all the bases.

"*I'm* sure as hell not retired," he said out loud. He started his car and pulled into traffic. He needed to find a pay phone.

At its peak, near the end of the seventies, the Walnut Towers housing project was home to almost two thousand people. Petrone had been there on the day in 1969 that the secretary of housing and urban development had cut the ribbon. The secretary had posed for photographs with various civic dignitaries in the center of the lobby not far from where Las Vegas's body was now sprawled. The city had condemned the structure in 1985 after years of problems with unsafe wiring and unsanitary plumbing systems.

The chief had personally assigned Larry Whittier as the lead homicide detective on the shootings. "It probably has something to do with the Kendall-Macnamara thing," he'd said to Petrone. "It's the fucking Brickyard. It's black guys, maybe it's Pointy Williams's people. You guys work together, see what you come up with." Petrone hadn't argued, though he doubted the shootings were directly related.

Linda Kaminsky, a crime-scene technician, was stripping off a pair of bloodstained gloves. It was eight-thirty in the morning. "What we got here is your basic firearms buffet," she said cheerfully. "That dirtbag"—she pointed to the body in the corner—"was shot twice in the mouth with what I'd guess was the nine millimeter that goes with the brass we found."

Petrone nodded glumly. He had never seen quite so much blood on a single floor. He pointed down at Las Vegas. "I take it *this* dirtbag here got it with a shotgun."

"That was part of it." Kaminsky grinned. "That dirtbag there took a load of double-ought in the upper back and head. You can't tell, what with the mess, but he was also shot once in the back of the head with this." She held up an evidence bag that contained a flattened lead bullet. "I found it on the floor underneath him. It might come from the nine, but I don't think so. Probably from a revolver. There's no brass to go with it, and these guys weren't cleaning up after themselves. My guess would be a .38, but the lab can tell you for sure this afternoon."

"Which one killed him? The .38 or the shotgun?"

"Jump ball, Sergeant."

Petrone nodded again. "What about the one in the car?"

Kaminsky's grin didn't falter. "The one in the car was shot once in the forehead with a medium-caliber handgun. Don't know if it was the .38 or the nine. We're still checking the alley for brass. I think the ME will tell you he was unconscious when he died, 'cause he's got a premortem knot on the side of his head as big as a cantaloupe. Somebody hit him pretty good, maybe through the car window, and then they shot him. None of the victims have any ID. We'll print all three of them at the morgue. I expect at least one of them had an arrest record. No cash or weapons found. Looks like a burn."

She looked around the trash-strewn lobby. "What it boils down to is that this was the scene of a no-shit gunfight last night, and these fellas came in second place. You need anything else?"

"Now that you mention it, I'd appreciate it if you'd give me the name-slant-names of the shooter-slant-shooters before you take off. And drop their photographs on my desk, and maybe tell me where I can find 'em. That would be very helpful. And I could use a Danish."

"There's a doughnut place a block down Walnut."

"Right." Petrone sighed. He lit a cigarette and stared at Las

Vegas's body. One of the uniforms at the door waved to catch his attention.

"Hey, Sarge," he called. "TV truck pulling up."

"Oh, Christ," Petrone muttered. He looked around for Whittier. He didn't have time for the press. He was meeting Lockhart in twenty minutes.

Kaminsky smiled at the pained expression on his face. "This keeps up, Sergeant Petrone, you'll be a TV star."

"I can't tell you how good that feels." Petrone spotted Whittier coming in the back doors of the lobby from the alley and walked quickly toward him. He had been pleased, that morning, to see him restored to something approaching normalcy. Now Whittier had a bulldog expression on his face and a blunt cigar, his trademark during his time in Narcotics, clenched between his massive jaws.

"TV people are outside, Larry," Petrone said. "If you don't need me, I'm going to meet with Lockhart."

Whittier nodded crisply. "I'll take care of everything here, Milos. You go catch your bad guys, I'll catch mine." He looked over Petrone's shoulder toward the front door and raised his voice at the uniformed officer standing there: "That fucker tries to cross that yellow tape, you shove his TV camera right up his ass."

Kaminsky laughed. Petrone grinned and slipped out the back door. The third victim was slumped in the front seat of a late-model sedan in the alley. Petrone paused for a moment, wondering how old the victim was. Twenty-one, maybe twenty-two, he thought. He shook his head, jammed his hands deep in the pockets of his overcoat, and walked away. "God, I love this country," he thought acidly. A woman staring across the tape blocking the alley gave him an angry look, and Petrone realized he'd spoken out loud. "Only in America, ma'am," he said pleasantly as he ducked under the tape and stepped onto the sidewalk. "Truly, we are the land o' opportunity."

Dink Reeves sat in his office waiting for the phone to ring. Pointy's call was forty minutes late already. Dink had showered and changed clothes three times since the attempted rip-off the night before. His scalp still stung from the powder burn he'd picked up from Las Vegas's muzzle blast. Beano-D sat in his chair next to the door looking at a pornographic magazine.

"How's your ear?"

"Still ringin'." Beano didn't look up. "Startin' to hear shit, though."

The streamlined phone on Dink's desk trilled softly. He lifted the handset carefully. "Yeah," he said quietly.

"Wassup? It go down all right? Sorry I'm a little late. Cassandra, she wanted to see *New Jack City*." Pointy sounded a little wired.

"It was a burn."

"What the fuck?"

"A burn." Dink sounded as if he were discussing the weather.

"You keep the money? You all right?"

"Everything's cool." Dink noticed the order of the two questions and felt a stab of anger. "There was no product."

"Shit."

"Danny, he saved everybody's ass. I slipped him a little extra for the week."

"Yeah, that's cool." There was a pause. "What about Las Vegas?"

"He's done." Dink tapped a brown cigarette on his desk. "I think maybe you oughtta be headin' back. Some shit's up."

"What kinda shit?"

"I got a call this afternoon." Dink lit the cigarette. "The thief, he's on his way back here."

Beano-D turned his magazine sideways and smiled at one of the pictures. "Look at *that* shit."

12

"I NEED TO KNOW that I'm not going to be pissing all over your people if I go straighten this thing out," Mackin said.

"I got no problem with making things right," Riles said cautiously. "He fucked you, he owes you. What you got in mind?"

They were sitting in Riles's office. The fact that Riles had a real office, instead of a regular barstool or a table in the back of an Italian restaurant, was one of the things about him that impressed Mackin. Riles even had a secretary. Her name was Francine. She was fifty-two years old and could type almost 120 words a minute.

Mackin noticed that Riles's passion for justice had cooled since their phone call. "What I got in mind is just that," Mackin snapped. "Making things right. The cocksucker didn't fuck me, Frank. He tried to rip me off. He tried to kill me. I don't think those cops planned to let me come back here and tell you that Williams set me up."

"Easy, Mackin, easy." Riles held up both hands in surrender. "I just want to know what's going on. We do some business with the guy, okay? I'm not saying that he's our number one earner. He's not high enough on the list to have a number, okay? But he's on the list. He helped us put this grocery thing together, all right? All the guys I work for, they're in love with the grocery business. They got me delivering truckloads of fresh seafood and prime rib to their kitchen doors."

Riles sighed. "It's not like I'm the king of the world around here, Mackin. I told you, you want him dead, I'll make a phone call. That's no big thing, business goes on. People understand. You want to drop a fucking nuclear weapon on the city, that's different. People are gonna ask me questions."

Mackin nodded. "Let's take a walk." He knew that Riles had his office swept for electronic surveillance twice a week, but he felt safer out in the open.

Riles told Francine he'd be gone for a couple of hours. "Call Judith and tell her I'll be home for dinner." Francine nodded crisply. Mackin thought she looked very efficient.

They walked toward the lake. An autumn chill was in the air. They both wore jackets.

"I hear you brought a girl up here with you." Riles smiled. "That's a little unusual for you, isn't it, mixing business and pleasure?"

"She's special, Frank. We're having a lot of fun."

"Take her by my place on Rush Street tonight. I'll call Lenny, you'll be on the house."

"Thanks." Mackin looked at the manila envelope in Riles's hand. "That for me, Frank?"

"If you want it." Riles looked dubious.

"I want to hurt him, Frank," Mackin said quietly. "I want to cost him some money. He's got to pay."

"I can get behind that," Riles said quickly. "How much? Twenty, thirty large? I'll call the son of a bitch, have cash delivered express in the morning."

"No." Mackin's tone didn't change. He took the envelope from the other man's hand. "I don't want him to give it to me. I want to take it from him."

Kenneth Bethune had listened to and obeyed his parents when they suggested he pursue a degree in accounting from Loyola after he completed a three-year enlistment in the army. "You'll always be able to make a good living," his father, an elementary-school teacher, told him gravely, and Kenneth's mother, abandoning her hopes that her only son would take holy orders, had agreed. So Bethune continued to live with his parents on Chicago's North Side for five years while he attended classes. He had served as a medic's assistant in the military, and it seemed natural to him to continue in that line of work at night and on weekends. That was in the early 1960s, as the profession of paramedic was gaining acceptance, and after completing six weeks of training Bethune found himself spending thirty hours a week hunched in the rear of a boxlike ambulance speeding from catastrophe to catastrophe.

Bethune soon became a familiar figure to many Chicago police officers, who learned to appreciate the young student's calm demeanor and unruffled professionalism in the face of tragedy. His future as a CPA became doubtful one cold night in a hospital emergency room, after Bethune and a Chicago cop had spent seven frantic minutes in the back of the ambulance

administering CPR to a woman whose Delta 88 had been re-
duced to fifty percent of its original size by a Kenworth tractor-
trailer truck that had jumped the median. Bethune and the
policeman were sitting in the hallway when the emergency-
room surgeon appeared, his greens splashed with blood, to tell
them the woman would live. "Nice work, fellas," the doctor
said laconically, then pushed back through the swinging doors
to attend to his patient.

Wordlessly, Bethune and the cop stood and walked out the
door, both of them pulling cigarettes from packs in their breast
pockets. "You're pretty good at this," the policeman said, his
breath billowing white in the chill air from Lake Michigan.
"You don't lose your mud. Ought to think about being a cop."
He pulled a deep drag from his cigarette—Bethune still remembered that it was a charcoal-filtered Tareyton—and disappeared into the night. Bethune never learned his name.
Eighteen months later, accounting degree in hand, Bethune
applied for a job with the Federal Bureau of Investigation.

That had been more than a quarter-century before, and now
Bethune was back in Chicago on his last assignment before
retirement. In the intervening years he had pursued everyone
from crooked defense contractors to corrupt FDA inspectors,
but his specialty had always been organized crime. Bethune
had been part of virtually every major Bureau offensive on the
mob from the pursuit of Jimmy Hoffa to the bugging of Paul
Castellano's Long Island dining room, and he was among the
original members of the FBI's successful, city-based Organized
Crime Strike Forces that had decimated the Mafia in the
early 1980s.

Now only ten weeks from retirement, Bethune's final respon-
sibility was closing down the operation of the Chicago Strike

Force. Chicago had always been the Bureau's toughest nut. From Al Capone to Paul Ricca to Sam Gianacana to Salvatore Capetti, the Chicago mob had always been so firmly entrenched that the FBI could do little more than wait for one of them to make a glaring mistake, as several of them had in the late eighties when they allowed their ownership of Teamsters president Roy Williams to open the door to federal investigators pursuing labor-racketeering charges. That had been the crack in the fortress wall that led to the Las Vegas skimming indictments, a major Bureau success, but as Bethune often pointed out to his superiors, that had also been "fifteen fucking years ago, and all those scumballs are dead."

Bethune was reading the daily transcript of the last of the Strike Force active wiretaps. It was eleven A.M. He closed the file folder, tucked it under his arm, walked down the hall to Daryl Mumford's office, tapped lightly on the ASAIC's door, and poked in his head.

"Gotta minute?"

"C'mon in, Ken." Mumford smiled and pushed the report he was reading to one side. "How's the family?"

"Good as gold." Bethune pulled out a cigarette and lit it, ignoring Mumford's automatic glance of disapproval. Smoking was absolutely prohibited in all federal office buildings. Bethune didn't much care. "Fran is in Sarasota. She says the house is almost ready. More importantly, I talked to the boat dealer yesterday, and the boat *is* ready."

Mumford smiled. He felt real affection for the older man, whom he thought of as a representative of a dying breed. Bethune was one of Bobby Kennedy's boys, and though the idealism of those days had worn a little thin, it was still a commodity the FBI needed more of. Rules or no rules, Daryl Mumford wasn't about to tell Ken Bethune to put out his cigarette. "How long?"

"Sixty-eight days." Bethune grinned. "Sixty-eight days, and the only perps I have to Mirandize will be the great, big sea bass I'll be hauling in every damn day, rain or shine."

Mumford laughed. Preliminaries over, he pointed to the folder in Bethune's hand. "What'cha got?"

Bethune tossed the folder on the desk. "Transcript of a conversation held day before yesterday between Francis Riles and Joseph Macchi. I saw your memo last month on the Thunderstruck thing, that little rat bastard Pointy Williams. Riles and Macchi are very interested in Williams. They talked for twenty-one minutes, and in the course of it Riles gave Macchi the scoop on those two cops that were shot last week. They were dirty, by the way, but I expect you already know that."

Mumford quickly scanned the transcript. His eyes were animated. "Jesus, this is wonderful, Ken. I hate to admit it, but I didn't know you still had any active taps."

"Macchi's the last." Bethune sucked hard on his cigarette and began looking helplessly for someplace to extinguish it. "Stupid bastard has his office phones swept every thirty days, always on the same day, so it's been kind of a pain in the ass to keep the tap active. Authorization expires in three days, and I don't think we're gonna get Judge Strukel to renew it. Macchi is small potatoes. We're getting some good intelligence stuff, but nothing indictable. Hell, with the Strike Force disbanded, I wouldn't know what to do with indictable material anyway." He walked over to the trash can and began looking for an empty soda can in which to dispose of his cigarette.

Mumford opened the bottom drawer of his desk, removed an ashtray, and slid it across the desk. "It's all here. The thief, the score, the shooting . . . this is just wonderful."

Bethune shook his head. "There's some good stuff there, yeah, but if you read carefully, you'll see the holes in it." He jammed the cigarette into the ashtray and leaned back. "Riles is very careful to avoid implicating either himself or Capetti in anything; it sounds like he's reading from the goddamn newspapers. He never mentions the thief's name. He never explains why in the world anyone would want to steal a quarter mil in food stamps."

Mumford thought of Janet Hassan's remarks about the grocery-store flowers. "I may have something on that from another source. The Staties over there—"

Bethune shook his head. "Don't want to know, Daryl. Don't care. Thunderstruck isn't a Strike Force op, 'cause there isn't any more Strike Force. The only thing that would interest me is a chance to put that bastard Riles, or better yet Capetti, in Marion Federal Penitentiary, and I don't see anything there that will do that. It's your baby, Daryl. I just hope that helps. Me, I'm going fishing."

Mumford nodded absently. "This car thing is interesting. . . . So this thief is coming back. It's almost enough to make you feel sorry for Williams. He's got street thugs trying to take out his operation, the Feds and the state people trying to indict him, and now this thief is coming back to fuck up his life."

Bethune smiled. "Ain't it great?"

Mumford, also smiling, looked up and nodded vigorously. "Better than terrific, Ken. Better than terrific." He flipped his Rolodex to Milos Petrone's number and picked up the telephone.

One hundred and seventy miles away, Deputy Sheriff Mike Milner looked from the note in his hand to the video console in front of him. Every cell in the Lounds County Jail had a security camera mounted high in the ceiling corner next to the television. There were fourteen cells in the jail, and each cell was monitored for fifteen seconds out of each minute. The lower-right corner of each monitor featured a digital display of the time and the cell number. He switched to cell nine. The camera said it was ten thirty-three in the morning.

"Barrett's in nine, right?" Milner gazed at the five men visible in the picture. They were sitting in the cell's bull pen, the common area outside the barred sleeping area. Two men were watching television, which produced the eerie feeling that they were looking directly into the camera. Two others, both serving a year for a series of DUIs, were playing an intent game of five-hundred rummy that had so far lasted four months. A fifth was crouched on the floor next to the cell door talking on the pay phone. "I don't see him."

The shift commander, a captain named Laura Henderson, glanced from a clipboard on her desk to the monitor. "Yeah, he's in nine, and nine is full up. Must be in his bunk."

Milner stood up. "I'll walk down there, then."

A small knot of worry was between Henderson's eyes. "Mike, we can't string the guy along. If he doesn't get hold of his family, we'll have to tell him ourselves. He's getting out tomorrow. Maybe he can make the services."

Milner nodded and, after Henderson deactivated the electronic locks, walked through the security doors into the cellblock. This errand was among the most distasteful parts of a jailer's job, and in eleven years of work in the jail Milner had only had to go through it twice before.

The doors on the cells of the Lounds County Jail were solid steel, not barred, with a slit cut at waist level for food trays and a screened hole at head level for conversation. Both the slit and the hole were covered with locked plates. Milner unlocked the cover on the hole in the door of cell nine. The sound of the key in the lock brought conversation in the cell to a halt, and when Milner opened the cover, he saw that the men who had been watching television were now looking at the cell door. The cardplayers were oblivious of the interruption. "Barrett!" Milner called out. "Got a message."

Malcolm Eugene Barrett, twenty-six, aka Malcolm Steel, aka Downtown Mal, was serving his fifth jail term in his fourth jail—Cleveland, Ohio, had hosted him twice—this time thirty days for drunk and disorderly. In the world Barrett inhabited he was accorded a certain respect for never having served penitentiary time. The night of his arrest Barrett had been far too drunk to be disorderly, but at the time it hadn't seemed wise to press the point. He had been drunk because he was celebrating the fact that four hours before his arrest, he and two of his friends had successfully burgled the largest home-appliance store in Lounds County. The cops never asked him about the burglary, and thirty days seemed a small price to pay for anonymity. Besides, the jail was overcrowded and the judge was cutting him loose the next day, nine days early.

When Milner called his name, he was on his bunk, intently reading an eight-month-old copy of *U.S. News & World Report*. He set the magazine aside and swung easily off the flat bunk. He was a big man, well over six feet tall and weighing more than 230 pounds. He was wearing jail-green pants and a white strap T-shirt. The trailing four inches of a surgical scar ran from his right armpit onto his chest under his shirt.

"Yeah, man," he said, smiling as he approached the door. "Y'all going to let this nigger out *today?*"

Milner's eyes were serious through the screen. "No, you don't juke and jive till tomorrow, Malcolm." He looked down at the sheet of paper in his hand. "Malcolm, do you have a brother named Lawrence Amos Barrett?"

"That's my little brother, yeah." Barrett's smile weakened slightly. "He sure as hell ain't in this county, though. You boys didn't 'rrest him, didya?"

Milner sighed. "Malcolm, I got a message here that you should call your aunt Miriam. It's important. You got the number?"

"Yeah, I got the number." Barrett's smile was gone and he looked disgusted. "He got 'rrested somewhere else, is what you're telling me, and Auntie Miriam's getting stuck with the bail?" The Barrett boys' mother had died when Malcolm was sixteen, and her sister had taken over the task of raising the two of them. Barrett gestured at the man crouched next to the door. "I'd call her right now, but this crazy motherfucker spends all day on the phone."

Milner angled his eyes down through the hole. "Lamont!" he snapped. "You talking to your old lady again?"

The man on the floor covered the handset mouthpiece and nodded. He wore a long, black ponytail and his thin arms were covered with an intricate network of jailhouse tattoos. "What's it to you, Milner? They put the fuckin' thing in here for us to use, didn't they?"

"We put it in there for *all* of you to use. You act like that phone is part of your ear. Get off it for a minute, Barrett needs to call his family."

"Be cool." Lamont murmured something into the phone and replaced the handset on the cradle. "Everybody round here's got a bad fuckin' attitude, man," he said as he walked over toward the gin-rummy game. "Need to dose this place or something. Shit."

Milner started to close the cover, then paused. "Malcolm, you need anything or you don't get through, you bang on the door. I'll come back." There was concern in his eyes as the cover snapped shut.

Barrett felt a tickle of real alarm. His experience told him that any news that made a jailer into a real human being was probably bad news, and there was no denying that his little brother was a little bit crazy. His right hand drifted unconsciously to the scar on his chest.

He quickly dialed his aunt's number. She answered on the first ring. "Hello?" Her familiar voice sounded even more frail than usual, and Barrett wondered if the chemotherapy was dragging her down again. He waited patiently as the phone control system went through its routine.

"This is a collect call from the Lounds County Jail in Lounds County, Indiana," said a flat, mechanical voice. "If you choose to accept this call, you will be billed normal toll and tariff charges plus one dollar. If you choose to accept this call, please press the pound sign on your phone."

There was a slight pause, and Barrett could imagine the delicate old woman reaching carefully to the face of the phone she kept next to her regular place on the sofa. There was a beep as she pushed the button.

"Malcolm? Malcolm baby, is that you?"

Barrett wasn't sure, but he thought his aunt was crying. "Yeah, it's me, Auntie Miriam." He forced himself to sound cheerful. "What's goin' on, Auntie? What's that fool brother of mine gone and done? He ain't in jail, is he? Is Las Vegas in jail?"

13

RODNEY carefully aimed the pistol and pulled the trigger. The plastic dart shot out of the child's gun and slapped into a centerfold pinned to the wall of Showalter's office at the club. The dart hung there for a moment, trembling, then fell to the floor. Rodney grinned. "Tit shot," he said.

"Her name is Alice," Showalter rumbled from behind his desk. "She used to dance for me."

Mackin smiled. "So that's the deal." He and Maggie had returned from Chicago that afternoon. He pointed to the sheet of paper he had received from Frank Riles. "Bottom line is, there's money up there. I'm gonna go up there and get some of it. You in or out?"

"In," Showalter said. He looked at Rodney, who was fitting another dart into the pistol. "How about it, bro? You in or out?"

"Fuck yes, I'm in. Got me a new old lady, she's spoiled and she's expensive. I'm in." Rodney fired again at the centerfold and winced. "Looked like that one hurt."

Mackin looked concerned. "Rodney, don't get me wrong on this, but—"

The younger man interrupted him. "You worried that maybe I don't want to knock this shithead down 'cause he's a black shithead? Black power, racial solidarity, all that sixties shit? Fuck that. Pointy Williams never did shit for me. We partners or what?"

Mackin nodded. "All the way."

"Then I'm in. Let's go make some money."

"You're an evil Negro, Rodney," Showalter growled equitably. "I feel better about myself when I think about you."

"Ain't nothing ought to make you feel good about yourself, you goddamn white-trash pornographer." Rodney pointed the gun across the desk and shot Showalter in the chest with his last dart. "I was a good little churchgoing boy when I met you two, and look at me now. I'm a goddamn unapprehended felon."

"Eddie will have wallet sets for both of you tomorrow night," Mackin interrupted. "I'd like you to drive up there the next day. There's a town called Easton, it's really just a suburb, that's only one interstate exit out of Williams's territory. Different jurisdiction, though. There's a Holidome just off the highway; get a motel room there and wait for me." He dropped an envelope on Showalter's desk. "There's a couple grand there for expenses. I'll be up day after that, probably." He stood up and headed for the door.

"Mackin." Showalter spoke from behind his desk. "When do I get my bartender back?"

Mackin smiled and opened the door. "Couple more days, Bo. We're having fun."

Rodney leered. "That Maggie, she's a hot little thing."

Showalter spoke again, his tone now serious. "What should we haul up there?"

Mackin wasn't smiling anymore. "Take a lot, Bo. I am. Might need it." He stepped out and closed the door behind him.

Rodney stood and walked over to where the darts had landed on the floor. He bent over to retrieve them. "Mackin is truly pissed at this Williams clown," he said conversationally. "I wonder if he'll kill him."

Showalter shook his head. "Not right away." He picked up the envelope and tucked it in his pocket. "Two grand here, five grand a pop for the wallet sets, so just getting up there he's out twelve thousand. He made twenty on the score, so he's still ahead, but he'll want to get *way* ahead. Can't do that if the sumbitch is dead."

"True." Rodney returned to his chair and loaded the dart pistol. "But once he gets ahead, I don't think he's gonna want Pointy Williams looking round for him." He aimed at the door and pulled the trigger. "Bull's-eye."

The Lakefront Hilton was generally thought to be one of the two or three best hotels in the state and featured prices to match. Nick Maloney was familiar with the limitations of a detective sergeant's expense account, and he wondered why Petrone had picked the hotel for their meeting. Maloney stepped through the pneumatic doors, glanced around the plush lobby, and headed for the door labeled CITY LIGHTS. He saw Petrone and another man sitting in a booth in the darkest corner of the bar.

"Sit down, Nick." Petrone pointed to a thermal coffeepot in the middle of the table. "We already ordered for you. Drink the coffee slowly, my friend. That pot cost seven dollars and eighty cents."

Maloney grinned at the detective. "Since when did you turn into a big spender?" He extended his hand to the other man at the table. "Nick Maloney. I'm with the *Times*."

"This is John Lockhart," Petrone said as the two men shook hands. "He's a big-time insurance flatfoot—"

"Loss-control manager," Lockhart interrupted with a pained expression. "I'm a *loss-control manager*, Milos."

"—but he used to be a real FBI cop kind of guy, and he's mostly okay." Petrone waved an arm around the elegant bar. "When you cease to be a real policeman and become a loss-control manager, your bosses put you in the Ritz."

"I know your work," Lockhart said to the reporter. "I mean your real work, not that public-relations-fluff Townsend Lake Strangler stroking that made Petrone here look like Dirty Harry Callahan. That labor-racketeering series you did a few years back was strong stuff. I was still with the Bureau, and that made some serious waves."

"Always nice to meet a reader," Maloney said. "That labor thing was kind of fun. You guys put Sam Jennerette in Leavenworth for an eighteen-year stretch after the wire services picked up on the story, and ever since he went up, he's been telling everyone who'll listen that he's gonna have me killed soon as he gets out. He sends me a Christmas card every year."

Lockhart looked dubious. "Sam Jennerette is not exactly a Cub Scout, Mr. Maloney."

"Nick." The reporter poured himself a cup of coffee. "In my experience, you don't have much to worry about as long as a gangster is *talking* about killing you. It's when they don't say anything that you start worrying."

"Nick has spent the past few years living off of the crumbs from my table," Petrone began.

Lockhart smiled at the reporter. "How do you put up with him?"

"I'm crazy about his wife. What've you guys got?"

Petrone pushed a two-inch-thick manila envelope across the table. "Don't open it in here, Nick," he said, his voice suddenly serious. "I've photocopied parts of seven different files. Everything in that envelope has been cleared for your use, background only, by the chief. This conversation is also background only, deep background. No direct quotes, attribution to 'departmental sources close to the investigation' or some reporter stuff like that. The photographs you can print, once you run the story."

"So what *is* the story?" Maloney slipped the envelope into his lap.

Petrone and Lockhart alternated in telling Maloney what they knew. The two men talked for almost forty minutes. Except for periodically refilling his coffee cup, the reporter sat absolutely still. Lockhart was surprised that he took no notes.

"So the way it looks," Petrone finished, "Pointy Williams hired a professional thief to heist a shitload of food stamps and set him up for a terminal waltz with Kendall and Macnamara. Somehow, Christ knows how, the thief, this Moffitt character, breaks the play and whacks both of them. If the wiretap stuff is on the money, he's now on his way back here to settle up. He may be here now, for all I know."

"Walnut Towers?"

Lockhart shrugged. Petrone shook his head. "I'm ninety-nine percent confident that he didn't have anything to do with that. We've ID'd the victims, and they're small-timers from out of town. Indiana. I'm not even certain the Williams organization is involved, though being the Brickyard it probably was. From what John knows about the guy, Moffitt would use professionals, not street hoods."

"From what I think I know about the guy," Lockhart said quietly, "he *wins* gunfights."

"So how long do I wait?"

"If you print it now, Nick, the son of a bitch will know we know about him." Petrone looked at the reporter. "Look, Nick, Pointy Williams is old news, he's been around fifteen years. That's one thing. This Thunderstruck thing, they've got a man under on Williams, and if you print that, you'll probably get a cop killed. That's another thing." Petrone hadn't given Maloney any details of the undercover operation and the reporter hadn't asked for any.

"You won't find a thing in that envelope that indicates that the department has a pervasive corruption problem, so Kendall and Macnamara are mostly old news, too. I truly don't give a shit about any of that. I want Moffitt for murder, and it sounds like he's on his way back here. You sit on this for a few days, maybe for a week or two, I've got a shot at nailing the bastard."

"No one else on the force is implicated beyond Kendall and Macnamara, you're sure?"

"I'm not absolutely certain that every single cop in the city is absolutely clean, no," Petrone said reasonably. "There's more than four hundred of us, for Christ's sake. But I'm sure that IA doesn't have any suspicions about anyone else working for Williams."

"Okay." Maloney stood up and tucked the envelope under his arm. "I'll talk to my editors, Milos. I'm sure they'll go along with a delay, but two weeks may be a little much."

"Do what you can, Nick."

The reporter reached across the table and shook Lockhart's hand. "Nice meeting you, John. Don't pick up any bad habits from this guy. He's got a thing for roaches."

"Don't you two start ganging up on me," Petrone said. "Life is tough enough without a laugh track."

"By the way, Milos." The reporter turned as he began to walk away. "I'm afraid I'm going to have to change the deal a little."

Petrone stared stonily at the reporter. "Don't start pulling my chain, Nick."

"This is bigger than I thought." Maloney gazed at the ceiling for a moment, deep in thought. "But . . . I'll continue to cooperate if you invite me over for dinner and convince Sarah to make roast beef. Say, Friday."

Petrone groaned.

"Hey, good idea," Lockhart said. "Count me in."

The bus station was in the Brickyard. Malcolm Barrett walked out into the rainy night with a single suitcase that held two changes of clothing, a carton of Kools, a seventeen-shot Steyr nine-millimeter pistol, and fifty rounds of ammunition. He found a pay phone and called his dead brother's girlfriend. She started crying as soon as she recognized his voice. "I'm at the bus station," he said shortly. "Pick me up."

He couldn't remember if her name was June or Julie or Jane. He'd only met her twice, both times when she'd appeared with Las Vegas at planning sessions for the score on Pointy Williams. The rip-off was originally Malcolm's idea.

He was tired of life as a small-time thief but felt no desire to be a street-corner dealer. He dreamed of setting himself and his brother up as major players. He had a connection in Atlanta who could supply him with limitless quantities of blow, cash only, no credit. "You're a good man, Barrett," the connection had told him one night, "but you be wastin' my time with your nickel-and-dime bullshit. You want to get serious, come back with fifty gs and we'll do a little business."

The fact of the matter was that $50,000 was almost equal to Malcolm Barrett's earnings for his entire criminal career. It was more money than he had ever thought about possessing at one time. The only way he could imagine obtaining that much money was to steal it, and the only person he knew of who might serve as a victim was Pointy Williams.

"We ain't from around here," he told his little brother. "No one knows who we are, where we're really from. When I was in Cleveland County Correctional, all I heard was 'Pointy Williams this' and 'Pointy Williams that.' This motherfucker got everybody convinced he's Supernigger. We do this right, maybe we can kryptonite the asshole."

It had taken months to put the operation together, Malcolm constantly trying to restrain his younger brother's rash impulsiveness: "Got to get him used to us, Las Vegas. Got to become part of the scenery round here."

Malcolm, Las Vegas, a cousin named Lock, and a friend named Eugene launched a small crime wave, carrying out a series of residential and business burglaries to finance the tease. Malcolm kept the other three away from the money and put together enough to buy six ounces of cocaine, three of them high-grade Peruvian flake that cost more than twice as much as common street dope. He also bought himself some new clothes, including two silk suits. "You want to be a player, you got to look like a player," he explained to the other three.

A bartender at a nightclub called Indian Jack's sent him to a bartender at Ma Rainey's, who set up a meeting with the assistant manager at Vingt-et-Un. Barrett distributed cocaine liberally during these sessions—not the Peruvian, he was saving that—and the Vingt-et-Un manager had already decided to get in touch with Dink Reeves when Pointy Williams himself approached the two men at the restaurant bar one night.

"I hear you are a man who likes French food and likes to party, Mr. Steel," Williams said, shaking Barrett's hand. "That means you're my kind of man."

"That's when I pulled out some of the Peruvian," Barrett told his brother. "We ended up at his office, stayed till five in the A.M."

On his next trip to the city, Las Vegas traveled with him. Malcolm sat in the dark elegance of Vingt-et-Un with Williams and casually dropped hints about the size of his action. "I'm like you, homes," he said one night, mimicking the style of his Atlanta connection. "I stay the hell away from nickel-and-dime shit."

Las Vegas spent his nights playing the slots at Ma Rainey's. He met June or whatever her name was the second night, and soon a romance blossomed.

"You stay here," Malcolm told his brother the next day. "Keep an eye on shit, find a good place for this to go down. I got this Williams fucker eating right out of my hand; gave him a half ounce of the flake last night and told him I might be willin' to do a three-key deal if we could do it fast. We be looking at seventy-five grand, cash, little brother, we don't fuck this up. We fuck it up, we be dead, so you fly low while I'm gone. I'm going home to take care of business, be back in three, four days."

In Lounds County three night later, he and his friends hit Shaken's Home Furnishings, and Malcolm's celebration put him in jail. Las Vegas, he assumed, had tried to go through with the deal on his own. Now he paced up and down the sidewalk in front of the bus station cursing himself for getting drunk that night, cursing his brother for not waiting, cursing the girl for taking too long.

She appeared fifteen minutes later. He threw his suitcase in the backseat and climbed into the passenger seat. She was still crying.

"You stop that, now," he said, not unkindly.

"Oh, Malcolm, it was terrible." She wiped her eyes with a crumpled, much-used tissue. "He and his cousin and Eugene got so amped when they found out you were in jail. They just sat around my apartment for two weeks just talking and drinking and talking, and then one afternoon Las Vegas, he started making phone calls. After a while all three of them went back in the bedroom for about half an hour, and then he got another phone call."

Barrett listened in silence.

"Around eleven o'clock they laid out all the rest of that special blow you left and started doing lines, and then they split. Las Vegas, he was so wired he couldn't hardly stay on the floor, and he kissed me and said he was gonna do a deal that was gonna make you proud of him, and they left, and that was the last time I ever saw him."

Her shoulders heaved, and she began to sob again. Barrett nodded, as much to himself as to the woman next to him.

"You hush now." June, he decided. "June, I'm gonna stay at your crib tonight, get some sleep. I'll take care of all this tomorrow. Count on it."

She looked at him over the tissue, alarm visible in her eyes. "What are you gonna do, Malcolm?"

"I'm goin' to fix everything, baby. I'm goin' to make things right."

14

RODNEY AND BO drove to Easton in the black man's car, a silver Taurus with a stereo system Bo believed could've served as the PA for Woodstock. Rodney was listening to Public Enemy's *Fear of a Black Planet.* "I know it makes me sound like an old fart," Bo said, "but I just don't get this new shit, this rap. You got any Delfonics?"

"Ain't new, and you're right, you're an old fart." Rodney's eyes shifted constantly from the road ahead to his mirrors to the blinking red light of his radar detector. He kept the car just below seventy miles an hour. "Rap been around since the seventies. Just what exactly we gonna do when we get where we're going?"

Bo shrugged. "Mackin picked up some dope in Chicago on this Williams guy; he's like any other operator. Does mostly cash business. I guess we'll just find the business with the most cash, walk in, and take it. First on the list is a joint called Ma Rainey's. Williams has some gambling action there. No big deal, in and out of town quick." He yawned and stretched. "I think Mackin's ready for a vacation."

"Wanted a vacation, should've taken off after the Milwaukee score. I did." Rodney touched his turn signal as they approached a service area. "Won't surprise me a bit, we have to kill someone before this is all over. Don't know why he went fuckin' around with a bunch of food stamps. Stealin' food stamps, that's coming way down in the world for a cat like Mackin."

Bo grinned. "Don't you let him forget it, either, but all he was doing was helping Riles out." He shook his head. "Food stamps, though. I know what you mean. Next we'll be hitting church poor boxes."

"I won't be hittin' no poor boxes." Rodney pulled up in front of a gas pump and handed Bo a twenty-dollar bill. "I got too much self-respect to be robbing poor boxes. Pay for the gas, bro, and grab us some sandwiches and coffee."

Rodney filled the gas tank as Showalter walked into the station. When he reappeared, the big man was carrying a paper sack and two large cups of coffee. He climbed into the car and handed Rodney an egg-salad sandwich and one of the cups. Rodney looked at him over his sunglasses. "Where's my change, man?"

"For Christ's sake, Rodney, the change was two dollars and sixteen cents."

"So where's my two dollars and sixteen cents?"

Showalter stared at him for a moment, then smiled. "I'm keeping it because when we went to the Raiders game a couple weeks ago, you kept my change after you paid for the parking."

Rodney shook his head. "Two wrongs don't make a right, Bo."

"I don't fucking believe this." Showalter dug a couple of bills and coins from his shirt pocket and set them on the console. "You never quit."

Rodney started the car. "We'll be there in about four hours. Maybe I'll buy you a cheeseburger. Turn the tape over."

"You sure you don't have any Delfonics?" Showalter turned the cassette and reinserted it in the tape deck. "Four hours of this, I'll be *ready* to kill someone."

"I think I'm going to move to Tempe, Nick." There was a touch of querulousness in the old man's voice, but only a touch. "My daughter's down there. The winters here, Lord God, it's too much for a man my age." He threw a torn bit of bread in the direction of the ducks.

Maloney barked out a laugh. "Like hell, Benny. The Seventh Cavalry couldn't get you out of this town." He'd almost said, "You'll die in this town," but the last time Maloney had seen Benny Freed had been at the funeral of Benny's wife, Rachel.

The old man seemed to read his mind. "Thank you again for coming to the funeral, Nick. Rachel always thought highly of you." He removed another piece of bread from the loaf on the bench between them and began to shred the slice between his fingers. His movements were controlled and precise. "I can't believe it was only three months ago, still summer. We used to come to the lake this time of year to feed the ducks together, you know. They're filthy birds, nasty dispositions, but Rachel thought they were so elegant on the water."

He threw more of the bread on the lake. "Old men's memories, Nick. What can this old man do for you?"

"Let's pretend that we were going to tip over a bank, Benny. Or maybe a museum or Fort Knox. Who do we call?"

Freed smiled at the ducks. "Felton Industrial Printing. I saw the stories in the newspapers. So slick and professional to steal just food stamps."

He squinted against the damp afternoon sunlight. Benny Freed was eighty-one years old and frail, but as far as Maloney knew, Freed carried more information about American crime and criminals in his head than was in all the computers of the Law Enforcement Assistance Administration. Freed had started his career as a croupier in Meyer Lansky's Colonial Inn casino in Hallandale, Florida, in 1938 and followed Lansky to Cuba the following year. He spent the forties and fifties organizing and operating gambling operations from Cuba to Toronto, working with some of the most dangerous men in the history of crime: Benny Siegel, Carmine Galante, Paul Ricca, Moe Dalitz. He was in Las Vegas the night Siegel was shot dead in Los Angeles.

"They knew about it at the Flamingo before the Los Angeles police knew," he once told Maloney matter-of-factly. "Guys were moving files out fifteen minutes after it happened. They knew about it at the Desert Inn. The whole damned town knew, Nick. No one was surprised, not even Meyer, and Meyer was Benny's best friend. With those people, you borrow that much money, keep it that long, it's like stealing. Meyer died in bed, I'll die in bed, because we never stole a dime from anyone."

Now Freed shook his head. "There isn't much I can tell you, Nick. It's been so long. I retired in '68. Sure, people still call me now and then, but I'm out of the game."

"C'mon, Benny." Maloney tossed a chunk of bread onto

the water and lit a cigarette. "You played cribbage with Joe Macchi once a week for fifteen years. You vouched for Capetti when he was just a kid, for chrissakes. People talk, especially to you."

"There was one man," Freed said cautiously. "I don't know his name, you understand. It was 1981, '82 maybe. Tommy Blue Eyes, the boy from Detroit? You remember, they found him in a drainpipe a couple of years ago. He was going to rob a bank in the Bahamas. The South Americans, they were starting to do a lot of their drug banking in the Bahamas, and everyone thought the banks there were full of cash. There was some talk, anyway. Always so much talk."

Freed massaged his knees with his gnarled fingers. "You have to excuse me, I can't be more specific. I wasn't really part of it, you understand. For me it was always gambling, never the rest of it, but I heard some talk. There was a man, a thief, who had worked with people in Chicago. Tommy Blue Eyes called Capetti about this man. He was supposed to be very good, a professional. Not a made man, you understand, not an Italian, but trustworthy. There was talk he had robbed guns from the army."

"Bingo." Maloney smiled. "That's the guy, Benny, the guy whose picture was in the paper. What was his name?"

The old man grimaced. "What do I know from names, Nick? People who know all the names end up like Benny, on a sofa with one eye on the floor halfway across the room. Me, I'm a gambler."

"So what happened?"

"Who knows? I know Tommy Blue Eyes didn't rob the bank. Later, I heard that Capetti wouldn't give him the thief's name, because you know Sal never really trusted Tommy. But I also heard that Tommy called it off because he was fighting that RICO thing. It wasn't the kind of thing you brought up to people over dinner, you understand."

Two ducks, one dirty gray and the other snow-white, swung gracefully across the pond from opposite directions. Maloney threw a slice of bread in the water between them. "You've been a big help, Benny. You think of anything else, give me a call."

The two ducks veered lazily toward the bread. Freed pointed. "Three to five on the gray one, Nick."

Mackin and Maggie Raynor were finishing lunch in his apartment. He had the blinds drawn. They were eating by candlelight. They'd spent barely a minute apart since their first night together. Maggie had made stir-fry.

"She can cook, too." Mackin smiled at her across the table.

She smiled back. "I'm a hell of a cook." She sipped from a glass of rosé. "And I already did most of the dishes."

"You're going to spoil me."

"Sure am."

They drank their wine. "I had a lot of fun in Chicago," she said.

"So did I."

"You didn't have to buy me all those things."

He smiled and shrugged. He couldn't remember ever being so comfortable in the company of a woman. "I like buying you things." He lifted the bottle and refilled her glass. "I'm going to have to leave town for a few days."

"With Bo and Rodney?"

He nodded. "They already left, this morning. I should take off tonight, maybe tomorrow morning. It'll only be for three or four days. Place called Easton. Business."

She spun her wineglass by its stem. "Mackin, I want you to know that I don't care what you do. I mean, I'm not dumb, okay? I've been around a little bit. However you make your money is none of my business. I won't ask you any questions."

He looked across the table at her. Her eyes glinted in the candlelight. "I'm not a bad person, Maggie, at least I don't think so. I don't let people push me around, but I'm not foaming at the mouth. I don't deal drugs, don't rape women, don't take food out of the mouths of starving babies."

She shook her head. "I don't want to know anything, Mackin. Your business is your business."

He grinned and spoke without thinking. "Want to come with me?"

"You bet." She reached across the table and took his hand. "Anytime, anywhere."

He made a show of looking at the grandfather clock. "We have a couple hours to kill before we have to leave. . . ."

"Race you to the bed."

Two hours later, Mackin lay with his arm draped over Maggie's sleeping form. Her quiet breathing was the only sound in the room. He didn't think about his decision to take her to Easton. It was no big deal. All his business would be in the city, and he trusted her. Bo and Rodney wouldn't like it much, but they wouldn't lose their minds over it, either.

Images from the unmarked police car in the Brickyard kept running through his mind. He remembered the way the big .45 had bucked in his hand when he shot the two cops, the way his ears hurt from the sound of the shots. He remembered the fear. The scene played itself out in his head in detail, just as it did every time he was drifting off to sleep. He pulled

Maggie closer and buried his face in her hair. It was the only way he'd found to make the images stop.

Rodney checked them into rooms at the Easton Holidome, two hundred yards from the interstate. "Not Mackin," Bo said. "He likes to have a couple of safe holes on jobs like this. He'll pick a place when he gets here."

Rodney lied on every line of the registration card, including make, model, and license plate of his car. "I did say it was silver," he told Showalter. The two men moved their bags into the rooms.

Showalter bought copies of the Easton daily paper and all the papers from the city. "The cop killings aren't front-page anymore," he said with satisfaction. "Only one of these is still running the driver's license picture, and it's about an inch square on page fourteen. We're in good shape."

Rodney drove to a service plaza and bought the largest and most detailed map of the city available. The two men spent the evening hours marking locations from Riles's information on the map. "I think, my dark-skinned friend," Bo said, "that you probably ought to handle the recon in this paradise next to downtown that Mackin calls the Brickyard."

Rodney smiled. "White boy scared of getting mugged?"

"Something like that."

They finished around eleven. Bo stood up. "I'm going to my room, gonna hit the hay. Mackin'll probably be here in the morning." Rodney was still awake and watching television at midnight when the phone rang.

"Hello," he said cautiously.

"Mackin. Just got in. I'm right up the road, little place called the Circle 7 motel. Room one sixteen."

"I saw the signs. Bo just went to bed. We worked out the map shit, figured out where Ma Rainey's is and that warehouse. Warehouse is only two exits away. You want me to drive over, show you what we got?"

"Tomorrow. Meet you for breakfast over there, say, nine. We're tired."

Rodney stared at his television and squinted. "We?"

"Maggie came along."

The black man didn't speak for four or five seconds. He sighed. "You are too much, Mackin. What she gonna be doin' while we're taking on your friend?"

"Shopping, I imagine. See you at breakfast." He broke the connection.

Rodney hung up the phone and scowled. Then he laughed out loud. "You dog, you." He used the remote control to shut off the television, rolled over, and went to sleep.

Mackin replaced the phone on the cradle and dropped his arm across Maggie's shoulder. They were in bed. He leaned over and kissed her neck. "I'm through for the day."

They had made love as soon as they reached the room and she was almost asleep. She ran a hand across his chest and smiled. "Good day?"

"I liked the way it ended." He pulled her closer. "Thanks for coming."

"I'm getting used to you," she murmured. "You don't need a keeper. I like that."

She raised a soft hand to his face and felt him grin in the darkness. "No, I don't need a keeper." He kissed her again. "Now sleep, wench."

It was Mackin who dropped off first. Maggie felt his body

settle into the rhythmic breathing of sleep. The room was black and silent. As she lay next to him, she thought about the first morning they had spent together and how much she liked to wake up with him. She suspected that he'd had second thoughts about bringing her to Easton, and the fact that he had brought her after all furthered her belief that this was more than a casual fling for him.

She smiled. They'd known each other only a few days, but she felt as if she already knew him well. He didn't need a keeper. He needed a haven, and Maggie had already decided that she would provide one. She neither knew nor cared what was chasing him. She assumed that one day he'd tell her, and she knew that when he did, it wouldn't change anything between them. She pushed her head under his shoulder and fell asleep.

Malcolm Barrett sat on a bus stop bench across the street from Pointy Williams's office on Amsterdam Street. He'd been there for twenty minutes, which he thought was long enough. He wasn't ready to be noticed. The lights were on in Pointy's office, but he had seen no movement in the window. He stood up and ambled toward the corner of Amsterdam and 113th Street.

He was dressed in dungarees and a stained flannel work shirt and was carrying a bottle of Mogen David wine wrapped in a paper bag. It wasn't very likely that he'd be recognized as the dapper, free-spending player who had entertained the boys at Vingt-et-Un. His pistol was tucked in the small of his back under a torn army fatigue jacket that he'd pulled from June's closet. He crossed Amsterdam at the light and continued walking until he found the alley that ran behind Pointy's building.

As soon as he entered the darkness of the alley, he set the bottle on the ground, pulled his pistol, and pushed it into the front of his pants. A half block down the narrow, brick-lined passageway he saw Pointy's Volvo parked at the building's back door. He didn't have much of a plan. He'd decided as soon as he got off the phone with his aunt that he had to find Pointy and kill him, but he didn't like the idea of returning to Vingt-et-Un. He walked down the alley to the car and saw a black metal fire escape that seemed to lead to Pointy's floor. Every few steps he stopped to listen and check his back.

Danny saw the black man from the back window on the second floor as soon as he entered the alley. He watched, curious, as the man shifted a pistol in his waistband and began to sneak through the darkness.

"Hey, Dink," he called over his shoulder. He was standing in the darkness of the back hall with his shotgun cradled in his arms. Beano-D was watching the front of the building from inside Grovner's Pawn and Loan. The two of them alternated shifts with the Conway brothers, a pair of heavies Pointy used for errands and additional security. "There's a guy with a gun playing Rambo in the alley."

Reeves joined him at the window. "Same guy Beano-D saw on the bus bench."

"Thought that guy was a wino."

"Winos don't have guns, Danny."

"What do you want me to do?"

Reeves thought for a moment. "Could be he's working for the thief. Could be he's part of the crew we danced with at the Towers, could be he's a fuckin' cop." He scowled. "Too much shit goin' on here. Unlock the fire-escape door. Don't bother him 'less he starts to come in. He comes in, you make like the sandman and put the fucker to sleep. Pointy'll want to talk to him."

Danny stepped to the door on the left wall and turned the handles on both dead bolts. "Where is Pointy?" He hadn't seen his employer since before the shootings at Walnut Towers.

"Plane gets in tomorrow."

They watched the black man in the alley approach the Volvo. He peered through the car windows, then pulled his gun and looked at the fire escape. The two men pulled back from the window.

Dink shook his head. "Ain't no cop. You want me to call Beano?"

Danny snorted. "Fucker's alone, no problem."

They heard metal grinding as the man in the alley pulled down the fire-escape ladder. Danny slid across the hall to a position next to the door. He would be behind it when it opened. He held the shotgun in both hands with the barrel pointed at the ceiling.

Dink drew his revolver and stepped out of sight into the office. "Bastard's got big balls," he whispered. The two men listened as the intruder attempted to climb the fire escape without making any noise.

Malcolm Barrett wasn't sure what he was going to do. The windows in the back of the office were dark, and the burglar in him liked the idea of a surreptitious entry. He thought he'd decide on a plan after he checked the upstairs fire door.

He climbed the stairs slowly. He could hear an occasional car pass the building on Amsterdam Street. His palms were sweating. At the top of the fire escape he reached out with his left hand and carefully turned the doorknob. The door was unlocked. He wiped his left hand on his jacket, shifted his gun and did the same with his right hand, then shifted the gun back.

He took a deep breath and tried to remember the layout of the office. He pushed open the door and stepped into the hallway. He felt only a whisper of air on his neck when Danny stepped out of the darkness and slugged him in the back of the neck with the butt of the shotgun. He collapsed on the quiet gray carpet.

15

MAGGIE wasn't sure whether or not Bo and Rodney were upset by her presence. She finally decided they weren't. The four of them were breakfasting at the Holidome.

"So who's running my bar?" Showalter growled at her, but he was smiling.

"Jesus, Bo, it's not like running General Motors." She was finishing a croissant. "Tina's covering my shifts. She needs the money. I made sure all the schedules were up-to-date before we left."

"Maggie's going back in a couple of days," Mackin said. "I'll drive back with you guys when we're done."

And that, Maggie decided, was her cue to say something the three men would find feminine and make herself scarce. "You know, I saw a brochure at the motel that said Easton has the biggest mall in the state. I think I'll go check it out."

Mackin reached into his breast pocket, removed a folded stack of currency, and shoved it into the outside pocket of her purse. "Buy yourself something nice."

She leaned over, kissed him, and slid out of the booth. "See you tonight?"

"Probably."

She walked out of the restaurant. The three men sat in silence for a moment. Showalter finally spoke. "I'm sure you've got a perfect explanation for bringing my bartender on this joyride, Mackin," he began.

"Cut it, Bo." Mackin kept his voice quiet. "It's no big thing. We drove up here in her car, in a couple of days I'll send her home. I like her. She doesn't have any idea what's going on, and she doesn't ask questions."

Showalter sighed. "That's all real reasonable, my man, but the bottom line is that we came here to do some very bad things, and having her around won't help."

"Won't hurt, either." Mackin turned to Rodney. "I'd like to do Ma Rainey's tonight."

The black man nodded. "I'll check it out this afternoon."

Pointy Williams was pissed off.

"Let me get this straight," he snapped at Dink Reeves. The two men were in Pointy's office on Amsterdam Street. "I go out of town for four, five days. While I'm gone, you almost get your goddamn head blown off in Walnut Towers, the thief is s'posed to be on his way back here, and some nigger you never saw before climbs my fucking fire escape with a piece."

"That's about it," Dink said. "Welcome home."

Williams stood up. "Let's take a look at this fire-escape-climbin' fool."

Dink led him to the office bathroom. Malcolm Barrett was tied to the toilet, his hands and feet bound. Masking tape covered his mouth. A small bloodstain from the blow to his head was visible on his collar. Barrett's eyes snapped up when the door opened. Williams recognized him immediately.

"Shit." There was real surprise in Williams's voice. He pulled Reeves back in the hall. "That's Malcolm Steel. That's the motherfucker set up the deal at the Towers. I thought you killed him."

Reeves shrugged. "Killed everyone there. He wasn't there."

Williams nodded. "I'll talk to him alone." He watched Reeves return to the office, then stepped back into the bathroom.

"Malcolm, Malcolm, Malcolm," he said chidingly. "Why you want to fuck with Pointy Williams? It wasn't enough all your people get killed, you have to come back here and die yourself. Who got it at the Towers was so important you had to come here? Cousin, maybe? A brother?"

Barrett's eyes flashed hate. Williams smiled.

"Brother. Well, your brother fucked up, homes, and now he's ice. Here's what I want you to think about: I'm goin' to spend the next few minutes with my people trying to figure out what the fuck to do with your body. Once we get that worked out, I'm comin' back in here to kill you personally."

He laughed and walked out of the bathroom. Malcolm Barrett immediately resumed twisting his wrists against the ropes that bound his hands. Beano-D had tied him well.

Rodney drifted into Ma Rainey's just as the lunch crowd started to break up. The club was in a large, dilapidated, one-story brick building on a corner in the Brickyard. He walked around the building, noting a utility pole sitting in the parking lot in the back. There was an entrance from the parking lot, but he walked all the way around and went in through the front door.

It was dark and cool inside. Rainey's was a long, narrow room divided by a waist-high partition. The bar ran the length of the left side of the room. A dozen tables were lined in front of the bar. That side was clearly the serious drinking side. Across the partition was the entertainment side of the club. Four pool tables squatted near the front door, and a stage ran across the far end of the room near the door to the parking lot. A PA system was set up on the stage, and photocopied flyers stapled on the walls advertised the appearance of a band called Reason's End. A sign over the bar said MAXIMUM CAPACITY—365. It looked like dozens of other bars Rodney knew.

Fewer than twenty people were in the club, most of them sitting on stools at the bar. The crowd was entirely black and Hispanic. Two bartenders leaned against the beer coolers chatting in low tones. The back wall of the bar, more than forty feet long, was lined with row upon row of full liquor bottles.

Rodney walked directly to the bar and pulled up a stool. A bartender approached immediately. "Draw," Rodney said, and threw a five on the bar. "I'd like the change in quarters."

The bartender returned with the beer and a handful of change. Rodney dropped another five in the tip jar and hefted the handful of quarters. "I'm looking for a chance to spend these," he said quietly. He smiled.

The bartender eyed him for a moment, then cocked his head to the back of the club. "End of the bar."

Rodney strolled toward the stage. The bar ended a few feet short of the back wall, and by turning as if he were walking behind the bar, Rodney came to a door covered with a stained green curtain. A beefy Hispanic man sat in front of the door on a barstool reading a comic book. A thin scar ran from the corner of his left eye to the lobe of his left ear. He looked up without curiosity as Rodney approached, his brown eyes as flat as agate.

"Bartender sent me back, friend," Rodney said.

The doorman glanced at the bartender, who offered a small nod. The doorman leaned back and returned to his comic book.

Rodney pushed through the curtain. It opened on a large room that appeared to run all the way behind the bar. The walls were covered with gambling machines, most of them video slots or video poker games. Rodney counted thirty-three of them. A dozen other men were in the room. "Shit fire," one of them said in an irritated voice, staring at the image on the screen in front of him.

Rodney selected a poker machine at random, dropped four quarters in the slot, and selected five-card draw. He bet the entire dollar. The machine dealt him a four-card straight, ten to the king, and another ten. He discarded everything but the two tens and drew a pair of deuces and a six. "Two Pair!" the machine flashed. "You Win!" A pile of brass game tokens erupted from the horizontal slot at the bottom. He carefully pocketed them, then continued playing on his quarters.

He ran out of quarters in less than ten minutes and walked back out to the bar. He discreetly pushed the tokens to the bartender, who pulled a heavy steel fishing-tackle box from a shelf under the bar. Rodney saw that it was filled with piles of currency and hundreds of tokens. The bartender dropped the tokens in the box, counted out four one-dollar bills, and handed them across the bar without a word.

Rodney drained his beer and looked around the room. A pay phone was in an alcove near the front door. He walked over, put the receiver between his jaw and shoulder, and reached into the front pocket of his pants. No one was paying any attention to him. He removed a set of diagonal cutters from his pocket and clipped the cord to the handset.

He stood in the alcove a moment, then walked back to the bar. "Phone's not working."

"Shit." The bartender scowled at the alcove. "Damn thing's broke all the time. Local call? You want to use the bar phone?"

"No, thanks." Rodney smiled. "Not important." He walked across the room and pushed open the back door. He squinted against the bright afternoon sunlight. This was going to be almost too easy.

Pointy Williams walked into Vingt-et-Un, saw Janet Hassan sitting in the bar, and turned on a thousand-watt smile. "Miss Howard," he said, and half-bowed. "I hope you missed me as much as I missed you."

"Mr. Williams." Janet inclined her head and smiled. "How was Florida?"

"Lots of sun, but not much fun without you. You're here early."

"Checking the schedule. Join me for a drink?"

Pointy thought about sitting down and decided against it. "I'm sorry, Janet. Rain-check me, I've got business." He leaned forward, brushed her cheek with his lips, and headed back into the restaurant.

He'd left Dink Reeves at the Amsterdam Street office with Malcolm Barrett still tied up in the bathroom. He was motivated not by mercy but by curiosity. He still wanted to know where Malcolm obtained the high-quality flake he'd been passing out.

He walked through the kitchen and greeted the staff, most of whom were cleaning up after the lunch rush. Vingt-et-Un had been favorably compared to the best French restaurants in the Midwest, in part because Williams paid the highest wages of any restaurant owner in the city. His profit margin was small but growing, and once or twice he'd even thought that one day he'd drop all his other interests in favor of the legitimacy of the restaurant. The thought never lasted long.

He closed himself in his office. He had a lot to think about. Most immediate was the man tied up in the bathroom, whom, Williams supposed, he would eventually have to kill. The return of the thief was a less pressing but no less serious concern. Williams wasn't overly worried about his own safety now that his crew was alerted, but there was a chance that the situation could complicate his relationship with the Capetti organization. Williams was the smallest player in the Consolidated Food deal and hadn't yet earned any significant income from the arrangement. He intended to earn a lot.

In the meantime there was the possibility that the thief would do something rash. He called Amsterdam Street and told Reeves to take Beano-D out on a collection run that night. "Let's not leave too much cash out there. Might tempt somebody to do some stupid shit."

Out in the bar, Janet Hassan finished her drink and spent a moment making small talk with the bartender. Then she gathered up her things and headed for her car. On the drive home she stopped at a pay phone, called the Thunderstruck support number, and left a message that Williams was back in the city.

"These files are bullshit," Lockhart said with disgust. He closed a thin manila folder and tossed it on top of a stack of similar folders on Petrone's desk. "Most of the intel is from the seventies."

Petrone was staring out his office window and tugging at his lip. "From Carl Ingers's day. I believe our friends Kendall and Macnamara cleaned out most of the more recent information we might have had about Williams's operation. We can put it together again, at least most of it, but it will take weeks."

Lockhart lit a cigarette. "So if you were going to take Williams down, where would you hit him?"

"The most recent information tells us that he's become quite the restaurateur. Owns a French joint called Vingt-et-Un that's probably a more valuable asset than just about anything else he's got. But what are you gonna get if you rob a restaurant? Credit card slips? No, if I wanted to hurt him, I'd hit the cash businesses, the dope and the gambling. That would be centered in the clubs, and there's no way to know for sure which club is the most likely target. There are dozens of bars in the Brickyard, and some of them are completely legitimate. The list of the ones that aren't is one of the things no longer in those files."

"What about the car thing?"

"That's more interesting and more frustrating. The wiretap said Williams stores his stolen cars in a warehouse. Hell, there are literally thousands of warehouses in a city this size. It would take months to determine which ones Williams owns or controls."

Petrone shook his head. "We're stuck, John, and I don't like it. I'm afraid we have to wait for our boy to announce himself."

Rodney came back to the motel room in the late afternoon. "It'll work. Corner building, long room, junction box on the outside, parking lot in the back. The game room's behind the bar. Big one. The cash is in a tackle box behind the bar, but they probably got a drop safe."

Mackin was lying on the bed, fully dressed. A football game was on the television, the sound turned off. "Which way does the back door open?"

Rodney thought for a moment. "Swings out, to the parking lot."

"Good. What about the phones?"

"Service pole next to the building in the parking lot. Lines enter the building right next to the junction box."

"Pay phone?"

Rodney grinned. "It's already out of order. Permanently."

Mackin nodded.

"Where's Maggie?"

"Shopping, dinner, a movie. I told her we'd be late." Mackin swung off the bed, opened the closet, pulled out the gun cases, and set them on the bed. "This one's for you," he said, handing over the smallest case.

Rodney opened it and removed a small shotgun. The stock was sawed down to a pistol grip and the barrel was only eighteen inches long. "Twenty-gauge." He sounded doubtful. "Haven't seen one of these for years. Not what I'd call serious firepower."

"Here." Mackin pushed across a handful of shells.

Rodney examined them for a moment and smiled. "I see. Got something else for me?"

Mackin pushed a .38 across the bed. "I doubt you need it. Bo and I will be carrying heavy metal. He's lining up cars. We go in when he gets back."

16

SHOWALTER showed up at eleven. Rodney drew a detailed diagram of the club and explained the layout. "We may not be able to get anywhere with the drop safe."

"Maybe we'll get lucky," Showalter said. "I gotta six-year-old Pontiac wagon parked on the back side of a shopping-center lot about a half mile from the club, so we're all set."

They loaded the gun cases in the trunk of the rental car. Mackin added a box of surgeon's gloves and three masks made from cutoff stockings. "Here we go."

They drove to the shopping center. The station wagon, a battered, green monolith of an automobile, was parked in a dark corner of the large lot. Mackin transferred the contents of the rental car's trunk into the backseat of the wagon and Showalter slid behind the wheel.

"What about the plates?" Mackin asked.

"Swapped the originals with a set I grabbed from some drive-way in the 'burbs." Showalter started the car and Rodney directed them to the back lot of Ma Rainey's.

They parked as close to the door as they could get. Showalter shut off the car, and he and Mackin pulled on gloves. "Two pair each," Mackin said. "Sometimes they tear."

Rodney stepped out of the car and slid the twenty-gauge under his jacket. "Give me two minutes," he said calmly. His dark face was impassive. "I'll go in through the front, make sure there's no heat in there. You guys come in the back."

Mackin nodded and glanced at his watch. "Two minutes. You won't be wearing gloves at first. Don't touch anything, wipe the wedges."

Rodney nodded and vanished into the darkness.

Mackin and Showalter each removed twelve-gauge shotguns from the cases and sat silently in the car. The sky threatened more rain. Mackin pulled back his cuff and looked at his watch. "Let's go."

They left the car and walked toward the front door. They paused at the side of the building long enough for Mackin to cut the phone line, then pulled on their masks. "Tally-fucking-ho," Showalter said.

Rodney kept the shotgun pressed tight against his side under his jacket and sauntered through the front door of the club. The doorman barely glanced at him. "Five-dollar cover," he said flatly. Rodney slipped him a bill and walked into the smoky darkness of the club.

There was a good crowd, almost three hundred people. The interior was full of noise, much of it coming from the frenetic performance of the band onstage. They were tearing through a cover of James Brown's "It's a Man's Man's Man's World."

Rodney pushed carefully through the crowd, heading for the men's room in the back. No cops were in evidence. Three bartenders were busily serving drinks. He saw a line of men waiting for admission to the game room. He walked past them and stuck his head in the men's room. No cops, no heat.

He walked back through the club. Besides the bartenders, two men were standing behind the bar. One was a trim man with intelligent eyes who wore a double-breasted jacket over a sports shirt with no tie. The other was a big man wearing a blue tank top and a plug hat. Management and muscle, he thought.

He strolled back beside the door and leaned against the wall, waiting. His hand was on the mask in his pocket. Precisely two minutes after he walked into the club, the back door burst open.

Mackin went through the door first, the shotgun at port arms in front of him. *"Everybody down!"* he shouted. *"Everybody down on the floor!"*

Showalter was directly behind him. As soon as he was through the door, he fired his shotgun into the air. Fist-sized chunks of ceiling tiles showered on the crowd. *"Down-down-down!"* Showalter bellowed through the nylon mask.

Rodney pulled the stocking over his head, slammed the butt of his shotgun into the stomach of the doorman, and leveled the weapon at the heavy man behind the bar. *"Hands up!"* he shouted. "Hands where I can see 'em!" Beano-D stared at him, then slowly raised his hands.

The club erupted into pandemonium. Dozens of women were screaming. The crowd surged away from Mackin and Showalter toward the front door, then surged back when they saw Rodney. Mackin fired another round, this one into one of the PA stacks next to the stage. A shower of fabric and bits of plastic flew across the stage. A feedback scream tore through the club and died in a burst of static. *"Down on the floor!"* Mackin roared.

The band immediately dropped to the floor of the stage. The patrons began to follow suit, some of the women still screaming. Rodney heard someone crying. Fine white dust from the blasted ceiling hung in the smoky air. He pulled on a set of gloves, removed a pair of wooden wedges from his jacket pocket, and kicked them under the front door. No one was coming in that way.

Showalter stayed at the back door. Mackin crossed the floor and threw a canvas carryall on the bar. "The registers and the tackle box," he said shortly. "Fast."

"Everybody, *shut up!*" Showalter shouted. The crowd gradually became silent, except for the crying woman.

Mackin saw Beano-D and the well-dressed man behind the bar. Neither had dropped to the floor. He pointed his shotgun directly at Beano-D's chest. "On the floor," he said calmly, "or die."

The well-dressed man put a hand on Beano-D's shoulder and slowly pushed him to the floor. He stared at Mackin levelly. "You're the thief," he said without inflection.

Mackin watched the bartender frantically emptying the tackle box into the carryall. He swiveled the gun to Dink Reeves. "Pop the safe," he ordered.

Dink shook his head. "No safe, man."

Mackin turned to Rodney and pointed at the bartender closest to the door. The big black man nodded and gestured with his shotgun: "Turn around." They were about thirty feet apart.

The bartender, a short, middle-aged man whose eyes were wide with fear, slowly turned and faced the mirror behind the bar. Rodney dropped the barrel of his shotgun an inch and fired. The load caught the short man in the small of the back. He bounced into the liquor bottles stacked behind the bar and fell to the floor in a rain of broken glass and blood. He gurgled in pain.

Several people on the floor began screaming at the sound of the shot. "*Shut up!*" Showalter shouted from the back door. His eyes behind the mask were wide with shock. Rodney racked the pump action of the twenty-gauge and pointed it at Dink Reeves.

"The safe," Mackin repeated.

Reeves dropped to the floor, pulled a carpet runner aside, and quickly opened a small safe set in the floor. Mackin gestured to the bartender. "Empty it."

The terrified bartender quickly filled the carryall. Mackin noted with satisfaction that most of the bills were hundreds. He snatched the bag from the bartender's hands and gestured at Rodney. "Out."

Rodney walked across the club quickly, stepping over the huddled patrons on the floor and constantly swinging the shotgun around him. He joined Showalter at the back door.

Mackin turned. "Everybody stay on the floor." He only had to raise his voice slightly to be heard over the muttering of the crowd. He started toward the back door.

Beano-D rose to his feet behind the bar. His hands were on his hips. "Pointy goin' to let me kill you for this."

Mackin turned. Beano-D made no move.

Dink Reeves slowly stood up. "Shut up, Beano." He looked at the bleeding bartender on the floor, still moaning, then at Mackin. "I never went along with ripping you off. We're even now, okay?"

Mackin stared at him. "Maybe. I'll think it over. You tell Pointy I said, 'Fuck you.'" He stepped quickly to the back door and jerked his head at Showalter and Rodney. "Go."

They went through the door. Mackin removed a pair of wedges identical to Rodney's from his jacket and jammed them under the door from the outside. The parking lot was empty.

"Power." Mackin headed to the car.

Showalter hurried to the outside wall of the club. He pointed at a large, gray box fronted with a glass cylinder and looked at Rodney.

Rodney shook his head. "That's the meter. The big one next to it."

Showalter nodded. He stood to one side of the box indicated by Rodney, pushed the barrel of the shotgun to within an inch of it, turned his face away, and pulled the trigger. The box exploded in a shower of yellow and orange sparks. The inside of Ma Rainey's went black.

Mackin pulled up in the station wagon. Showalter and Rodney climbed in, and Mackin pulled smoothly onto the street. Rain began to spatter the windshield.

"Are you out of your fucking mind?" Showalter turned and shouted at Rodney. "What the fuck did you do that poor bastard for? We didn't have to kill anybody!"

"We didn't kill anybody, man." Rodney grinned from the darkness of the backseat.

"Take it easy, Bo." Mackin pulled onto the interstate access ramp and accelerated into the late-night traffic. "Guy's not dead. They don't let him bleed to death on the floor, he'll be fine in a couple of days. Show him, Rodney."

Rodney broke the shotgun, removed one of the shells, and handed it to Showalter. The big man examined it intently. "Handload. I don't get it."

"Convincers," Rodney said. "Less than half a normal powder charge, no shot."

"No shot? Something hit that guy. The poor son of a bitch was bleeding all over the floor."

"Rock salt," Rodney said. "Make you scream, make you bleed a little bit, hurts like holy hell, but it ain't gonna kill anyone."

Showalter stared at him. "Rock salt? You shot that guy with a half-load of rock salt?" He burst into laughter. "Son of a bitch," he said, shaking his head. "Everybody in that bar thinks you're a stone killer, and you shot him with rock salt. I don't believe it."

"It worked, didn't it?" Rodney grinned again. "You light off a shotgun in a crowded room, most people gonna do whatever you tell 'em to do."

Showalter shook his head. "My brother took a load of rock salt in the ass when he was fifteen. Chasing some local nooky. Couldn't sit down for a week. Rock salt."

Mackin patted the carryall. "How'd we do?"

Showalter unzipped the bag. "Hard to tell in the dark. Lotsa cash in here, though, mostly C-notes. I figure at least twenty, maybe twenty-five grand."

The interior of the club descended into chaos the moment the lights went out, as many of the more than three hundred people in the room rose from the floor and surged toward the doors. There was a lot of screaming. Dink Reeves fumbled in the darkness behind the bar until he found the bouncer's flashlight, a nine-battery club that lit half the room when he turned it on. It took almost two minutes to get everyone reasonably calm and quiet.

"Go see what that motherfucker did to the front door," Reeves snapped at Beano-D. He could tell from the confusion at the back door that it had been secured from the outside. The club's windows were covered with black wrought-iron grating. "Everyone just shut up and hold still," he yelled into the crowd. "We'll get you out of here in a minute."

One of the bartenders rose from the floor next to the wounded man. He looked as if he was in his early fifties. "I ain't no doctor, Dink, but I don't think Phil is hurt that bad." He shook his head and used a bar towel to wipe traces of blood from his hands. "He's hurt all right, he's a hurting unit and he's bleeding a little bit, but I don't think he's dying."

"We'll get him to the hospital soon as we can." Reeves picked up the phone and started to dial, then cursed and slammed it down onto the cradle. "Phone's out. Check the pay phone, but that's probably out, too."

"It is," the bartender said quietly. "Went out this afternoon."

Reeves glanced at the older man. "You takin' this pretty well, George." He smiled. "Just another night at Ma's?"

"I was worried 'bout Phil when that boy shot him," George said seriously. "It looked pretty bad. Years ago I was tending bar at AJ's when a couple boys come in and stuck us up; they shot old Mike Jebboe dead. Mike didn't even do nothin', he was just standing there with his hands up and one of those boys shot him right in the belly, so I was worried 'bout Phil."

George glanced at the wounded man, who was keening in pain. A cocktail waitress was pressing a towel against the wounds in his back. "I think Phil's gonna be all right, though, and if Phil's gonna be okay, I guess there ain't much to get your water up over. I've been robbed before, three times, matter of fact."

George turned his gaze to Reeves. "Probably be robbed again someday. But it ain't my money."

Reeves nodded. "You're a sensible man, George. It ain't my money, either. But the guy whose money it is, he's gonna be real pissed off 'bout this."

At the dark front of the bar, Beano-D was kicking at the wedges under the door. He held his pistol in his right hand and cursed softly and viciously as he hammered at the wedges with the heel of his boot.

Milos Petrone barely made it out of his car before Maloney collared him. The reporter's brown hair was slick with rain.

"Deal's off, Milos." Maloney pointed over his shoulder at the front of Ma Rainey's. More than two hundred people, most of them patrons who had been inside during the robbery, were milling on the sidewalk. Some were sitting on the curb, their chins hunched down inside their coat collars. Several had police blankets wrapped around them. Uniformed officers were taking statements. A team of paramedics was wheeling a black man on a gurney into the back of a waiting ambulance. Light bars from several vehicles created a strobe effect in the darkness. "Enough witnesses are consistent enough on the leader's description. He said some things on his way out. This was your guy. He's back."

Lockhart climbed out of the passenger side of Petrone's car. He shook his head. "Hard to believe, Nick. This guy isn't the stickup type, at least, not a bar. The Bank of England, maybe, but not a bar."

Petrone sighed. "This isn't about money, John. It's payback." He pushed his way past the police lines, found a uniformed sergeant, and identified himself.

"No homicide here, Sergeant," the uniformed officer said. "Guy on the stretcher looked like hell, all the witnesses thought he got shot to doll rags, but it turned out they shot him with rock salt. Paras say he'll be okay."

Petrone walked into the club and found Leonard Hamilton from Robbery. "Hey, Len," he said bleakly, staring at the blood and shattered glass on the floor behind the bar.

"Milos." Hamilton was crouched over the open safe in the floor. "What brings you here?"

"Same guy, Len."

"Same guy that did Felton?" Hamilton looked surprised.

Petrone nodded. "Yup."

"Talented bastard." Hamilton straightened up. "Burning bars *and* shotguns in a crowded nightclub. I suppose we really ought to catch this guy. You sure?"

"Surer than I want to be." Petrone pulled himself onto one of the barstools. "What've you got?"

"Three-man crew, two white, one black. Leader was a Cauc male, maybe thirty-five, maybe forty-five. Six to six-five, one-ninety to two-thirty, depending on the witness. Cool, calm, collected, didn't fuck around."

"That's the guy who ran the burning bar, killed Kendall and Macnamara."

"Jehoshaphat." Hamilton said it the way Petrone said "I'll be damned."

Hamilton came around the bar. "Second perp black male, maybe thirty, thirty-five, five-nine to six-one, one-seventy to two-ten, short hair, burly. He shotgunned the bartender with rock salt, if you can believe it."

"I heard."

"Third perp white male, forty or fifty, six to six-three, two-hundred to two-thirty, also stocky. It's all a guess. The white guys came in wearing masks, the black guy put one on before anyone really noticed him. They used wedges on the doors and blew the building's power on the way out. No one even glimpsed the car. Very, very slick. These guys ever decide to do banks, the FBI will have a chance to earn their keep."

"They *have* done banks." Lockhart appeared beside Petrone. Rain was beaded on his coat. "And jewelry stores and fur warehouses and military bases . . . Shit." He shook his head. "This is not a good thing, Milos."

"We have one more day," Petrone said.

"Don't get you."

"Tomorrow's paper is already on the press. Maloney can't get anything out till the day after."

They walked back to their car. Nick Maloney was leaning on the fender. "Care to comment?"

"Nick, we've got to work something out on this."

"Can't do it, Milos. You know that as well as I do. The guy is definitely back, and it sure as hell doesn't look like you need to worry about scaring him off." Maloney shrugged. "Hell, Milos, I'm not sure I'd sit on it even if my editors let me. This is bigger than all of us, it's an honest-to-God gang war. Partner, couple of days from now you're going to have a hell of a lot more than the *Times* to worry about."

Petrone grimaced. "Tell me about it."

"I have one thing for you," Maloney said. "It isn't much, but I confirmed that this Moffitt character gets some of his work from Sal Capetti's people in Chicago, and that he has been for close to ten years, at least. Your buddies at the Bureau shake the Chicago tree hard enough, maybe a name will fall out."

"Somehow I don't think so," Petrone said.

✶   ✶   ✶

Mackin wheeled the station wagon into the shopping-center parking lot and pulled to a stop next to their rental car. The three men quickly transferred their weapons and the bag into the sedan, then wiped down the wagon. Fifteen minutes later they were back in Rodney's motel room.

There was $26,400 in the carryall. Mackin gave the other two men $9,000 each and took the remainder himself.

"Thank you, sir." Showalter folded the thick wad of bills and shoved them into the front pocket of his jeans. "A profitable evening for all concerned. We hurt Mr. Williams this night."

"Not enough." Mackin stretched across the bed and slipped his share of the money into the nightstand drawer. "Not enough."

Showalter raised his eyebrows in mock surprise. "Do we plan to strike the enemy again, Captain? Dare we enter the lion's den twice?"

Mackin nodded. "One more time." He was hungry. He picked up the phone to call Maggie.

A slight grimace passed over Rodney's face. "You think it's smart to hang around here, I mean, with Maggie being along and all? Maybe we ought to just get the fuck outta town, head on home. We can come back and bang on Williams later."

Mackin shook his head as he dialed. "One more time."

17

"YOU MADE the Chicago papers." Riles's voice was emotionless. It was two days after the score at Ma Rainey's. "You're on page eleven of this morning's *Trib*, page three in the *Sun-Times*. The headline says 'City Faces Chicago-Style Gang War.' " It was eleven o'clock in the morning.

"You ought to see the papers here. I told you it might get hairy." Mackin's eyes scanned the parking lot of the grocery store. "The son of a bitch should never have tried to fuck me."

"I imagine he's a little clearer on that now."

"You getting any heat?" A tall man with blond hair got out of a late-model Honda and started walking toward the automatic doors of the grocery store. He was wearing sunglasses with wire frames and smoked lenses. He looked at Mackin as he walked across the parking lot. Showalter got out of the

Chevy and leaned against it, his arms folded across his chest and his eyes fixed on the blond man's back. Mackin shifted his weight so that his jacket fell slightly open.

"Nothing serious. Sal has seen the paper. He wants me to keep an eye on things, on our interests."

"I've got no wish to fuck anything up for you guys. This is about me and Pointy Williams, no one else."

"A guy who works for Williams, guy named Reeves, called me up. He asked if maybe I could talk you into going home. He seems like a reasonable guy. He wants to let bygones be, and all that shit."

"I think I met him. What'd you tell him?" The blond man had reached the sidewalk in front of the store and was wrestling with a grocery cart. After a few seconds of tugging, he swore and wrenched it free. He shot Mackin an embarrassed grin and disappeared into the store.

"I told him that I didn't know you that well, and that he and his people brought this on themselves when they set you up. He said that he didn't have anything to do with the two cops. That whole thing was Williams's idea, according to Reeves. I believe him. He seems too smart for a chickenshit thing like that. So, anyway, I told him that if I talked to you, I'd ask you to think about lightening up."

Mackin didn't respond. Showalter looked in the direction of the phone, raised his wrist, and tapped his watch with his finger. Mackin nodded.

Riles sighed. "So how far is this gonna go?"

"How the fuck should I know? I'll keep going till I'm done. Fucker pissed me off, Frank."

Mackin waited. Showalter was slowly pacing around the Chevy, his head rotating slowly as he monitored the parking lot. Riles exhaled into the phone.

"Whatever." Riles's voice was resigned. "Look, this pay phone stuff is neat-o and secure and all that shit, but if Sal wants me to get hold of you in a hurry, we could have a problem. Give me a number."

"I'm at the Circle 7 motel in Easton. Ask for room one sixteen. Rodney and Bo are in the Holidome, room two forty-eight."

"All right. You do whatever you gotta do. Be careful, Mackin. The way you're going, someone's going to get killed."

"Already happened, Frank. I'll keep in touch." Mackin hung up the phone and headed across the parking lot to the car.

Ricky Cento sat in a chair upholstered in green vinyl and watched his boss play cards. The Ma Rainey's robbery had disturbed him. He was supposed to meet with Dink Reeves that afternoon. Frank Riles had spent twenty minutes on the phone with Macchi earlier that day. Ricky was nervous.

Joe Macchi stared at his cards for a long moment, then removed two and set them facedown on the table. "Do me right in the crib," he said threateningly, "I'll go out this hand."

"How about some shit in the crib instead?" his opponent said. He pushed two cards across the table. "I've got a barn burner over here. Maybe I'll go out this hand." Anthony Pellanta was sixty-one. He had served as Macchi's consigliere for sixteen years. In recent years that service had primarily consisted of acting as Macchi's cribbage opponent.

Macchi laid a card down. "Four."

Pellanta immediately laid down a four of his own. "Eight for two." He moved his peg on the cribbage board. "Seen the papers?"

Ricky tensed. He couldn't help it. Neither of the older men noticed.

Macchi snorted. "The robbery at the nigger club? Fuck yes. Been on the phone with Chicago about it every day for a week." He laid down the seven of hearts. "Fifteen for two."

"The robbery I'm talking about was just the day before yesterday, Joe." Pellanta set down the eight of diamonds. "Twenty-three."

Macchi slapped the eight of hearts onto the table. "Thirty-one for four," he said triumphantly. "Riles called me, it's that business with the two police I told you about. We knew something was going to happen."

Pellanta sighed and laid down the nine of spades. "Nine . . . Joe, are we involved with this business?"

"No. Not yet. If we have to get involved, we wait for Chicago to tell us. This is their deal. Frank's running it." He laid down the nine of hearts. "I'm killing you, Tony, killing you. Eighteen for two."

Pellanta played the nine of diamonds. "Twenty-seven for six and one for the go." He moved his peg seven places. It ended up well short of the end of the board. "Damn." He leaned back. "Joe, we aren't in a good position to get into a shooting war with the blacks, you know that."

"We won't." Macchi was studying his hand. "Fifteen for two and four hearts is six. Frank called me this morning; all he wants is that if the thief needs help, we help. Frank doesn't think the thief will need help."

"He'll need help soon. The whole city is looking for him."

"He's not in the city. He's in a motel in Easton. I told you, Riles called me today. He'll probably move soon, what with the newspapers and TV people making such a deal over this. Count your fucking hand, Tony."

Cento was staring at the legal pad on Macchi's desk.

*　　*　　*

The warehouse sat two miles outside of the city at the end of a small industrial park next to the interstate. Mackin saw that Williams, or whoever was working for Williams who had picked the location, had done a good job. The building was no more than two hundred yards from the interstate, but was shielded from the highway by a thick noisebreak of pine trees. The only access to the warehouse was by way of a long, narrow frontage road that branched away from the interstate access ramp. The building and parking lot were surrounded by a chain-link fence.

Mackin and Rodney were crouched in the cool darkness of the trees. Their car was parked in the lot of a self-storage complex a half mile up the access road. Rodney was examining the warehouse through a pair of high-powered field glasses. It was six-thirty in the evening.

"Not a soul. No interior lights on that I can see, no movement. There ain't nobody in there, Mackin." Rodney handed the binoculars across to the older man.

Mackin scanned the warehouse. "No cars in the parking lot, either. The way I understand it, Williams has a crew working the street almost every night. They'll snatch two or three high-dollar cars, 'Vettes, Benzes, Caddys, whatever, bring 'em here. Two or three guys, tops, will be inside to handle the money, park the cars, and fix whatever cosmetic damage was done to the cars during the thefts. The thieves are mostly kids, and they're paying them a few hundred bucks for each car. They're selling the cars overseas for eight, ten grand apiece."

"Sounds illegal to me." Rodney grinned in the failing light. "Probably the kind of thing that we ought to put a stop to. Hand over that thermos."

Mackin passed a coffee-and-whisky-filled steel thermos to the black man. He looked up at the rapidly darkening sky. "No sign of rain, thank Christ."

Bo Showalter appeared out of the shadows next to them. He, too, was carrying field glasses. "No, no rain, and you're right— thank God. Crawling around in the mud is already too much like humping the boonies. I kept looking for fucking claymores wired to the trees."

"What did you find?"

"Three doors, basically front and back fire exits and the big door for the loading bay. There's no way to be sure without going inside, but my guess is that it's a standard single-bay warehouse with a small office in one corner. That's how the windows look, anyway. The office is where the money proba- bly is."

Showalter looked quizzically at Mackin. "This is your party, boss, and I'm all for recon and all that military shit, but from here it looks like we can walk out of these trees and right through the back door. No one can see us from the interstate, and the next complex up the frontage road is vacant. We're pretty much the only life-forms in the area. Fuck, let's do it."

Rodney passed the thermos to Showalter. "You think there's a shitload of money in there, Mackin?"

"Probably not." Mackin sounded distant. He was thinking about Showalter's suggestion. "Maybe five, six grand to pay the thieves and buy parts."

"Shit." Rodney looked surprised. "If there's no money in there, why in hell are we gonna rob the place?"

"We aren't going to rob it." Mackin raised the glasses back to his eyes. "We're going to burn it down."

*   *   *

Ricky Cento was sitting in his downtown apartment staring at his television and worrying. The Miami Dolphins were systematically destroying the Green Bay Packers at the Orange Bowl. As Cento chewed at his lower lip, Dan Marino dropped back and rifled a pass twenty-five yards downfield to Mark Duper. "How many times have we seen that?" Dick Enberg's voice was conversational. "First and ten Miami, on the Green Bay twenty-one yard line."

Cento wasn't worrying about the game—he had two hundred on Miami and knew the money was already as good as in his pocket—but he was very worried about another of his income streams. Dink Reeves had told him the night before to shut down his burgeoning cocaine operation. Cento had expected to receive a full kilo of the drug from Reeves, the biggest delivery of his short career.

"Not this time, baby," the black man told him. "Not after what happened at Ma's." There was a lot more to it than the bar robbery. Cento suspected that Reeves was involved in the Walnut Towers shooting, but there was no way he could know that for the first time in years the Pointy Williams operation was strapped for product. Pointy's months-long fixation on the mythical Peruvian connection had caused him to neglect older, more reliable suppliers, and Reeves was working the phones in an effort to rebuild bridges. "No one's gettin' anything but the major street guys, Ricky. Sorry. Maybe next month. It's best to lay low right now."

They had met in Carlisle's, a midtown restaurant and club that catered to a yuppie crowd. It was just before the dinner rush, and the two merged inconspicuously in the crowd of after-work executives. They were sitting in a booth near the bar.

"I *told* you that he was looking at Ma Rainey's," Cento said. "Safe should have been fucking *empty* when he hit. You shoulda had that big Beano motherfucker and about six of his guns behind the fucking bar, wasted his ass the second he showed up."

Reeves shook his head. "Beano-D was there, Ricky, and so was I. We were 'bout ten seconds away from dumping the safe when they showed up. Don't be thinkin' we weren't paying attention. Your tip was right on."

Cento nervously drained his drink and motioned to the cocktail waitress. "Bourbon and Coke." He pointed at Reeves. "You?"

Reeves shook his head. An untouched Pepsi sat on the table in front of him. They waited for the waitress to return to the bar.

Cento hadn't given Reeves very much, just the fact that the thief was interested in Williams's gambling operation. He had hoped that Reeves and his people could quietly solve the problem before it got any further out of hand. Now Reeves was telling him to put his own operation on hold, which was precisely what Cento wanted to avoid.

Reeves leaned across the table. His brown eyes were flat and serious. "Ricky, you hear about that business at Walnut Towers?"

Cento nodded. "That you?"

Reeves didn't look away. "We had some people there. Did the thief have anything to do with that?"

"No way, man." Cento shook his head violently, though he kept his voice low. "Way too soon, y'know? It happened way too soon. From what Macchi told me, the son of a bitch wasn't even in town yet. Whatever happened at the Towers ain't part of this thing."

Reeves held Cento's eyes with his own for a moment, then looked away. "That all depends on what thing you're talking about," he had said.

Now, alone in his apartment, Cento was trying to figure out what would be the best move for Ricky Cento. He saw two things clearly: the presence of the thief in the city was bad for everyone's business, including that of the Macchi organization. "What little fucking business we do," he sneered aloud. Ever since Kendall and Macnamara had been killed, every cop in town was looking to clobber someone. The thief had to go away. The other thing he saw clearly was that if Joe Macchi even got a hint that Ricky Cento was playing both ends, Ricky Cento would end up in the lake.

On the screen Don Shula was shaking his finger at one of the referees. A graphic appeared that said Miami was up by sixteen. Cento spent the next thirty minutes alternately staring at the television and staring at his phone. It was the pain of the lost kilo of coke that made up his mind. He called the number Dink had given him.

The phone at the other end was picked up almost immediately. "Yeah?"

"Dink Reeves." Cento was surprised. No one but Reeves had ever answered the phone before.

"Dink ain't round tonight. You want to talk to Pointy?"

Cento thought furiously for a moment. His arrangement with Dink was entirely private, and Reeves had assured him that Williams knew nothing about it. "Yeah, put Pointy on. It's about the thief."

Williams came to the phone quickly. "Who the fuck is this?" he snapped.

"Don't worry about who this is." Cento tried to keep his nerves out of his voice. "This is the same person who tried to save your ass at Ma Rainey's, the one who told you the thief was coming back. You want to know where he is?"

"I'm listening."

"Circle 7 motel, room one sixteen. It's in Easton. He may not be there much longer." Cento dropped the phone in the cradle, fell back on his couch, and sighed. "Done is done," he said aloud. He headed to the kitchen to refill his drink. As he picked up his glass, he saw that Miami had won by nine points.

"Hell with it," Mackin said suddenly. "Let's do it." The sun was dropping behind the trees and the three men could feel the cold from the damp, leafy ground seeping through their clothes. There had been no movement at the warehouse for more than an hour. "We've got everything in the car, right?"

Showalter nodded. He was breathing into his cupped hands to keep them warm. "Yeah, it's all in the car, but it ain't a lot. We got the toolbox, a siphon kit, a machete, and enough styrofoam cups for an American Legion picnic. We're looking at a couple of hours' work."

"We got tampons, too, Bo," Rodney said sternly. "Don't be forgetting the damned tampons. Can't be a modern-day, serious criminal 'thout styrofoam cups and a box of fucking tampons in the trunk of your car."

Mackin grinned. "Rodney, you're laughing now, but we're going to school you with those tampons."

"I hate to be a downer," Showalter said, "but I'm seeing some logistical problems here."

Mackin lowered the field glasses and turned to him. "Like what?"

"Like, how the fuck we get in there? I'm not quite the young stud I was twenty years ago, and we could be here all night if you're going to wait for me to climb a ten-foot fence."

Rodney laughed. "You fat old fuck, I told Mackin we shoulda left your sorry ass in Kansas City. I'll tell you what, though; we've been here better than two hours and haven't seen a single, solitary person. I think I should just walk on down there with the bolt cutters and whack that lock right off the gate. I mean, fuck it. Go big or stay at home, y'know?"

Mackin thought for a moment. "There's probably only two or three people showing up to work here tonight, and only the first ones to arrive would know anything was wrong if the lock was gone. We could probably introduce ourselves before they had a chance to cause any trouble. Hell, they're gonna be car guys, mechanics, so it's not like they're professional muscle. Why not? Let's do this shit, go back to the motel, get some sleep, and head the fuck out of here tomorrow."

"Tallyho," Showalter said. He and Rodney disappeared into the darkness down the access road toward the car. Mackin used the last of the failing light to check the load in his .45. He carefully retracted the slide a half inch, then allowed the spring to pull it back in position. He dropped the magazine out of the butt and tapped it twice against his hand. As he reloaded the weapon, he wondered what Maggie was doing.

Pointy Williams hung up the phone and stared at the top of his desk. The phone call was literally too good to be true, and it wasn't unreasonable to believe that there would be a warm reception for whoever showed up at the Circle 7 motel. On the other hand, the call had been intended for Dink, and Williams knew that Dink had some connections who had provided some pretty good information about the thief. He pulled out a telephone book, opened the yellow pages to *Motels*, and found the Circle 7. He looked up at Beano-D, who was watching *American Gladiators* from his accustomed place next to the door.

"Homes, I got something for you," Pointy said.

"There are twenty-nine automobiles in here," Rodney said happily. "Not one of them is more than two years old, and not one of them came off the showroom floor for less than thirty grand. Hell, some of 'em got *keys* in 'em."

"Forget it," Mackin said. "Last thing we need is you getting picked up in Kansas City driving a hot car from this town."

Even Mackin was surprised at how easily Rodney's suggestion had worked out. He had watched from the trees as Rodney and Bo drove up to the locked gate. Rodney had removed a set of bolt cutters from the trunk, cut the padlock, and opened the gate, then waved Mackin down. Bo parked the car behind the warehouse. Mackin left the gate closed behind him. The three of them had made a careful search for any signs of an electronic security system, without results. "What are they gonna do if someone breaks in?" Rodney asked. "Call the cops?" They used the bolt cutters to lever up the big loading-bay door enough to allow Mackin to slip beneath it, and he let in the other two men through one of the fire doors.

Showalter was spreading his tools on a canvas sheet in the middle of the warehouse floor. "Somebody look around for buckets or tubs, shit like that. Anything that can hold gasoline. Plastic is okay, it won't be in long enough to make any difference." He was assembling a siphon unit from a six-foot length of corrugated, one-inch plastic hose and a small hand pump.

"I used one of those things when I was a teenager back in the seventies," Rodney said. He headed for the back of the warehouse to find a bucket. "Gas crisis and all. Used to siphon gas from my uncle Keith. He was a mean bastard."

Mackin collected the six packages of styrofoam cups in a pile. Each package contained two hundred cups. He picked up the machete and attacked the pile.

"Chop it as small as you can." Showalter was examining the gas cap cover on a year-old Lincoln Town Car. He walked up to the driver's side window, reached in, and punched a button. The gas cap popped open. "There we go." He dropped his cigarette to the floor and carefully squashed it with his foot. "Gennulmans, the smoking lamp is out."

"What in the fuck are you doing?" Rodney appeared with a pair of plastic buckets in his arms. He was kicking a galvanized double-mop bucket along the floor in front of him. The bucket was mounted on wheels and was complete with an awkward-looking wringer with a long handle.

Mackin looked up from his efforts. "What's it look like I'm doing? I'm chopping up these goddamn cups."

Showalter shook his head when he saw the buckets. "Is that it?"

"That's it." Rodney dropped the plastic buckets. "You need more? What're we doing here?"

Showalter was still eyeing the buckets. "Making napalm."

18

DINK had Danny with him and no one seemed to know when he'd be back, so Beano-D took the Conway brothers to Easton. Ralph and Wayne Conway grew up in the projects—for a couple of months Wayne had dated a girl who lived in Walnut Towers the year before the building was condemned—and both had gone to work for Pointy Williams in their teens. They were inseparable. The two had quickly worked their way up from runners to street-corner dealers, where Pointy left them for a couple of years. They impressed Williams with the brute animal ferocity they displayed when protecting their territory, and after they'd worked for him long enough to prove they were no more dishonest than any other drug dealers, he began to use them for special assignments.

Now Ralph was talking to his brother. "You see what's goin' on here, bro? This motherfucker is the motherfucker who stuck up Ma's. He's some kind of bad sumbitch, and we ain't gonna take no chances with him. We pop the door and go in shootin'."

Wayne nodded. He'd spent his life doing whatever his brother told him to do, and if he hadn't killed anyone yet, it wasn't his fault. He thought he'd killed a guy once, invested four minutes in *trying* to kill him with a chain, but he'd found out later the son of a bitch spent eleven days in intensive care and lived.

The Conway brothers carried pistols from the cache in Williams's office. Beano-D carried a special gun, a ten-year-old Ingram Mac-11 submachine pistol. It wasn't much bigger than a car radio and had a twenty-round magazine jutting from its handgrip.

"At least three guys," Beano-D said to the brothers as they sped down the interstate to Easton. "Two honkies and a nigger. The tall honky, dark hair, he's mine."

Showalter pointed at the fragmented pile of styrofoam and cellophane at Mackin's feet. "Mix that shit with gasoline, let it set up for a few minutes, you get napalm. Jellied gasoline. Or what you get is so close to napalm it doesn't matter. It sticks to what it burns, and it burns forever." He grinned wolfishly. "Old Marine Corps trick."

"We be here forever if you plan on mixing that shit up in these," Rodney said, gesturing to the buckets. "I've got an idea." He disappeared into the back of the warehouse. A few seconds later he called out, "Hey, Bo! Pop the trunk on one of those cars."

He reappeared dragging a five-foot-long roll of clear industrial plastic sheeting. "There's a little spray-paint operation back there. Probably for touch-up work if they have to fuck up a door to get in the car."

"What do you have in mind, bro?" Showalter looked a little confused. He had opened the trunk of a brand-new, white Cadillac.

"There's your bucket, you stupid honky slug." Rodney pointed into the trunk. "Just line it with some of this plastic."

"I'll be damned." Showalter shook his head. "You know, you may be criminal black scum, Rodney, but you're *smart* criminal black scum."

The two men spread a large sheet of plastic across the floor and walls of the car trunk. Mackin dumped the mass of styrofoam and cellophane into the trunk, and Showalter began to siphon gas from nearby cars into the galvanized bucket.

Showalter spent almost an hour transferring gas from various cars into the bucket and from the bucket into the trunk of the Caddy. Rodney opened a dozen cans of automotive paint from the back of the warehouse and set one can in the backseat of each of the most expensive-looking vehicles. While they worked, Mackin poured enough gas into two soda bottles to fill each about halfway.

"See if those windows will open, Bo. It's getting kind of thick in here."

Showalter nodded. He had poured almost eighty gallons of gas over the styrofoam in the trunk and was stirring the mixture with a mop handle. Fumes from the trunk rose almost five feet in the air. He walked over to the back window. "Sealed shut." He walked over to the toolbox, picked up a wrench, and smashed the window.

Mackin dropped a few chunks of styrofoam into each bottle, then inserted a tampon into each bottleneck. "Watch this," he said to Rodney. When the material of the tampon touched the gasoline, the fabric swelled to fill the top of the bottle. "Best Molotov cocktail in the world. The tampon maintains the seal across the top of the bottle, so when the son of a bitch lights off, it doesn't just burn, it blows up."

Lights flashed across the front window of the warehouse. "Company." Rodney looked between the bars on the front window. "Two guys, and they don't seem too worried. Probably think we're their partners."

The two men, both black and middle-aged, were smiling when they walked into the warehouse. One of them carried a slim attaché case. Both were wearing open-neck shirts over slacks. The man with the attaché case was wearing a checked sports coat. A hint of gray was in the hair over his ears. He stopped speaking in midsentence when he saw Mackin.

"Who are you?" He seemed more surprised than alarmed.

"Oh, shit," said the second man.

Mackin had produced his .45 and had it pointed somewhere between the two men. "Check 'em out," he said to Rodney. "Evening, gentlemen," he said to the new arrivals. "Don't pay any attention to us. We're just here to fuck up your lives."

Ralph Conway wheeled his Chrysler into the parking lot of the Circle 7 motel and drove slowly past room 116. Lights were on in the room. It was eleven-fifteen P.M.

"Park over there," Beano-D said from the backseat, pointing to a dark area near the empty swimming pool. "Shut off the lights, leave the engine on." He hefted the Ingram and looked over the parking lot. The lights were on in the motel lobby, but the only lobby window that overlooked the back parking had its curtains drawn. Three other cars were in the lot, and none was close to room 116.

"This motherfucker makes a lot of noise," Beano-D said,

holding up the machine pistol. He was guessing; he'd never actually fired the Mac-11. " 'Less Superman is in one of those rooms, nobody be givin' us any trouble. We ain't gonna fuck around with knockin' on the damned door, okay? I saw this cocksucker work in Ma Rainey's, and the way to deal with him is just knock down the door and kill him."

"You got it, baby." Wayne had opened a road atlas and was laying out three lines of cocaine. "We just knock down the door and *kill 'em all*, right, bro?"

"Yeah." Ralph watched the razor blade in his brother's hand flash over the small pile of white powder. "*Yeah.*"

"You ain't knockin' shit down," Beano said to Wayne. "You stay right in this car, cover our ass when it goes down. These are serious motherfuckers we're dealing with here."

"Goddammit, Beano-D," Wayne began.

"Don't give me no hard time, homes," the big man said.

Wayne grumbled as he offered the atlas to his brother. The three men each snorted a line, then Beano and Ralph got out of the car.

"Stay right here," Beano-D said to Wayne. He looked at Ralph. "Let's go, homes." They started across the parking lot toward Mackin's room.

"That's it," Showalter said, a hint of pride in his voice.

"Christ, I hope to God that's it." Rodney's eyes were watering. He snapped the gas cap off a Corvette he had pushed in front of the garage-type loading door. "Let's get the fuck out of here." The warehouse smelled like a refinery. Gasoline fumes were so thick that it was difficult to see the building's far wall.

The white Cadillac, its trunk still holding fifteen gallons of the gas/styrofoam mixture, was parked in the middle of the warehouse floor. One of Mackin's Molotov cocktails sat in the semiliquid mess in the trunk. Ropes of gasoline-drenched plastic sheeting connected the Caddy's trunk to the open trunks of five other cars, each of which also held a dozen gallons of the mixture. Additional plastic fuses ran from those trunks to the front seats of three Corvettes, including the one Rodney had moved. Each was parked across one of the doors.

Showalter wasn't entirely pleased with the consistency of his mixture—"Looks more like gasoline goop than napalm," Rodney had observed as he poured the contents of his cans of paint in and around the cars he'd selected—but Showalter had no doubt that it would burn. He'd used a mop to spread gallons of it across the warehouse floor and over almost all the cars. He joined Mackin and Rodney at the loading door.

"Both the windows are broken," Showalter said. "We leave this big fucker open three, four feet, we'll get plenty of draft." He looked at Mackin. "All set."

"You do the honors, Bo." Mackin picked up the remaining Molotov cocktail, jerked the loading door up to waist level, and ducked outside. Rodney joined him. A few seconds later Showalter appeared, trailing another long, twisted sheet of plastic outside the warehouse and carrying one of the plastic buckets. Mackin handed him the gas-filled bottle.

Showalter faked out twenty feet of coiled sheeting, enough so that he was sure that he was in clear air with no chance of igniting the whole warehouse when he lit the fuse. He used gasoline from the bucket to liberally soak down the sheeting, then wrapped one end around the bottom of the bottle. He walked a few feet away and lit a cigarette. "Start the car."

Rodney and Mackin sprinted over to the Pontiac. The two

men who had arrived earlier were on the grass inside the fence, their arms and legs bound with layers of duct tape. Mackin judged the distance between their bodies and the warehouse and decided they'd be safe. He leaned over them.

"There's going to be a big bang in there in about five minutes. You won't be hurt. Next time you see him, you tell Pointy Williams, 'Fuck you.' And you tell him I said *now* it's over."

The two stared back at him, their eyes wide with fear over the strips of tape that covered their mouths. Rodney started the car. "Let's go," he yelled at Showalter.

Maggie Raynor stood under a hot shower and relaxed. She'd spent most of the day exploring the mall. At lunch she'd picked up a local paper. Mackin's picture was on page fourteen. She didn't read the story. She wasn't looking for any excess moral baggage.

For most of her life things had just happened to Maggie, and mostly they were bad things. Mackin, she'd decided, was a very good thing. Her only concern was that nothing bad happen to him. She got out of the shower and began to dry herself. She had just started to hum "Hey, Jude" when she heard a loud, tearing impact from the direction of the door. She swung the towel around her body and stepped out of the bathroom.

Showalter was puffing furiously on the cigarette. When a third of it had burned away, he carefully trimmed the coal. Then he crouched over the bottle and, with infinite delicacy, inserted the filter end deep between the neck of the bottle and the gasoline-soaked tampon. Satisfied, he lumbered toward the car, waving his arms. Mackin leaned back from the passenger's seat and opened the back door for him.

"How long?" he asked as Rodney pulled onto the frontage road.

"I figure three, maybe four minutes. There's a little bit of a breeze, so maybe two or three minutes." Showalter smiled. "Man, I haven't done anything like that in years."

Rodney covered a fast half mile before he turned on the car lights. Mackin was checking out the contents of the attaché case. They sped through three intersections before they reached a main road with a traffic light.

"Looks like around five, six thousand," Mackin said.

"The really smooth way to do it would've been to have one of them little boxes that starts your car from across the parking lot," Showalter began. "We could've just pressed the button, and a spark from either the ignition or the engine—"

A deep, rumbling roar welled up behind them. Even Rodney craned his neck around for an instant as a gigantic orange fireball rose over the trees behind them. Mackin smiled.

"Well, maybe one or two minutes," Showalter said, smiling, too.

Beano-D looked at Ralph and nodded. They were standing just outside the door to room 116. The two men stepped back and Ralph, the heavier of the two, raised his right foot and kicked the door.

Their first surprise came when the hinges tore out of the jamb and the entire door fell into the motel room. Beano-D stepped through the door and swung the barrel of the pistol in a short horizontal arc. The room was empty. He saw shopping bags on the bed and a carryall bag on the floor.

"What the hell?" A blond woman stepped out of the bathroom with a towel wrapped around her body. Beano-D pulled the trigger on the Ingram. It made a loud sound like ripping canvas and twisted violently in his hand. Bright brass shell casings filled the air.

All twenty rounds fired in less than a second. More than half of them were wide of the target. Seven of them stitched their way up Maggie Raynor's torso. The last one hit her in the throat. Blood instantly soaked the white towel. She made a sound somewhere between a loud exhalation and a grunt and slipped to the floor.

"Motherfucker." Beano-D stared at the gun in his hand. That was his second surprise. "This fuckin' thing is empty." He jammed the machine gun into his waistband and pulled out his nine-millimeter. "Check the bathroom," he said to Ralph, but they both knew no one else was there. Beano reached out without thinking and grabbed a purse sitting on the nightstand.

Ralph stepped over Maggie's body and peered into the bathroom. He used the barrel of his weapon to push aside the shower curtain, then quickly stepped back into the bedroom. He shook his head at Beano-D, his eyes wide with cocaine and fear.

The Chrysler screeched to the door. Wayne motioned for them to get in. In twenty seconds they were back on the interstate.

"Nothin'," Wayne said excitedly. "No lights come on, no windows opened, *nothin'*. We're clean, homeboys."

His brother ignored him. "Wrong room?"

Beano-D shook his head. "I saw the bag the motherfucker used at Ma's. On the floor. Right room." He let out a deep breath. "Check the purse."

"How many were there?" Wayne was almost bouncing in his seat. He leaned far over the wheel. "Man, you shoulda *seen* you motherfuckers knock down that door. That was some kind of shit."

"Well, at least you got his bitch." Ralph pulled Maggie's red leather wallet from the purse and opened it. "Looks like . . . Hey, this is cool, homes. There's a bunch of fuckin' hundreds in here."

"Bitch? All you killed was a fuckin' bitch?" Wayne looked shocked.

"Shut the fuck up, Wayne," Beano-D hissed. He turned back to Ralph. "Keep the cash, lose all the rest of that shit soon as we get back."

"Just a bitch?" Wayne slumped in the seat.

"Hell, that oughtta get his attention." Ralph was trying to sound encouraging.

"We already had his motherfuckin' attention," Beano said.

19

PETRONE was standing in the parking lot almost two hundred feet away from the burning warehouse and still felt heat from the flames on his face. The fire had involved the entire building. A fire department captain was supervising the actions of the crews from four pumper trucks. Two hoses arched silvery streams of water over the chain-link fence onto the burning building, while the other two systematically wet down the grounds around the building and the trees surrounding the property.

"Wow." Lockhart, standing next to Petrone, shook his head. "Wow."

"Found two guys tied up just inside the fence," the captain said to Petrone. "They're okay, I guess. We haven't made it all the way into the building. There's only two fire doors, bars on the windows. Whoever lit this fucker up parked a Corvette across each doorway. Corvette's got a lot of 'glass in the body.

Real hard to light, but once you get it going, it burns like hell's gymnasium."

"Glass?" Petrone looked at the captain.

"Fiberglass," the captain said tersely. " 'Bout all you can do is watch it burn, try to keep it from lighting anything else up. No one'll be going through those doors for a couple hours. I can tell you right now some kind of accelerant was used all over the building, 'cause it's just a fucking sheet-steel warehouse sitting on a concrete pad. The guys we found say there's nothing in there to burn except cars, and cars all alone sure as hell wouldn't be burning like this."

Lockhart heard a long, low-pitched whooshing sound from the warehouse. A bright yellow fireball rose above the burning building for an instant, then vanished. Bright colored dots danced before his eyes where the flame had been.

"What was *that?*"

"Gas tank, I'd guess." The captain pulled out a handkerchief, cleared his throat, and spit into the cloth. He stared at it for a moment, then carefully folded the handkerchief and returned it to his pocket. "A couple of my guys made a run at one of the windows with a hydraulic saw, but the heat drove 'em back. They said the fucking building is *full* of cars. That's the third one to go up."

"Jesus." Lockhart thought for a moment about dozens of gas tanks holding hundreds of gallons of fuel. "Maybe we ought to back up a little."

The captain shrugged. "Nothing to worry about. That's as bad as it'll get. That stuff you see in the movies, automobiles blowing up like the fucking space shuttle, that's Hollywood shit. Your typical car isn't gonna do that unless you put an explosive device in the tank. Hell, those cars in there probably wouldn't be doing what you just saw if the bastards hadn't taken off all the gas caps." He shook his head. "That's a guess, but this isn't—someone really wanted to burn this bastard, let me tell you, and whoever he was knew exactly what he was doing. Be here all night."

The captain walked toward the closest pumper truck and began shouting instructions to the hose crew. Lockhart looked at Petrone. "What do you think?"

"I think this has gone far enough," the detective said quietly. "You see that over there?" He pointed to the lead truck, closest to the flames, where Nick Maloney was interviewing one of the firefighters. "Nick's gonna write another story. That's okay, that's his job, but the story he writes is going to get me pulled in front of my boss, and the goddamn mayor, and everyone else in town worried about crime. Worried about a goddamn gang war. I'm not really looking forward to that."

Petrone jammed his hands deep in his overcoat pockets. "But what really has me cranked is that this son of a bitch comes to my town and thinks he can raise all this hell and cause all this destruction and start a goddamn riot every time he turns around, and he's right. *He's right.* There's not a god-damn thing I can do about it."

Petrone blew out his breath in a controlled sigh. "That really has me cranked, John."

The headlights of a car bounced across the parking lot and stopped, illuminating the firefighters for an instant before they extinguished. Petrone looked at the car. "My, my," he murmured to Lockhart. "The man, hisself."

Pointy Williams climbed from behind the wheel of his Volvo and stared at the burning warehouse. His face was expression-less in the dancing light of the flames. Petrone touched Lock-hart's arm. "Let me talk to him alone." He walked across the parking lot and stood at Williams's side.

"Hell of a fire, isn't it?"

Williams's head turned slowly. He stared at the detective. "I know you?"

Petrone nodded. "Milos Petrone. Sergeant Milos Petrone now, but I was a plainclothes officer, just started in Homicide, when I picked you up after Carl Ingers got smoked."

Williams nodded. "I remember," he said tonelessly.

"Looks to me like somebody lost an awful lot of money here tonight. Fire captain said that warehouse is full of cars, real expensive cars."

Petrone crossed his arms. "I've been told the cars were stolen, so it's not like the guy who parked 'em in there is going to be able to file an insurance claim or anything. The guys from Auto Theft'll probably be down here for a week trying to read vehicle identification numbers."

"Who told you that?" Williams was still staring at the warehouse, and there wasn't much interest in his voice.

"Hell, you know how it is, Pointy. You mind I call you Pointy? I've been reading so much about you this week, files and wiretap transcripts and newspaper stories, I feel like we're old friends." Petrone turned back to the burning building. "Yeah, you know how it goes. I'm a cop. Sometimes people tell cops things. As a matter of fact, I got told that maybe those cars are—were—yours."

"I just stopped to watch the fire," Williams said calmly. "Don't know nothing about this."

"You're sure taking it well, if the cars were yours. There's maybe two dozen vehicles in there. Figure ten thousand apiece, you're out a quarter mil in inventory, almost as much as went in that printing-plant robbery last week."

Petrone stepped in front of Williams and stared levelly into the black man's eyes. The bantering note had left his voice. "I know it's the thief, Pointy. I know you set him up with a couple of corrupt cops, and I know he got away. I know he's the guy who took down Ma Rainey's the other night. How much did he really get? Thirty, forty grand?"

Williams stared back at the cop for a moment, then shook his head. "Not that much. Maybe twenty, twenty-five."

"I spent the morning on Thursday watching the ME's people bag three kids at Walnut Towers," Petrone said conversationally. "Your wheels are coming off, Pointy. There's blood in the water and the sharks are circling."

The black man turned and pulled open the door of the Volvo. "Fuck that," he spat. "Fuck you, Petrone. I'm still rolling. You do your fucking job, arrest the crazy motherfucker. You got his picture, for chrissakes."

"I don't know," Petrone said dubiously. "I don't think he looks much like that picture anymore. Besides, the guy seems to be on my side." He grinned and pointed at the fire. "He's done a wonderful thing here, fr'instance, to reduce the size of the city's vehicular theft problem."

The Volvo started with the sound of gnashing metal. The window rolled smoothly down. "Maybe I take care of this shit on my own, Petrone." Williams's voice was calm again. "Maybe I'm takin' care of it right this fuckin' minute. I do, you'll read about it in the papers." He put the car in gear and pulled away, the car window rising soundlessly as he left.

Petrone turned back to the burning building and saw Maloney talking to the fire captain. "You're right about the newspapers, Pointy. You are oh so right about that."

✳   ✳   ✳

Rodney saw red emergency lights in the Circle 7 parking lot from two blocks away. "Trouble." He pulled into the Holidome lot and shut off the car.

"Could be nothing," Showalter said.

Mackin tapped Rodney on the shoulder. "Check it out, bro." His face and voice were expressionless. "We'll be in the room."

Rodney stepped out of the car and began the walk to the other motel. Showalter and Mackin entered the Holidome. They didn't speak until they were in the room.

"Don't jump to any conclusions," Showalter said.

"She's dead." There was no emotion in Mackin's voice.

"You don't know that. We're clean, there's no way Williams could've found us."

"Sure he could." Mackin walked to the dresser, opened a bottle of bourbon, and poured three fingers into a plastic glass. "My fucking picture has been in the paper almost every day."

"So maybe it's the cops. Maybe they're just holding her for questioning."

"She's dead." Mackin drained the glass and poured another one. "Those were ambulance lights."

Showalter sat down. "Let's wait for Rodney, man. Let's be sure."

Mackin stared into his glass. "I'm sure."

Phil Walinski had been a cop in Easton for seventeen years, long enough to remember when the interstate was brand-new and his city was little more than a pleasant town that still had four miles of undeveloped lakefront inside the city limits. In the midseventies, his years in the patrol division, Easton's biggest crime problem had been auto theft and auto burglary. Now he was a shift commander in the detective division who spent as much time worrying about drugs and random murder as he did about crimes against property. The dead woman on the floor of the motel room was the city's twenty-first homicide victim of the year.

"Maybe we'll hit an even two dozen before Christmas," he said to Henry Rader, a crime-scene specialist attached to the local State Police barracks. "Never done that before."

"Phil, old buddy, you get up to much more than two dozen a year, you're going to have to talk your city commission into hiring a forensics specialist." Rader was crouched on the floor. He was a heavy, middle-aged man with wire-rimmed glasses and thick blond hair. His thick fingers were delicately guiding the tip of a mechanical pencil into an empty brass shell casing. He raised himself from the floor with visible effort. "This is a first, my friend."

"First what?" Walinski looked out the open door. An ambulance was backed up to the room door, its own rear door open, but the vehicle's lights and engine were off and the driver was leaning against its fender smoking a cigarette. A uniformed officer was keeping a handful of spectators away from the crime scene. "And why should we hire someone when we've got you?"

"You should hire someone because your wonderful little community is turning into a snake pit, and the proof of that proposition is that we are standing amid the aftermath of Easton's first machine-gunning."

Walinski's head snapped around. "What the hell?"

"Indeed." Rader smiled. "Not, I grant you, much of a machine gun. My guess would be a Mac-10 or Mac-11, which is probably the closest thing to a purse machine pistol ever devised by the demented mind of man, but a machine gun, nonetheless."

Rader looked over to the detective who had examined the body. "How many times was she hit, Lou?"

"Five or six times, boss." Lou was on his knees looking under the bed. "There's some more brass under here, the shit is everywhere, but I don't see a purse. No personal stuff at all except for the clothes in the closet. Room was rented to a Mr. and Mrs. J. Raynor. No sign of the mister."

"Probably the perp." Walinski shook his head. "A machine gun. Ain't that a pisser."

"Rotten little weapon." Rader pulled a large plastic bag out of his jacket pocket and dropped the casing into it. "Became very popular in the eighties as a fashion accessory with the dope crowd, but it's more effective as a prop than as a tool. The cyclic rate is far too high and the weapon tends to be poorly constructed."

"Run the numbers on all the cars in the lot, Lou," Walinski said. "Get the name of the desk clerk that checked them in."

Rader looked around the room. "This Ingram fires a .380 cartridge; in Europe they call it the nine-millimeter short or nine-millimeter Kurz, but there's no comparison to a real nine like that." He pointed to the weapon in the holster on the uniform's hip. "This is a low-power, low-velocity cartridge that really isn't what you think of as a mankiller."

Two paramedics wheeled the body out of the room and into the ambulance. Bloody blond hair protruded from beneath the gray blanket. A thickset black man in the crowd outside the room turned slowly and walked away.

"Killed the fuck out of her," Walinski said.

"The marketplace advantage an Ingram possesses is price, because like any other low-quality instrument they are remarkably inexpensive," Rader said. "Still, for a reasonably priced automatic weapon, it's tough to beat the Uzi or the Schmeisser."

"Henry, give me a break, okay?" Walinski leaned out of the door of the room and spit into the parking lot. "Enough about how shitty the gun is. It's a machine gun. I guarantee you the newspapers are going to make it sound like she was killed with an armored regiment."

"Well, of course." Rader blinked behind his glasses.

The warehouse fire made CNN the next morning. Salvatore Capetti sat in his living room and watched without expression as video images of the blaze danced across his television screen. A reporter on the scene was saying something about a gang war. Nick Maloney's story had again been picked up by both Chicago papers, and the *Chicago Tribune* ran it just below the fold on page one. Capetti read it carefully, twice. Then he picked up the phone and called Frank Riles.

Twenty minutes later the two men were in Capetti's backyard. Riles opened the conversation.

"Williams's people sent ten thousand, cash, for the printing-plant thing, Sal. It ain't much, but it's a gesture."

"It must stop now, Francis," the old man said sternly. "Look at this."

He pointed to a single paragraph near the end of Maloney's story. Riles had already seen it at breakfast, but he read it again. "The fact that the week of violence began with the robbery of almost $250,000 in food stamps has caused several investigators to theorize that organized crime might be attempting to move into the grocery industry. However, police and Justice Department sources say that the so-called Macchi organization, repeatedly named by federal investigators as one of the controlling bodies in the city's underworld, is virtually moribund and has been for several years. The possibility that the violence is linked to the Chicago mob, said to have been headed for more than a decade by Sal Capetti, was labeled 'sheer speculation' by Daryl Mumford of the Chicago FBI office, as were reports that the investigation would act as a catalyst to revive the Midwest Organized Crime Strike Force, currently slated to be disbanded next month."

Capetti tapped the paper with a long, bony finger. "Ten years, Francis. Ten years I've been responsible for taking care of our business, and never once have those parasites at the Justice Department come close to me. To us. Now, in a week, everything goes to hell and I see my name back in the papers. What's our exposure?"

"On paper, nothing," Riles said quickly. He'd been thinking about the question all morning. "The feds can subpoena the whole world, all they'll find is that Hookright sold twelve percent of Consolidated to a real estate investment company for one hundred and forty thousand dollars. That's what all the papers say, and the real estate people are mostly clean. There's nothing written down that indicates who really controls the company."

"But Mr. Hookright knows, is that not so?"

Riles shrugged. "Sort of, I guess. Little Wayne Hookright's had his head buried so far in a pile of cocaine for the past year that there's no telling what he remembers, but yeah. He knows he did the deal with me, personally, even if he really doesn't know how much control he gave up, and that's not good."

Capetti slowly lowered himself into a garden chair made of white wrought-iron and patted the seat of the chair beside him. Riles sat down.

"Three, four years ago," Capetti said reflectively, "all my people wanted to be John Gotti." He turned to Riles, smiling, and patted the younger man's knee. "Except you, of course, Francis. You have always understood. But the young men, they wanted to work for a Teflon don, because someday they wanted to be Teflon dons. Where is Gotti now? Who is taking care of Gotti's people?"

Capetti shook his head. "I never liked Gotti, Francis. Of course, it is not important to like someone to do business, but it helps, and I never liked Gotti. I liked Paul Castellano very much, but Paul was stupid. He let his subordinates run wild. He lived in an ostentatious mansion. He did not take care of business, and so the Justice Department put a microphone in his dining room and indicted him, and then his people killed him."

"That's New York, Sal," Riles said quietly. "That's *Godfather* shit. All those guys are crazy."

"Sure it's New York, and New York has been a mess since Gambino died, but the lesson is still there for the wise man. They called me, you know, about Paul."

Riles looked surprised. "I didn't know that, Sal."

Capetti nodded. "Yes. They went to the other families, they had to. Paul was the biggest man in New York, and not even a Teflon man could kill the biggest man in New York without permission. I met with them when I flew down to Florida that time."

"What did you tell them?"

Capetti shrugged. "What could I say? Paul let them bug his house; good Lord, it was out of control. He had to go. Everyone was at risk." He turned to look directly at Riles. "I don't want people making calls like that about me, Francis. I tell you this formally: It must end. This thief must go home. No more newspaper stories."

Riles nodded. "Sì, Don Salvatore," he said quietly. He stood up and motioned for Ray to get the car.

⁎   ⁎   ⁎

Rodney walked into the motel room, looked at Mackin, and shook his head. Mackin was sitting on the bed. He nodded.

"I'm having a look around," Showalter said shortly. His face was tight with anxiety. "Be back in a minute." He shoved a pistol in his waistband, covered it with an unbuttoned flannel shirt, and walked out the door.

Mackin smiled. "Bo likes to be doing something," he said. "All the time."

Rodney stared at Mackin for a moment, then walked to the dresser and poured two drinks. He handed one to Mackin and sat down in the chair across from the bed. The two men were silent for a moment.

Mackin finally spoke. "How bad was it?" He was staring into his glass.

Rodney shifted in his chair. "It was bad." He looked in the direction of the curtained window. "I couldn't see much, but there was a lot of blood. A cop outside the room told someone in the crowd that she'd been shot more than once."

"Goddammit." Mackin didn't raise his voice, but his fingers tightened white around the glass. "Goddammit."

"She was a nice kid."

Mackin shot off the bed and walked to the dresser to refill his drink. "That helps. C'mon, bro. You're being too quiet. Tell me what a fuck-up I am. Tell me how stupid I was to let her come along."

"What's done is done," Rodney said quietly. "What do you want to hear? She was a nice kid. It looked like it went down real fast. She probably didn't feel anything."

Mackin slumped back onto the bed. "That doesn't make me feel any better."

Rodney sighed. "I'm not trying to make you feel better,

Mackin. I'm making conversation. You're gonna have to carry this cross all by yourself."

"Goddammit," Mackin said again. "I don't even have a picture of her, can you believe that? I get the girl killed and I don't even have a photograph of her."

"Things are bad," Rodney said carefully. "Maybe we ought to think about not letting them get any worse. Maybe we ought to just get the hell out of here and deal with this shit at a later date."

Mackin was still staring at his glass. "I really liked her, Rodney. I mean, I really, really liked her a lot. We just seemed to fit. Been a long time since I met someone who made me feel that way."

"Take it easy on this thing, Mackin. You didn't even know her a month."

"I knew enough." Mackin leaned over and carefully set the empty glass on the floor. "I knew enough to know for sure that I didn't want to get her killed. Isn't that some kind of rule? First rule, don't get your lover killed." He croaked out a sour laugh.

"Now's the time for thinking," Rodney said. "Let dealing with the pain wait. Right now we have to decide what the fuck we're gonna do."

"I know what I'm going to do. I know exactly what I'm going to do." Mackin pulled his .45 and checked the load.

Rodney scowled. "Goddamn, Mackin. Don't be thinking for a second that this gangbang can't get any worse. I'm sorry about Maggie, I truly am, but there's no reason for you or me or Bo to join her. Let's get out while we still can."

Mackin set the pistol on the bed next to him. "It's not like that, Rodney. It's not like she was a player. She was special. I can't walk away from this, and you know I can't. It was a shitty thing to do, bringing her here. She deserves more than me just walking away."

Rodney stood up and sighed. He set his glass on the dresser next to the bottle and turned to the bed. "Does she deserve you dying, bro? You think that will make everything better?"

Mackin picked up the pistol and stared at it. "I don't plan on doing the dying."

20

THE LOBBY of Vingt-et-Un was large enough to hold thirty prospective diners and often did; the restaurant was among the most popular in the downtown district. The right lobby wall was broken by a door that led to the softly lit bar, which could accommodate another two dozen people. As tables became available, patrons were collected and seated by a hostess, who stood at a small podium on the lobby's left wall.

For four nights a week, that podium was Janet Hassan's station. Tonight the rain had chased downtown shoppers into the restaurant, and she had a full bar and two parties of five in the lobby. Half her mind was directed toward keeping straight the list of waiting customers, the other was analyzing her employer's strange behavior.

Pointy Williams had spent the night before closeted in the restaurant's small office with Dink Reeves and Beano-D. Tonight Reeves and Beano-D were sitting in the bar. They'd been there for almost three hours. Dink's was a familiar face to Hassan—he was in the restaurant a couple of times a week and sometimes ate there. Beano-D, though, had appeared in the past only long enough to pass a whispered message to Reeves or Williams. Hassan was sure that his continued presence was a sign of trouble. Williams himself had entered the restaurant early, shortly after dark, and immediately closed himself in the back office. The line lights on the phone at the cashier's desk indicated that he was making calls.

He'd hardly spoken to Hassan as he walked by. She glanced down at the large purse on the shelf of the podium. Inside was her service revolver, a massive .41 magnum with a four-inch ribbed barrel, which her superior officer, Caroline Reese, allowed her to carry in the bag after a quiet conversation with Petrone.

"I'd be happier if you checked out a snubbie, Janet," Reese had told her. "That's a hell of a big piece to trigger off in a crowded room if, God forbid, something really does go down."

"I'd like to stick to the .41, Captain," Hassan said quietly. "It's my carry weapon, it's what I qualify with. I'm comfortable with it."

"I'm aware of your ability, Janet," Reese had said. Hassan was on the State Police combat pistol team. "Just remember we're talking about a real restaurant and real people, not Hogan's Alley and mechanical targets."

Now Hassan picked up a pair of menus and walked to the door of the small bar. "Richardson party?" A young couple smiled and rose from one of the two booths on the wall. Hassan saw Beano-D sitting on a barstool. He stared at her without interest. Dink Reeves was talking on a cordless phone. As she led the couple out of the bar, she saw Petrone come through the restaurant's front door and stride across the lobby.

"Don't mind me, miss," he said politely. He flashed his tin. She thought he looked tired and tense. "I'm here to see the owner about something." He slid past the Richardsons and headed to the back of the restaurant.

She turned and saw Beano-D start to stand up. Reeves reached out and put a hand on his shoulder: "It's cool."

From the backseat, Mackin pointed to the parking lot of a market across the street from Vingt-et-Un. "Park there. Wait ten minutes, no more. If I'm not out in ten, just leave. Go home." He pulled his .45 from the holster under his arm and checked its load.

Rodney was driving. "This is fucked, Mackin." He parked and turned to look over the seat. "You don't even know if the motherfucker is in there. If he's in there, we oughtta just wait for him to come out, do him outside. You ain't thinkin' here, bro."

Mackin didn't bother to argue. "I'm tired of fucking around with this man, Rodney." There was no emotion in his voice. "That's his car. He's in there, I can smell him. I'm going to walk in there, kill him, and get out. Then we all go home." He opened the car door and stepped out into the rain.

Rodney turned to Showalter. "Thanks for all the fuckin' help, homes," he snapped. "I don't think I could've talked him out of this without all your support."

Showalter shrugged. "I know him a little better than you do, Rodney. He ain't in the mood to negotiate, and I'm not gonna argue with him. He's gonna do what he's gonna do. Best thing we can do is exactly what he says, wait ten minutes."

Rodney pounded on the steering wheel. "Goddammit, I'm the only person here thinkin' straight. We are an eyelash, a fucking *eyelash*, away from being dead or locked up. It's a goddamn miracle we're still in business, and we're pushing our luck right off the table. I say put this fucking Ford on Seventy West right now. Haul ass."

Showalter leaned his head back on the seat. "I've been down this road before, Rodney. Years ago, before your time, Mackin and I took down a military armory for a shitload of guns and munitions."

"You have told me that goddamn story two hundred times."

Showalter smiled. "Not the whole story, bro. See, it was my score, and one of the first times Mackin and I ever worked together. I knew these Marines from 'Nam, the kind of guys you could do business with. It was a contract job, the buyer was this fucker from England who wanted the shit for some pissant war in Africa. I set it up with these Marines, and we all hit the armory around three o'clock Saturday morning of Christmas weekend."

He grinned at the memory. "Went like clockwork, got paid and all. One of the inside Marines was a master sergeant named Tompkins. Fucker drank like a sailor, and two nights after the score I hear he's sitting in the NCO Club blasted out of his mind talking to his buddies about how he had the scoop on the armory robbery, wink-wink-nudge-nudge. So he had to go."

His smile vanished. "Tompkins, he didn't know Mackin from Batman, couldn't touch him, but he sure as hell knew me. Mackin and I had just started working together, and the sensible thing for him would've been to just split. But he didn't. He stayed right there with me in South Carolina, place crawling with state cops, FBI, Naval Intelligence—for all I know the fuckin' CIA was looking for us. It took us eight, nine days to fix everything. And I'll tell you something, bro, that time in South Carolina was way worse than this."

Rodney wasn't mollified. "That may be, Bo, but I'll bet you weren't trying to fix everything with Mackin's picture on the front page of the fucking newspaper every day."

Showalter frowned and didn't answer.

Petrone walked through the kitchen and knocked on the door of the restaurant's office. "It's Detective Sergeant Petrone, Pointy." He opened his badge case flat and pushed it under the door. "Uncock your rocket launcher and let me in. I just want to talk."

He heard a desk drawer open and close. The door unlocked and opened. Williams handed him his badge. He was sitting behind a desk cluttered with invoices, menus, and a calculator. "What the fuck you talkin' about, rocket launcher?"

Petrone leaned his haunch against the corner of the desk. "Report on my desk this morning said a woman got machine-gunned in Easton last night. Said she got zipped up like a pair of cheap pants. I figured you and our boy Moffitt had graduated to heavy artillery."

Williams's expression didn't change. "Yeah, you right. Last night I shot that woman all to hell with a machine gun, week before that I put a bomb in the mayor's car, next month I'm gonna blow up the fuckin' White House. Hell, few years ago I took a vacation, caused that earthquake in L.A. There ain't shit happened I ain't responsible for."

Petrone raised his hands in a gesture of defeat. "Okay, Pointy, okay. I came by because I thought maybe the fire gave you second thoughts."

"I don't know shit about the fire, don't know shit about those cars, don't know shit about shit. I just leased the fucking warehouse. It's s'posed to be full of pinball machines, Petrone. Those boys stealin' cars, it ain't my problem. Talk to Simons. Leave me alone."

Petrone nodded. "I know you're not going to ask us for any help, and I also know that there isn't anyone else you can ask. I thought maybe you might think about leaving town for a while, give us a chance to catch this Moffitt character."

"Ain't nobody chasing Pointy Williams out of this town," the black man snapped. "Not you, not Moffitt, not Sal fuckin' Capetti. You got that? You want to arrest me, you arrest me, but you better charge me and it better stand up, because—"

A woman screamed in the lobby.

Dink Reeves, still on the phone to Danny, was looking directly at the front doors of the restaurant when Mackin walked in. He immediately recognized the thief's eyes and stopped speaking in midsentence.

"What's going on?" Danny, still sitting on Malcolm Barrett at the office on Amsterdam Street, could tell that something was wrong.

"Thief just walked in," Reeves said quietly.

Beano-D swiveled on his barstool. He stared at Reeves for a second, then turned his eyes to the lobby. Mackin, his hair tousled and wet from the rain, was standing just inside the door behind a group of four shoppers. The shoppers were loaded with bags from department stores and were taking off their coats. Beano-D couldn't see Mackin's hands.

"Motherfucker," Beano-D said, loudly enough to draw shocked looks from the other patrons in the bar. He saw that Mackin was scanning the lobby. He pulled his pistol from his waistband below the bar, covered it with his jacket, and stepped into the lobby.

"Dink, what the fuck is going on down there?" Danny was agitated. "You need me down there?"

"Stay where you are, Danny. Everything's cool." Dink broke the connection and stood up. Beano-D had moved out into the lobby, his jacket over his gun hand, and was staring at Mackin. Dink slipped out of the bar and headed toward the back of the restaurant.

Beano-D locked eyes with Mackin and let his jacket fall to the floor. The two men were twenty-five feet apart, and the four customers stood between them. "I tol' you I was gonna kill you, motherfucker," Beano-D said, and started to raise his weapon. One of the women in front of Mackin saw the black gun coming up and screamed. The family of five sitting on one of the benches in the lobby watched in horror. The mother threw her arms around the two smallest children and pulled them close. Beano-D leveled his weapon at Mackin and fired.

At the sound of the scream Williams bolted out of his chair. He jerked open a desk drawer and removed a silver revolver. "Lobby."

"Stay here," Petrone began, but the black man had already pushed past him and was running through the kitchen. "Goddammit, Williams, drop that gun," Petrone yelled as he, too, began to run, but the other man was already around the corner. A gunshot ripped through the restaurant and now the screaming was general. Petrone flipped his jacket open and pulled his weapon. Pointy was turning into the lobby as Petrone reached the restaurant floor.

✻   ✻   ✻

Janet Hassan's instincts started screaming the second the man with wet hair walked through the door. She watched in fascination as he looked over the lobby and saw Beano-D. Two things hit her simultaneously, an intellectual recognition that the man at the door was the face from the driver's license, and more viscerally that the jacket over Beano-D's right hand almost certainly covered a gun. Her own hand dropped below the podium and unsnapped her purse. She automatically shifted her feet to even her weight and wrapped her hand around the butt of the magnum. She began to lift the weapon as Beano-D dropped his jacket, her eyes flashing between Beano-D and the thief. She hardly heard the screaming. She wondered where Petrone was. She wished she had her badge.

Mackin held his pistol under his jacket in his right hand as he walked through the restaurant doors. He was behind four people bundled in raincoats and laden with shopping bags. As soon as they were inside the restaurant, they began to remove their coats. He stood behind them, just inside the door, and scoped out the lobby. He saw Beano-D walk out of the bar and began to wonder if he'd made a mistake. Out of the corner of his eye he saw the hostess, a good-looking girl in a pantsuit uniform designed to look like a man's tuxedo, begin to move in an alarming way. Someone screamed. He started to lift his gun.

Beano-D said something, pointed his weapon, and fired. Mackin cringed into his jacket. One of the people in front of him, a short, heavyset older woman still half in her coat, fainted and dropped to the floor. Something hit the wall next to Mackin's head. As he raised his pistol, he saw Beano-D framed in the light from the door to the bar. Directly behind the black man, in the line of fire, a pair of young women were hugging each other at the bar, their eyes squeezed shut in terror. Pointy Williams ran out of the restaurant and into the lobby. Mackin ignored Beano-D and swung his weapon toward Williams. One of the old woman's companions stepped in front of Mackin screaming.

"Shit," he said.

Petrone reached the lobby two seconds after Williams, his weapon out but pointed at the floor. The people in the restaurant behind him were crawling under their tables. He saw Williams and the thief spend a frozen moment staring at each other. A big black man had a pistol leveled at the thief and was beginning to walk across the lobby. The thief was standing behind a clump of people—Petrone couldn't tell how many, but one of them was on the ground and apparently hit. In the quiet light of the lobby, Petrone could see a tendril of blue smoke drifting from the barrel of the black man's gun. Petrone reached out, grabbed Williams's shoulder, and pulled him back toward the dining area. "Drop that goddamn gun," he rasped, his eyes flitting over the tableau in the lobby.

His stare with Mackin broken, Williams lowered his weapon, turned on his heel, and began to walk to the back of the building. He shoved his pistol in his waistband as he went. Petrone didn't bother to yell at him. He raised his gun toward Beano-D. "Freeze!" he yelled, and realized no one was paying any attention to him. From the corner of his eye he saw Janet Hassan's hands appear holding a gun. She yelled something and Beano-D triggered another shot. Petrone fired.

Janet Hassan's first concern was for the citizens in the lobby. She saw Petrone fire. Beano-D kept walking. The father of the family on the bench was shielding his wife and children with his body. She still couldn't see the thief's hands. She raised the magnum in a two-handed grip, centered the sights on the middle of Beano-D's chest, and leaned forward slightly. "Freeze, Beano!" she yelled. "Police!" She wondered if he believed her.

Beano-D was walking slowly across the lobby. Someone popped a cap behind him. He ignored it. The bitch at the podium, the piece of trim Pointy had been trying to fuck since summer, yelled something at him. He ignored her. He held his gun stiff-armed in front of him. The thief was standing in the doorway, a gun in his hand. "You're a dead motherfucker," Beano-D said, and Janet Hassan shot him in the chest under his upraised arm.

The impact stopped him. A puzzled look spread across his face. He turned slowly toward the podium. The bitch had a gun. Her lips were moving, but Beano-D couldn't hear what she was saying. He couldn't hear anything. He tried to pull the trigger, but he couldn't. He couldn't make his hands or arms do anything. He felt something wet running across his stomach.

"Drop the gun, Beano, now!" Hassan had regained her sight picture. Beano-D began to turn, the gun still held in front of him. She shot him again. The last thing he saw was a jet of bright orange flame erupting from the barrel of her gun. He folded up and fell to the floor and died.

At the faint but unmistakable sound of the first shot from across the street, Rodney looked at Showalter. "Well?" he said angrily.

Showalter unholstered his pistol. "Start the car."

Mackin saw a man in a gray suit grab Pointy Williams's shoulder and spin him back into the restaurant. He backed against the door. He knew he couldn't make it across the lobby. Beano-D fired at him again, this time well wide. He was stunned to see the girl in the tuxedo suit produce a huge revolver and aim it at the black man. She shot Beano in the chest and the man's pink shirt turned dark with blood. "Fuck this," Mackin said. He pushed through the doors and out into the rain.

The Taurus pulled up in front of him. There was another shot in the building behind him. He jumped into the backseat. "Go." He hadn't made it six feet into the building.

Petrone stared at Beano-D's body for a moment, then swung around to look for Pointy Williams. Several diners in the restaurant screamed as he turned toward them, and he realized he still held his weapon. "I'm a police officer," he said loudly. No one appeared to be reassured.

Janet Hassan stepped around the podium and walked to Beano-D. She used her foot to push the nine-millimeter pistol away from his hand. He was very clearly dead. She saw Petrone looking over the dining floor, his revolver in his hand. "Clear, Sergeant," she yelled. She picked up the nine-millimeter from the floor, walked back to the podium, and put the guns on the shelf. Petrone was still looking around.

"Sergeant!" She repeated it until he turned to her. "*Clear, Sergeant.*"

Petrone glanced at the gun in his hand. "Oh. Right." He carefully uncocked the pistol and returned it to his holster.

Hassan picked up the phone and dialed 911.

Mackin, Showalter, and Rodney slipped into the Holidome one at a time. Mackin went directly to the room. Bo and Rodney killed thirty minutes in the bar. Showalter was the first one back to the room.

"Everything's cool," he said. "The lobby, or whatever you call it, looks right, no cops or obvious house security. Rodney's on his way."

"The desk people here have never really seen me." Mackin was sitting at the room's round table with a bottle of bourbon in front of him, but his glass was dry. "But, hell, I didn't think the desk pukes at the other place saw me, either."

What bothered Bo most was that Mackin's voice was so conversational. "Could've been a maid, Mackin. Could've been another guest. You said Williams had juice with the cops. Anything in that room tie to Kansas City?"

"You mean, besides Maggie's body?" Mackin smiled. "Some clothes, some cash, a bag or two. Fingerprints, probably, but I guess they've had those since Atlanta. Maggie's car was in the lot, but it has California plates. I don't know."

Rodney tapped lightly on the door and walked in. He was fingering a folded message slip from the desk.

"She didn't have much family," Bo said cautiously. "A sister, I think, but they didn't get along. She wasn't in Kansas City long. I don't think they'll get any closer than the bar, if that far, and if they do, I'll just tell 'em that she took off with a customer. We could come out of this okay, we get the fuck out of here tonight."

Rodney cleared his throat. "There was a message at the desk. From Riles. He left a number. I called. He wants a sit-down. Tomorrow. Someplace called Momo Amusement, on the west side. Says Williams will be there. No guns."

Mackin looked up and nodded. "I fucked that whole thing up, too. Capetti's probably ready to hang my balls on his bedroom wall. Give me the address, I'll take a cab over there. You guys go home. Now."

Rodney looked uncomfortable. "He says you can bring one guy to the meet. He says he figures you'll bring me, 'cause Bo likes to be the outside guy."

"No shit." Mackin seemed only mildly interested. "I guess that means he's not going to kill me right away. I'll go alone."

"Fuck you will," Showalter growled. "I got a scoped .227 Herret in the trunk that'll shoot the nuts off a polar bear at three hundred meters. Anybody fucks with you, they'll die before they hear the shot. Let's do the sit-down, make this right, then go home."

Showalter turned to Rodney. "How about it?"

Rodney sighed. "In for a fucking penny."

21

FRANK RILES sat in the backseat of his car and read the newspaper story about the murdered girl in the motel room. "Oh, shit," he said aloud.

"Problems, boss?" Ray had driven the two of them from Chicago. It was two-thirty in the afternoon and the steel gray sky made it feel like twilight.

"Fucking Williams found the fucking motel and wasted Mackin's fucking girlfriend. Shit, shit, shit."

"Who's Mackin?" Ricky Cento was sitting next to Ray in the front seat.

"Mackin, Ricky, is the thief who started this whole shitstorm." Riles was still reading. "Pointy Williams tried to kill him, which pissed Mackin off. Now it looks like Williams killed Mackin's woman, which I'm sure has *really* pissed Mackin off. This is way out of hand. You're going to have a busy night, Ray."

The driver nodded. Riles closed the newspaper and looked out the Lincoln's window. It was raining. He wondered how Williams had found the motel. The car glided to a stop in front of an elegant, red-brick building.

"Eight seventeen Racine." Ray was looking at a discreet sign next to the door. "Turcotte Arms Luxury Apartments."

"We're heading for the seventh-floor penthouse," Riles said. "There's a private entrance around the corner. I have a key. Let's go. You, too, Ricky."

"Who lives here?"

"Business partner." Riles used the newspaper to shield his head from the rain. They walked around the corner to a door covered with a steel gate. Riles produced a key, unlocked the gate, unlocked the door, and led the three of them into a small, well-appointed reception area. Elevator doors were on the far wall.

"That goes straight up to Hookright's apartment," Riles said to Ray. He handed his driver the key. "This operates the elevator. I'll wait here, you take Ricky with you."

Cento looked nervously at the elevator. "What are we doing here, Mr. Riles?"

Riles picked an overstuffed armchair and sat down. "Dissolving the partnership."

"You missed," the chief said, "but you still have to fill all this shit out." He pushed a stack of forms across his desk. "You've been through this before."

"No, I haven't, actually," Petrone said. It was the morning after the shooting. "I have drawn my weapon a total of six times in my career, but that was the first time I ever fired it off the range."

"No shit." The chief lit a cigarette. "Well, it looks like you could spend some more time in the basement. Yours was definitely an air ball."

"I was practically falling down. It was a one-handed snap shot."

The chief scowled. "For Christ's sake don't put that in the report. That's all the shoot team needs to hear, a detective sergeant firing snap shots in a crowded restaurant lobby. I'm supposed to put you on immediate administrative leave, but for the time being, let's fuck that."

"It was kind of heavy, Chief. Hassan was solid. She did it by the numbers."

"Looks like it. Two shots at an armed moving target, both in the kill ring, could cover the entrance wounds with a coaster. I'll take that anytime. She'll sail through the hearing, don't worry."

Petrone picked up the paperwork and rose from his chair. "I got a bad feeling about this, Chief. Walking into that restaurant like that, that was right out of *High Noon*. First, I think something really pissed off our boy, and second, I don't imagine that he's going to stay for the rest of the party. I think maybe the only thing he wants to do is kill Williams, and Williams probably won't be keeping office hours for a while."

The chief nodded. "I got a pickup order out on Williams and Reeves, but even if we find them, I won't be able to hold either one of them long. That fucking Ralph Simons'll pop 'em out of the cooler before we have time to loosen our ties."

"Do me a favor, Chief." Petrone looked thoughtful. "See if you can get the guys in Easton to send over a copy of whatever latents they found in that motel room, along with an inventory. Maybe the girl was somehow involved in all this."

The chief nodded. "I wish Moffitt would kill Williams or Williams would kill Moffitt. Sure as hell quiet things down."

"This sucks." Showalter was sitting in the front seat of Rodney's Taurus. The car was parked in an alley a half block from the front door of Momo Amusement. "This is an impossible shot."

"You keep that fucking rifle in its case and in the backseat," Mackin said. "You're legal that way. Cop comes along and asks, you're a hunter on your way to Arkansas. You're lost and looking at the map."

"I don't like going in there without a piece." Rodney didn't sound nervous.

"You don't have to. Riles wants to see me, not you."

"I *really* don't like you walking in there without a piece," Rodney said.

"Riles says no guns, there won't be any guns."

Showalter was shaking his head. "Mackin, if something goes down, it's gonna take me forever to get a shot."

"Nothing's going down, Bo." Mackin's voice was flat. "Riles knows you're out here somewhere, watching. That's why he said what he said to Rodney. He wants us to know that he knows there are people here tonight who will remember what happens. He sure as hell doesn't want you chasing him back to Chicago."

Mackin turned to Rodney. "I'm going in."

"Right. Of fuckin' course. We just walk in there and party." Rodney sighed. "Let's dance."

✻   ✻   ✻

The truck bay at Momo Amusement was long and narrow. Ricky Cento set up the last of five folding chairs around a cheap rectangular conference table, lifted a shotgun from the table, and walked over to where Frank Riles stood at the window. "All set, Mr. Riles."

Riles nodded without speaking. The window was small and cracked. It opened onto a tiny alley behind the building. Ray walked in through the front door. He was wearing a long overcoat made of dark blue wool.

"Alley gate is shut and locked," he said to Riles. "The only way in is through the front door. There's no one around."

"What time is it?"

Ray looked at his watch. "Nine-thirty. Half hour to go."

Riles nodded again. "Cento."

Ricky Cento turned. "Yessir?"

"Joe tells me good things about you. Says you're solid. That's why you're here. Here's what I want you to remember: No matter what happens in here, you don't do a goddamn thing with that shotgun until I tell you to. *No matter what.* Pointy Williams shoots me in the head with a fucking crossbow, you don't move unless my corpse tells you to. You got that?"

"I got it, Mr. Riles."

Riles turned from the window and gazed at the conference table. "I know about your side bet with Dink Reeves, Ricky," he said quietly.

Cento became intensely aware of the weight of the shotgun in his right hand. He felt his underarms grow damp with sweat. He had already seen one man die that afternoon. He said nothing.

Riles walked over to Ray and leaned against the wall. He looked at the younger man questioningly. "I don't really have a problem with that. Macchi, he's a great old guy, but maybe not the best guy to work for if you want to make a little money." He smiled. "All that Mustache Pete shit about drugs and Lucky Luciano. Am I right?"

Cento stared at the two of them. He was petrified. He knew there wasn't a round in the chamber of the shotgun. Ray was staring levelly at him, his hands in his coat pockets.

"Now would be a very bad time for you to start lying to me, Ricky." Riles reached under his coat and Cento sucked in his breath, but the older man was reaching for a cigarette. "So am I right?" He flipped open his gold lighter and stared at Cento over the flame.

"I've done a little business with Reeves, yeah," Cento choked out. "I mean, yes, sir. But I haven't done nothing to fuck Joe over, Mr. Riles. I ain't stole nothin', honest to God."

Riles made a patting motion in the air with the hand holding his cigarette. "Take it easy, Ricky. I believe you." He smiled and pointed casually at his driver. "Hell, if I didn't believe that already, Ray would've killed you when you walked in."

Riles shook his head. "What I don't know, Ricky, is whether or not you were the guy who gave Williams the Circle 7 motel. That is something that I've wondered about."

Cento stared pleadingly at the two men without speaking.

Riles ignored him. "See, Mackin, the guy Williams wants to kill—you're gonna meet him pretty soon—he's a smart motherfucker. Pointy Williams, on the other hand—you ever met Williams, Ricky?"

Cento shook his head.

"Well, I've only met him a couple times, but I know about him, if you know what I mean. I've done business with the guy, a lot of business, and I know about him. And Williams isn't smart enough to have found that motel all on his own. The only place in town with Mackin's phone number was right here, and I'm pretty sure Joe didn't give it up. So I gotta admit that I've wondered if maybe you didn't help Williams a little bit."

"Look, Mr. Riles," Cento said quickly, a note of desperation in his voice, "maybe I did a little business with Dink on some stuff—"

"Quiet, Ricky." Riles looked like a stern schoolteacher. "Don't interrupt me. What I'm telling you is, *I don't want to know* if you gave Williams the motel." Headlights flashed on the pinball machines stacked against the far wall, and Riles walked back to the window. "They're coming," he said to Ray.

"See, if you gave up the motel, I'd probably have to whack you." Riles was still staring out the window. "Or I'd have to tell Mackin that you ratted him out, and then he'd whack you. So what I'm going to do is stop wondering, Ricky. I'm going to let bygones be bygones. That's the whole fucking problem we have here, is no one wants to let go of the past. The motel is the past, Ricky. Someday Joe Macchi will be part of the past. Guys like you and me, we have to worry about the future."

He turned and looked directly into Cento's eyes. "I'm letting go of the past, Ricky. I don't want to know about the motel. Maybe someday you can do me a favor."

Cento slowly exhaled. "Anytime, Mr. Riles. Anything at all."

Riles nodded. "Rack a round into that pump gun. You remember what I told you."

There was a short knock at the door. "That's Mackin and his guy," Riles said to Ray. "Let them in, pat them down."

Mackin and Rodney were already sitting at the table when Dink Reeves arrived. He submitted to Ray's search without comment and sat down across the table from Riles. "Pointy be here in a minute," he said quietly.

He turned to Mackin. "You about two hundred twenty pounds of bad news, aren't you?" There was no animosity in his voice.

Rodney grinned. Mackin's expression didn't change.

Reeves nodded. "Riles said you were a badass. Makes any difference, you're way ahead on this thing. Ma Rainey's made a noise, but that warehouse thing, that was big-time. You cost us a whole lot of money."

"I was way ahead of this thing when I made it out of that police car without a bullet in my head."

"Let's wait for Pointy," Riles said calmly. "We'll get it all worked out."

The six men in the room waited an uneasy ten minutes. Ray stood motionless before the door. Cento was across the room in the shadows, the shotgun cradled under one arm and pointed down. Mackin sat at the far end of the table, with Rodney on his right. Reeves sat alone on the long side of the table across from Riles. The chair at the head of the table was empty. Ray's ears picked up the sound of a motor a full second before the splash of headlights hit the front window.

"He's here," the driver said. Riles nodded.

Pointy Williams knocked twice and pushed open the door. He stood in the doorway, staring at Mackin.

"He clean?" Williams asked Riles shortly.

"He's clean." Riles motioned to Ray. "And now Ray is going to make sure you're clean, and then we're all going to sit down and work this shit out." Riles was sitting alone on one of the long sides of the table. His arms were crossed on the table in front of him. He watched without visible interest as Ray expertly ran his hands over Williams's clothes.

The driver paused when he reached the black man's left

jacket pocket, then reached inside and removed Williams's cigarette case. He opened it, looked inside for a moment, and handed it back without comment. "He's clean," he said to Riles.

"Goddamn right I'm clean," Williams snapped. He pulled out the chair at the head of the table and dropped into it. He was wearing the same brown silk suit and white shirt he'd been wearing during the encounter at Vingt-et-Un. "Didn't carry a piece for four, five years before that crazy son of a bitch came to town." He pointed at Mackin. "Past five days I've had one of my clubs robbed, a couple punk niggers tried to rip me off for seventy-five thousand cash, and I watched two hundred thousand dollars' worth of cars burn to the fucking ground. Last night that cocksucker came at me right in my own restaurant and killed one of my people."

Williams turned angrily to Riles. "How are you goddamn Italians gonna make all this right?"

Reeves spoke before Riles could reply. "I told you already, Pointy. He didn't do Beano-D. That bitch Janet did Beano, and she had a badge to go with her gun. She was a fuckin' cop, homes."

"Yeah, she was a cop, Pointy." Riles stared levelly at him. "The thing of it is, you two"—he used both hands to point toward Mackin and Williams simultaneously—"have turned this town into Dodge City. For all I know they're talking about you on CNN right now. The people I work for want all this to stop, and tonight we're gonna make it stop."

Mackin spoke for the first time. "How?" He was staring at Williams. "This piece of shit set me up. He killed a girl who had nothing to do with this situation. I don't know if I can let that go by."

"Maggie, wasn't that her name?" Riles turned to Mackin. An edge of anger entered his voice. "Maybe you'd like to explain to us exactly why you brought her along on this little field trip? You're supposed to be a fucking pro, you told me you were going to handle this thing like a pro, and you bring along some citizen broad who gets caught in the line of fire. What do you want from me? Sympathy?"

Mackin, eyes bright with rage, stared without speaking.

"And you." Riles pointed at Williams. "We do a deal in good faith, I provide you with a service because I am led to believe that you run a good organization. It turns out every two-bit kid with a gun is trying to get a piece of your ass and the cops are waiting right outside your door. You set up my man here, try to get him killed, for what? For twenty thousand dollars? What the fuck were you thinking of? We're setting up to do major business in this town and you're nickel-and-diming everything away. And now I hear you were actually hitting a little bit on the broad who gunned your man in the restaurant. Hitting on a cop."

Pointy shot a vicious look at Riles. He opened the silver case, pulled out a cigarette, and lit it. "So everyone is a fuckup but the Italians," he said savagely. "No one's got their shit together but the hoods from Chicago." He glowered at Riles, stood up, put his hands on the table, and leaned forward. "Well, you ain't in Chicago, Riles. I'm here to listen to how you plan to fix everything that fucked up this week."

Riles nodded evenly at him. "I've had a bad week, too." There was weariness in his voice now. He tapped once on the table with the knuckles of his right hand. Ray, standing directly behind Williams, removed a silenced .22 automatic from his overcoat pocket, stepped back toward the door, and shot the black man in the back of the head. The gun made a sound like a tiny firecracker.

Williams's eyes bulged. He opened his mouth as if to speak. A trickle of blood emerged. His arms buckled and he fell face first on the table. His cigarette, still smoldering, rolled toward Riles. Ray stepped to the table and carefully shot Williams again, this time in his upturned left ear, then stood with the pistol hanging in his hand and pointed at the floor.

"I've had a bad week, too," Riles said again. He picked up Williams's cigarette and turned toward the rest of the men at the table. "Let me tell you about it."

"You know, in a way I feel like all this is maybe my fault," Riles said. His eyes were squeezed shut in fatigue and he was rubbing his forehead with one hand. His other hand held Pointy Williams's cigarette, still smoldering. Williams's corpse lay sprawled across the table from the waist up, his dead eyes wide with surprise. Blood dripped from his mouth and added to the crimson halo around his head. The loudest sound in the room was the rain pounding on the roof.

Mackin, Rodney, and Dink Reeves hadn't moved since the instant the gun appeared in Ray's hand. Riles saw with approval that all three of them had their eyes fixed on him intently. No one in the room was looking at the corpse except Ricky Cento, who was standing behind the group at the table. The shotgun, Riles noted, hadn't moved. Ray walked easily over to the window and used the silencer on his pistol to lift one of the torn curtains. He peered outside for a moment, then returned to his place behind his employer.

"I mean, I kind of brought everybody together here." Riles looked hard at the cigarette in his hand for a moment, as if wondering where it came from, then stubbed it in the ashtray. "Menthol," he said with distaste. He removed one of his own from the pack on the table in front of him and lit it. "And I think the problem we have here is that everyone has forgotten why we all got together."

A thin finger of blood was slowly stringing across the table to Riles's elbow. He ignored it. "This whole thing was about *business*. Everyone was supposed to make money. That's what I do. That's what I am. A businessman. A week ago I was the golden boy. I put the people I work for into one of the biggest deals of my life, a basically legit deal, and the whole food-stamp thing, that was icing. Just icing. Everything was fucking hunky-dory."

He pointed at the corpse. "Then this guy decides to pull a cheap rip-off, and the next thing you know everything has gone to hell in a handcar. You want to know how bad this is?"

He didn't seem to be speaking to anyone in particular, and nobody answered him. He pulled on his cigarette.

"Here's one way to see how bad it is. This kind of work, the hard stuff, I haven't had to do anything like this in almost twelve years. And the reason I had to handle this personally is that you cowboys have pissed off the wrong people. Fuck the cops. Fuck the FBI, fuck the Justice Department. Those people are bullshit. *You guys have pissed off Sal Capetti.* You ought to be dead, and you're walking around."

The stream of blood had found a small irregularity in the surface of the table and started to form a second pool.

"But like I said, it could be that all this is my fault. Sal isn't looking to run up his score. As far as Sal is concerned, everyone here is even. It's done. We all go home."

Dink Reeves broke the silence. "This is my home, Riles."

He spoke without emotion. "You telling me that Sal Capetti be runnin' shit in the Brickyard now?"

"Fuck, no." Riles sounded exasperated. "Your action is your action, Reeves. I had to do what I had to do. This isn't about territory. No one's looking to step on your toes. It's over. Maybe someday we can do business again. From what I hear, you understand reality a little better than our late friend."

Reeves reached into the breast pocket of his sports coat. Ricky Cento stiffened slightly, but Ray didn't move. Ray had patted down Dink, and Ray knew that whatever else Dink might have in his coat, he didn't have a gun. His hand emerged holding a pair of dark sunglasses. He carefully opened the earpieces one at a time and slipped the glasses over his eyes. It was pitch-black and raining outside, but nobody in the room found the gesture affected. He stood up. "What about the grocery thing?"

Riles snorted. "The fucking grocery thing, I dropped it in the garbage. What grocery thing?"

Reeves nodded. "I'm out of here." He walked to the door. Ray slipped his pistol into his overcoat pocket and stepped aside.

From the doorway, Reeves turned back and looked at Mackin. "Man says we're even. That good for you?"

All emotion had left Mackin's face. He nodded twice. Reeves vanished into the dark rain.

"Ray, go get the car, please. Ricky, for now I want you to wait outside. When we're done here, clean this up." The two men left the room. Riles looked down at the blood on the tabletop and sighed. "Mackin, could I have a minute?"

Mackin looked at Rodney and nodded. The black man stood up and walked to the door. "I'll get the car," he said quietly.

It was the first time he'd spoken since he'd walked into the room. "I'll be outside." He didn't look at the body on the table as he left.

Mackin and Riles were alone. Riles lit another cigarette and handed it across the table. "If I know you, Mackin, you've got Bo Showalter waiting out there in the fucking rain with a rifle or a bazooka or some shit to cover your ass." He tried to make his voice light. "Bo really gets into that commando shit, doesn't he?"

Mackin tried on a weak smile and decided he didn't like it. "It's cool, Frank. Bo wasn't going to do anything unless he knew for sure that this got out of hand."

Riles nodded. Silence lay heavy in the room. "I'm truly sorry about the girl. Maggie, right?"

Mackin nodded as he took the cigarette. "Maggie Raynor," he said dully. His eyes were fixed on what was left of Pointy Williams.

"Is that . . ." Riles caught himself. "Is she going to come back on you? You need a hand with your back trail?"

"No. No, I don't think so. We weren't together long."

"Oh, Christ, Mackin." There was real pain in Riles's voice. "Why did you bring her here? Why in the name of God did you bring her along?"

Mackin slowly shook his head. "I don't know, Frank. Don't know. Getting old, maybe. Slipping." He raised both hands to his face.

Riles stood up and removed a thick, white envelope from his coat pocket. He set it carefully on the table in front of Mackin. "This is the last of the money from the Milwaukee score. There's twenty thousand in there. Take a vacation, Mackin. If it makes any difference, you're all right with Sal.

There's no problem." He reached out his hand as if to touch the other man's shoulder, then withdrew it. "You were right, what you said to Reeves. You were ahead on this thing when you made it out of that fucking car alive."

Mackin nodded a last time and picked up the envelope. He joined Riles at the door. "I'm sick of the rain," he said.

22

DINK REEVES walked into his office on Amsterdam Street and sat behind his desk. Danny walked in from the hall and joined him. He wasn't carrying his shotgun.

"Conway brothers are keeping an eye on things," Danny said. "The fire-escape dude's still in the bathroom. I think maybe we better kill him or give him some water, or something."

Dink nodded.

"Where's Pointy?"

"Pointy's dead." Dink looked the other man in the eyes. "Man from Chicago shot him twice in the head. Thief is goin' home. This"—he gestured around the office—"this is all ours now, we tough enough to keep it."

"Motherfucker." Danny crossed his arms. "Chicago comin' after the Brickyard?"

"Man says no. Says our business is our business. You in?"

Danny nodded. "Pointy was getting a little loopy, Dink. I mean, I liked him and all, but he wasn't taking care of business. I'll hang, if you're running shit."

Dink nodded back at him. "Bring that motherfucker in here. Keep his arms tied, pull off the gag."

Two minutes later Danny, shotgun in hand, led Malcolm Barrett into Reeves's office.

"Pointy Williams killed your brother," Dink said quietly, "and tonight someone killed Pointy Williams."

Barrett stared at him without speaking.

Reeves pulled out one of his scented cigarettes and lit it. "I ain't gonna 'pologize for your brother bein' dead, 'cause your brother fucked up, but I need to know how you stand."

Barrett shrugged and licked his lips. "My beef was with Pointy," he croaked. "I got no problem with anyone else. You sure he's wasted?"

"Watched it happen." Reeves took a deep drag from his cigarette. "Ballsy fuckin' play, homes, walking up those fire-escape stairs. You straighten up, fly right, maybe I find a place for you. You lookin' for work?"

Barrett's cracked lips broke into a grin.

The police found the Volvo two days later. A plainclothes officer on his way to an early briefing ducked into a bagel shop across the street from police headquarters at six o'clock in the morning. On his way out he noticed that the silver car's trunk was unlocked and ajar. A ring of keys dangled from the trunk lock. The cop stopped on the sidewalk, curious, with half of a cinnamon-and-raisin bagel protruding from his mouth. Without touching the vehicle, he squatted on the curb and angled his gaze into the trunk opening. In the artificial glow of the streetlights he saw Pointy Williams's left shoe, a soft leather slouch loafer, and an ankle clad in gray silk. The rest of the body was covered by a blanket.

"Holy shit," he muttered around the bagel. He started back into the bagel shop to use the phone, then looked across the street at the dirty gray stone of the courthouse.

"Hell." He ran across the street. Ten minutes later a harried-looking shift sergeant told him to call Petrone at home.

That night Sarah Petrone made dinner for John Lockhart and Nick Maloney. The insurance investigator was leaving town the following afternoon.

"You seem awfully sure it's all over," Sarah said to Lockhart. She nodded in the direction of her husband at the other end of the table, who was busily reducing a plate stacked with sliced meat and mashed potatoes. "Milos thinks this could go on for a while. Bodies stacking up like cordwood, he says."

Lockhart pushed his plate away and leaned back in his chair. "Remind me," he said to Maloney, "to marry a bank president."

"Vice president," Sarah said. "There's plenty more roast beef, and in honor of having guests I broke every rule of Milos's diet and bought a chocolate cake."

Lockhart looked aghast. "Diet? Diet? This man is on a *diet*? Sarah, do you have any idea how he eats when he's out of the house? It's appalling. It's like watching the firebombing of Dresden."

Maloney burst into laughter.

"I've heard. I'm afraid my husband lies to me about many things." Sarah turned to Maloney. "Do you think it's over, Nick?"

"Depends on what 'it' you're talking about, Sarah." The reporter had finished his meal and was playing with an unlit cigarette. "We're talking about two different things here. John's in town to catch this Moffitt guy for being the thief of the century, but with Williams dead the Moffitt guy is almost certainly gone. Hell, Moffitt probably killed him. On the other hand, Williams's murder complicates our local situation a little bit. Nature abhors a vacuum, et cetera, et cetera. I imagine a few more bodies will turn up as his operation comes under new management, but I don't think Mr. Moffitt will be involved."

"Moffitt probably didn't kill Williams." Petrone had finished eating and dropped his napkin on his plate. "They told me just before I left the office that the bullets that killed Williams were fired by the same gun that was used to kill Wayne Hookright. They both look like professional hits, two in the head with a silenced .22, so whoever killed Hookright is the same guy that killed Pointy. They closed the books."

Sarah walked into the living room and returned with an ashtray for Maloney. "Who's Wayne Hookrat?"

"Hookright," Petrone said. "Grocery-store guy; a couple of tenants found his body in the Dumpster behind the Turcotte Arms apartments a couple of days ago. The usual, two in the head. Found six grams of cocaine and enough prescription bottles for a pharmacy in his penthouse. This thing seems to revolve around grocery stores, believe it or not, and if we spend the next six months poking at it, we'll probably figure the whole deal out."

Sarah set the ashtray down in front of the reporter. "Will you spend the next six months working on it?"

Maloney lit a cigarette. Everyone looked at the detective.

"I'd guess that the chief will leave me on this for another two, three weeks. We can't just walk away from a double cop killing, but no, this won't last for another six months. People forget. Lead story on the news last night was that nine-year-old girl going for the liver transplant; that'll be a three-ring media circus for the next month. There were three homicides in the Brickyard last week that had nothing to do with any of this, and they'll require attention and resources. There are only two people I really want to arrest, Moffitt and the guy with the .22. I'm sure they're both gone."

"As I will be," Lockhart said. "Sarah, I would love a piece of cake, and I'll even help with the dishes."

"Think you can catch this clown from your desk in Hartford, John?" Maloney was grinning.

"Not going to Hartford." Lockhart beamed at the slab of cake Sarah deposited before him. "Going to Chicago. If your guy Freed is right, some wiseguy in Chicago knows the thief, probably even knows his name. I've got an old buddy in the Bureau office out there, guy named Ken Bethune, who's an organized-crime specialist. I'm gonna talk to him, see what he can come up with."

"What about the girl, the dead one?"

"Maggie Raynor," Maloney said. "She was a stripper from San Diego. All anyone out there remembers is that she took off four or five months ago with a guy whose name might be Bob or might be Bill. He was moving to, depending on who you talk to, either Omaha, Nebraska, Aspen, Colorado, or Kansas City. There's a sister in Massachusetts who's married to an aerospace engineer and doesn't want to talk about dear little Maggie."

"She's the key," Petrone said from the end of the table. "Find out where she's been lately, and you'll find out where Moffitt is."

"I'm already pushing my travel budget pretty hard," Lockhart said, "and it's going to be tough to justify. My company didn't insure Felton Printing, so my bosses aren't going to let me run completely free on this. Let's see what I come up with in Chicago. Hell, I'm not even convinced the killing is related. No one at the motel could ID Moffitt as the man with the girl."

"It's related," Petrone said. "She was with him. She's why he freaked out and walked into Vingt-et-Un, John, I'm telling you. I saw the man's eyes. He was crazy."

"So it's over." Sarah poured herself a cup of coffee. "Nick will write us a book and explain it all."

"I just might do that, Sarah." The reporter stubbed his cigarette. "How about you push that cake over to my side of the table?"

"Me, too," Petrone said. "I love chocolate."

"Not in a million years," his wife said.

Epilogue

RODNEY AND BO drove Mackin to Chicago and dropped him at O'Hare. He bought a ticket for Charlotte, North Carolina. He rented a car at the Charlotte airport and spent his time driving slowly down the coast. He saw one story on the "gang war" in the back of the *Charlotte Observer* the day he landed, but it didn't include his photograph and he didn't see any further press attention. He spent his days exploring small coastal communities and prowling through used-book stores. He didn't find anything he liked.

He flew back to Kansas City from Miami after twelve days. He called Showalter from the airport when he arrived.

"Everything cool?"

"Totally," Bo said. "Nothing's come back on us. Chicago

has called a couple of times, they're still getting a little bit of heat, not serious. Nothing at all here."

"I'm going home. I'll call you in a couple of days."

"I'll pick you up, man." Bo sounded concerned. "Lot to catch up on. Rodney broke up with that expensive girlfriend. I hired three new dancers. Hell, let's get drunk."

"I'll take a cab. Call you in a couple of days." He hung up.

Mackin found a cab and directed the driver to his apartment building. He ignored the cabbie's efforts at conversation.

The shades were drawn in his apartment and it was dark. He tossed his keys on an antique organ desk next to the door, set his wallet on top of them, and pulled off his coat. He got a tall glass from the kitchen and poured four fingers of straight bourbon. He swallowed half of it at once, pulled his gun from his suitcase, and set it on the desk.

He walked to the bookcase in the living room. Mackin was an unorganized collector, concentrating on favorite authors rather than on a country or an historical period. He was proud of his Graham Greenes. He picked up a 1940 British first edition of Greene's *The Power and the Glory*. Right next to it was the first American edition of the same novel, retitled *The Labyrinthine Ways* and published by Viking, and next to that was the 1946 Viking edition with the original title. He was the only collector he knew who owned all three.

The compact solidity of the book pleased him. He ran his hand over the cover and remembered how Maggie had held one of his books on a sunny morning, their first morning together. He opened the book and his eyes fell on the epigraph, a couplet from John Dryden. *Th' inclosure narrow'd; the sagacious power / Of hounds and death drew nearer every hour.* He winced, closed the book, and returned it to the shelf.

He walked into his bedroom. An elastic, black silk ruffle that Maggie wore in her hair lay in the middle of the floor. He automatically reached down and picked it up. He was tired. He started for the bed, then realized the sheets would smell like her. He walked back into the living room. On his way to the couch he dropped the ruffle in the trash. He wondered if he would sleep.